Hun

Veslor Mates – Book Six

By Laurann Dohner

Hunter Raze

by Laurann Dohner

When her parents died in her youth, Anabel Brick — along with her sister, Jessa — was raised as an orphan of United Earth. While her sister became an Alien Research Specialist, Anabel's skills were put to a different use. She's a tool for U.E. and its military fleet…a spy…a killer. Her current mission also turns out to be her last. If she succeeds, if the criminals don't take her out first, she'll remain marooned on the deep-space planet. Any rescue effort too dangerous to attempt for a single operative. Anabel always knew her life wasn't going to have a happy ending.

Little does Anabel know, the hunter is about to become the hunted.

Raze and his hunter grouping have suffered too much loss. All they have left is each other and the anticipation of hunting prey for the rest of their lives. It does give them a sense of peace to track, capture, and sometimes kill vile beings who harm others. Now his grouping has been commissioned by other Veslors to find Anabel and return her to her family safely. Finding the female is easy; Raze and his grouping brothers are the best at what they do. Subduing a woman who's more than human is another matter.

2

Little does Raze know, rescuing Anabel could have dire consequences for everyone...Veslors included.

Veslor Mates Series List

The Gorison Traveler Incident

Mission: Guardian Angel

The Breeding Experiment

Mission: Planet Biter

The Torid Affair

Hunter Raze

Hunter Raze by Laurann Dohner

Copyright © November 2021

Editor: Kelli Collins

Cover Art: Dar Albert

ISBN: 978-1-950597-21-5

Hunter Raze

Veslor Mates – Book Six

By Laurann Dohner

Prologue

The alarms blared as smoke filled the air from the circulation vents. Anabel made it to her private crew cabin and sealed the door. She yanked open the emergency cabinet located to her immediate left and put on a breathing mask, sucking in fresh oxygen to stop coughing.

The deck under her vibrated and for a split second, gravity becoming unstable on the massive space freighter. It went back to normal before she began to float. It was a warning that she was nearly out of time.

She ran to her bunk and dropped to her knees, pulling out the heavy locker located underneath. Conveniently, her arm bled a little where she'd hit it while fleeing, and she reached up, ran her fingers over the cut, then carefully inserted two of her bloodstained fingertips into the locking mechanism. It clicked, the lid opening.

The hidden compartment at the top fell open, since she'd used her DNA to verify ownership instead of her fingerprints, revealing a slim data pad and two modified weapons. She shoved the weapons into her deep jumpsuit pockets and turned on the pad. It instantly connected to the network.

She tapped in new orders, sending her message to both hidden rockets. The information was too important to risk sending just one. The rockets were equipped with obstacle avoidance navigation systems, but by using both, she could be certain her handler would receive at least one of them.

"Kurt, it's way worse than we suspected. Gemini isn't just sneaking in survey crews to scope out planets before they bid. The crew of the *Soapa Six* are on their way to kill the existing indigenous aliens, so they can classify a planet as unclaimed. I have proof. There're over ninety thousand defenseless inhabitants on their next targeted planet."

She reached down and yanked up her jumpsuit leg, exposing her ankle. She pressed three fingers in the right spots and flinched from the slight pain as the skin split apart, ejecting the small data chip. She used her sleeve to clean the chip of blood.

The small injury tingled as it automatically began to heal. It was one feature of her synthetic legs that she appreciated. She slapped the data chip onto the pad, a small corner of the screen displaying the information she'd stolen as it began to upload to the rockets.

"Read the logs I copied from the captain's quarters. This freighter was sent to a planet called Biter eleven months before New Worlds company stationed a survey team there. I think Gemini was responsible for sabotaging that survey team after they were outbid, because they were afraid the team would find proof that aliens had recently been slaughtered on the planet. And it wasn't the work of one person, or payback by some corporate exec that Gemini threw under the bus. It's how these assholes *always* operate. The owners of Gemini are regularly murdering aliens on their home worlds to gain unclaimed planet rights."

Another explosion went off and the deck under her vibrated again. She knew exactly where it had originated from—since she'd set the bombs herself. The emergency pods near the shuttle bay were no more.

"I couldn't let them kill off another entire planet of aliens." She stared at the data pad screen through the clear glass of her breathing mask. "I did some sabotaging of my own."

Anabel saw that the data chip had completely uploaded and confirmed the information had been accepted by both rockets' onboard computers. She quickly detached the chip and opened the secret compartment on her lower leg again, inserting the chip into the same hiding spot.

"Put Gemini out of business. Make sure they can't murder more aliens or sabotage other survey teams. I've got enough proof to bury their asses, Kurt."

Tears filled her eyes, but she blinked them back; hopefully her handler would never notice. "I blew up every shuttle to prevent the crew from reaching the surface. That's not happening on my watch. I'm certain the crew isn't aware that I'm uploading all this, but they'll probably know when I launch the rockets. Then again, maybe not. I'm betting the bridge is too busy trying to save the freighter to worry about monitoring exterior sensors. Soon, *Soapa Six* will no longer have life support and the lower cargo hulls are breaching as I speak. I gave myself twenty minutes before this freighter becomes a death trap."

Her voice choked up slightly. "I'm going to try to make my way to a life pod to reach the targeted planet's surface. If any crew members have the same idea, I'll take out as many as I can. I tried to block all access to the pods, but I know there're a few talented hackers onboard."

Anabel took a deep breath. This was the last message she'd ever send. There was so much to say but so little time. The launching of the rockets would have alerted the bridge that someone onboard had likely betrayed them. They would have sealed off the ship to find the traitor and hampered her escape. That meant attacking first and sending her message last.

"I always bitched about my job...consider this my resignation, since I know you won't be allowed to come after me. Maybe Gemini specifically chose a planet outside of fleet jurisdiction so that United Earth wouldn't bother verifying their claim, and the other survey companies would avoid bidding on it. It's something you might want to dig deeper into their files to seek an answer to. Are there other out-of-bounds planets that Gemini or other companies are trying to claim? That's now *your* job to figure out. Or maybe pass it off to the higher-ups. These greedy idiots are going to start a war with aliens at some point if they aren't stopped. That should light a fire under the big bosses' asses."

Gravity went wonky again, but still Anabel didn't float. Though her body did feel lighter than normal. The freighter listed to the right, making her slide a few inches across the floor. "You were a great handler, for an asshole." She smiled. Kurt would know she didn't mean that last part, but he wouldn't be the only one viewing what she'd sent. "I enjoyed arguing with you." Then she sobered. "No guilt. No regrets. Just please send my sister my death notice, okay? That's the only promise I'm holding you to. Do it for me. Tell her that I'm sorry and I love her."

He'd understand what she couldn't say. Kurt knew to watch out for her baby sister. He'd make certain he was the one to notify Jessa—and he'd tell her a good enough lie about how she'd died that her sister wouldn't get herself arrested searching for answers. Jessa had to be one of the best hackers ever created by the fleet. Kurt would look out for her sister, keep tabs on her. For Anabel. Because he was a good friend.

The freighter deck leaned farther. "I have to go. It's been real." She ended the transmission and ordered both rockets to launch, verifying they'd successfully gotten away before she smashed the data pad on the hard corner of the open trunk. She couldn't risk losing her pride and attempting to send a secondary message before the rocket flew out of signal range.

Like pleading with Kurt to send help...or making him feel even more guilt when they both knew he wouldn't be allowed to do so. The big bosses wouldn't take the risk. The freighter had flown into hostile space. The risks were too great.

Kurt's job sucked as much as hers did. They were both puppets being controlled by arrogant masters sitting safely behind desks on Earth. People like her didn't get rescued if shit hit the fan. Fleet and United Earth just covered up how they'd *really* died.

Anabel got to her feet, bent to grab the go-bag she kept packed inside the locker, and straightened. The door chimed as she approached it, and she paused, glancing at the corridor monitor.

Two security officers stood outside her door with their blasters drawn.

12

"You figured out who set those bombs, huh?" she murmured to herself. "That was fast." Part of her was impressed. She hadn't believed they could be so competent.

She withdrew one of the small but powerful modified weapons, aimed it at the ceiling, and shot out the lights. Then she threw herself against the bulkhead next to the door. The vid screen showing the hallway cut out and she saw a red light flash on the panel beside it. Security had overridden her cabin lock.

The door slid open.

The first officer entered with his gun at the ready, failing to notice her just inches away in the darkness. Anabel braced her back and kicked out hard, sending him flying across the room. The corridor light was enough to see him slamming into her open trunk hard enough to flip over it, where he landed with a loud thud.

The second officer rushed in, and she threw out her hand to knock his weapon to the side even as she fired hers. The deadly laser hit his chin, taking off most of his face.

Anabel fled the cabin, pulling her second weapon. The mask helped her breathe in the smoke-laden corridor. She ran fast, not surprised when laser fire hit the wall behind her as she passed an intersecting corridor. Every security officer on the ship would be gunning for her if they'd identified her as the saboteur.

She ran faster, tucking her head to avoid hitting the ceiling. She had surprise on her side with her synthetic lower legs. Once she got going, she could pick up inhuman speed with those babies. The downside was, if she wasn't careful, not only could she elongate her stride with the bounce they generated, but she could gain height. That wasn't good on a freighter. Knocking herself out by slamming her head into a ceiling would prove deadly in her current situation.

She made it to a level access panel, stopped, and gave it a vicious kick. Her shoe split where the material met the sole but she ignored it, ripping off the now damaged metal plate to reveal a ladder. She pocketed her weapons, adjusted the bag on her arm so it didn't fall to another deck, and began her climb.

She swiftly went up a level and kicked again, this time with her undamaged shoe. The exit panel went flying. She peered out, groaning when she saw a security guard under the metal plate. The heavy panel had obviously hit him head-on. He rolled and grunted beneath it, trying to get free. She ignored him and ran to the left, toward the emergency pod station that she'd hacked hours before, ensuring it only opened for her.

The hack was successful. She gained access, the doors sealing behind her as she studied the four oval hatches. She walked to the third from her right, tapped in the new code she'd created, and unsealed it. She tossed her bag inside the dark circular pod—but not before she heard laser fire hitting the entry door to the small room.

Security had already discovered she'd blocked their access and were attempting to use lasers to damage the lock. They'd eventually succeed. The freighter was old, the doors made of lower-grade material than they should be.

She climbed into the emergency pod and the auto-lights came on, revealing space for only the six seats circling the wall. She twisted and sealed the hatch, quickly reaching into her hair bun to withdraw a data device that doubled as a harmless-looking hairclip.

Fleet always provided the neatest tools.

She inserted it into the access port and heard a series of clicks in the otherwise silent pod, the program on the hairclip doing its job to override the autopilot. She just needed a few more seconds…

"No time like now to find out if my authorization hack worked in the captain's quarters. If not, I'm dead," she muttered under her breath.

"Pod online," a computerized voice stated clearly. "Hello, Captain Mase."

Relief hit hard and fast. The onboard computer thought she was the captain. When she'd broken into his cabin, Anabel had switched his image and voice with her own, to gain access to the main computer. It would do whatever she ordered—while locking the real Mase out of secure areas, thinking he was a lowly maintenance worker.

"Prepare for launch."

Anabel threw herself into a seat and buckled in. She hooked one of the straps of her bag with her foot, then pulled out her weapons, flipping on the safeties before stashing them inside the small storage compartment in her armrest. She removed her breathing mask and shoved it in with her weapons, before sealing the compartment.

"Launch in sixty seconds, Captain Mase."

"Emergency override," she stated, keeping her voice calm. "Launch now. Initiate the transfer of new landing coordinates to the autopilot after launch."

The pod engines activated and the circular pod shook hard. The pressure of her body being shoved back into the seat and the simultaneous loss of gravity had her wanting to puke. The pod had probably launched into a rapid spin as it shot out of the side of the freighter.

She closed her eyes as the lights flickered, knowing what was coming. It wouldn't be pleasant.

The engines cut off, the pod going instantly silent. The automated piloting system would be recalculating where she'd programmed it to go with the hack. It took only seconds before the engines kicked on again.

Her body violently lurched to the left and slightly upward. She'd have been brutally thrown around the spherical walls if she hadn't belted in. Her heavy bag yanked on her leg where the strap snagged on her ankle, but at least it didn't go flying. Her stomach rolled and she swallowed down bile. She had no idea how long the pod would take to reach the planet designated as M736. It could be hours or days. She hadn't had time to do the calculations, too busy sabotaging the freighter. But she knew they'd been close to the planet. Too close. It's why she'd had to rush her plans.

Captain Mase and the rest of his eighty-seven-man crew would hopefully be dead within hours. Life support would blow in another five minutes, if her guess was right. The rest of her explosive charges were set to go off after that, destroying critical parts of the hull on every level to buckle the entire freighter.

She'd been unable to access every pod section to blow them up like she had the shuttles. There were a few talented hackers onboard who

16

might gain access to the remaining pods. And they might feel generous enough to take other crew along with them. Doubtful, since everyone working on the freighter had been ex-convicts, but still a possibility if they were smart enough to think ahead. Numbers were good to increase survival rates if a crew got marooned on an alien planet.

She'd browsed the employee files she'd stolen from the captain's quarters. No one on that ship could claim anything close to innocence. The majority were long-term crew who'd helped kill alien races in the past. There had only been three new-hires, Anabel included, and all had violent criminal histories. Only *her* identity had been forged by United Earth and the fleet to make her look like a dangerous ex-convict. No guilt surfaced over killing the crew.

Besides, it wasn't as if she'd *asked* to work undercover missions. That choice had been made for her after her parents died, when she was ten. Sometimes her job involved killing bad guys.

Anabel took deep, calming breaths. *Ninety thousand.* That was the number she focused on. Not eighty-seven criminals and their captain. The innocent aliens on the nearby planet were more important than a bunch of killers hired by a heartless corporation capable of ordering mass extinction. Gemini would be taken down with the proof she'd transmitted to her handler. Kurt wouldn't let her sacrifice be for nothing.

Her only regret was her younger sister. Tears filled her eyes, and this time she let them flow. Jessa would be all alone with Anabel gone. It tore her up knowing the pain her sister would feel over being told of her death. It would also kill her baby sister's dreams for their future. They'd planned to eventually settle together on a quiet planet when their United Earth contracts were fulfilled.

Not that she really believed the big bosses would just let her go. She'd done too many missions, knew too much. She'd seen what happened to other operatives when it came time for their contracts to expire. They either agreed to work longer...or accidents happened. Deadly ones.

That was something it had taken her years to realize. Retirement was a lie, something to keep them in line as they carried out missions. There was no such thing as freedom for people like her.

Anabel had given her sister the only gift she could by pretending to agree to their retirement plans—hope.

Her death would be the end of that.

"I'm sorry, sis," she whispered. "So damn sorry. Kurt won't be allowed to tell you I died while stopping a company from murdering entire worlds of aliens...but I know you'd understand if he could."

Kurt would make certain that her baby sister got her letter. It was a vid, actually. Which was important. Jessa hadn't been allowed to actually see Anabel—in person or in vids—since the fleet had separated them as children.

She wanted her sister to be able to look into her eyes, even if it was just on a recording. To see her face while hearing her voice at the same time. It would give Jessa a memento to hold onto forever. Her sister would also know how much she loved her. She'd made that abundantly clear in the recording.

Anabel had faith that whatever cover story Kurt came up with would also give her sister closure. Either Kurt himself or someone on their secret team would visit Jessa, to give her the news in person. Maybe even hug her, like Anabel hadn't been able to do since childhood.

Emotion choked her at realizing that would never become a reality. She wasn't ever going to get the chance to see her sister in person again. Her life, and any future opportunity to sneak a visit to her sister, was over.

Anabel reached up and wiped at her tears, closing her eyes.

"I'm not dead yet," she muttered. "I might be marooned on a planet until I die, but I'll make damn sure I'm the only human left standing if some of those fuckers from *Soapa Six* make it to the surface. My job isn't finished until then."

Chapter One

Three months later

Anabel avoided laser fire and picked up her pace, dodging thick red tree trunks as two ex-crew members from *Soapa Six* hunted her. She saw a huge, familiar purple plant and gritted her teeth. Her time on KP—as she'd dubbed the planet—had taught her all about the killer plants. Most of the vegetation was deadly, in fact.

She threw herself down, sliding under dozens of purple leaves that were larger than her entire body, and twisted to the side to avoid slamming headfirst into the wide base of the plant where it emerged from the ground. She still hit the base with her upper body hard enough to knock the air from her lungs. The entire plant began to shake and tremble. The massive leaves lowered to the ground. She curled her body tightly around the six-feet-diameter trunk to avoid touching them.

"Where'd that bitch go?" one of the crew members from *Soapa Six* panted.

"I don't know," his companion panted back. "I think Dodge is right. She's a cyborg. No one human can run that fast."

"I don't care *what* she is. I'm going to find her, fuck her, and kill her."

"You heard Dodge. He wants us to bring her back alive. She's the only damn woman on the planet. At least, the only fuckable one. No way am I touching those reptilian aliens. My dick would probably be ripped off by what passes for their pussy. Their goddamn scales look sharp as hell."

"That cunt is the reason we're stuck on this planet until Gemini sends another freighter to pick us up. I fucking *hate* this goddamn place."

Anabel smirked. Their company wouldn't be sending a rescue.

"Look at the dirt," the other man said, lowering his voice. "The bitch is hiding under that plant."

She was grateful for her modified ear, enabling her to catch the slightest whispered word.

"Go around to the other side of it to see if she crawled out," the guy ordered.

"We're gonna get her!" Eagerness filled the other man's voice.

Anabel hoped they'd never encountered one of these plants before and would crawl in after her. She coughed, making sure they knew where she was. The purple base of plant trembled again. It was definitely awake.

"She's in there," yelled the guy who'd circled around. "Come out, bitch!"

"I can't," she rasped. "I broke my ankle."

"Crawl under there and get her," the other ordered.

She smiled. "Yeah. Come get me. I'm hurt."

"You're gonna hurt so much more by the time we're through with you," he muttered low, thinking she couldn't hear him. "Go in there, Kevin. Drag her out."

"I'm going." Kevin sounded happy to do so...

Until he screamed. "It's got me! The fucking plant has me!"

She reached up and covered her ears, keeping her body snug against the base. Laser fire sounded. Kevin's screams turned to shrieks of terror and pain. She couldn't see him from where she lay on her side, facing the tree. But she didn't need to watch to know what was happening. Those large leaves were wrapping around their next meal, crushing him to death. She'd seen it happen to an animal on her second day on the planet.

His screams abruptly stopped, but his friend kept firing his laser.

"It won't do any good," she muttered. "Leaves are too thick. You're just pissing it off and making loud noises. Big mistake in this part of the valley..."

The dirt beneath her began to thump lightly. "Here they come."

She released her ears and gripped the base as best she could, drawing her knees in tighter and hanging on as the vibrations grew stronger. The laser fire halted. She imagined the remaining crew member finally felt or heard the approaching pack of shredders, what she'd named the beasts.

"Fuck!" More laser fire sounded.

Then there were high-pitched screams, mixed with animalistic whistles. The laser fire stopped once more. Anabel heard disturbing tearing and crunching noises, and she sealed her lips tight, breathing through her nose to avoid puking. The man was being eaten.

The shredders were vicious. The size of rhinos from Earth, they looked like screwed-up hairless wolves with eight legs. The two front limbs acted like arms with deadly claws to grab their prey, bringing it closer to their razor-sharp teeth.

Anabel had a love/hate relationship with the shredders. She loved when they killed one of the crew for her, but sometimes they migrated into the area beneath her home base, where they'd hang out for a couple weeks while birthing babies. That meant she had to stay in place, therefore hindering her job.

She'd looked for a better place to sleep, but her cave was the safest. It was too high for the wildlife to reach. It also gave her a great vantage point to see danger coming. There had been some major storms that had rolled in over the months. They'd also hindered her mutual hunt for the crew. It was suicide to go out in the pouring rain, since they resulted in flashfloods.

A good hour passed before the pack of shredders began to wander away. Anabel remained stuck there, since the purple leaves still touched the ground. The plant, even while eating its catch, would always be looking for another meal.

It grew colder as the sun went down. At last, she heard the plant closing, the way they did at night. The leaves would lift toward the sky, presumably to catch any overnight moisture in the air.

She waited another good half hour after the leaves rose above the ground before she began to belly crawl along the dirt, very careful not to make any noise that would alert the plant to her presence. Once she was outside of its range, she got to her feet and glanced around.

The two moons always gave off enough light for her to see by. She walked to where she spotted an alarming amount of blood on the ground. Nothing of the crew member remained but small pieces of his clothing and boots. Shredders didn't waste meat. She located his weapon, but it had been crushed.

"Damn," she whispered, her hope of salvaging it dashed. She walked around the purple plant, maintaining a good distance. The other man's weapon was visible, part of the stock sticking out of the rolled leaf that contained his body, but there was no way she could reach it without brushing up against other leaves.

She spotted a small bag on the ground and tiptoed closer, keeping her gaze on the leaves. If they so much as twitched, she'd leap back. The plant didn't move, so she quickly scooped up the bag and backed off fast. She clipped it to her belt and started jogging toward the mountain cliff.

Anabel hadn't gone far before she heard a noise, coming to a halt and going absolutely still. She moved only her eyes, her senses straining to locate the direction of the sound. It was a bit to her right and up high. She very slowly turned her head and saw movement near the top of a tree.

The size of the moving shadow told her it was one of the gorilla-like tree beasties. They didn't seem to eat meat, but they'd beat living creatures to a bloody pulp if they came too close to any tree they'd claimed as their home, especially if they had babies up there. She'd seen it happen twice before.

She very slowly began to walk, keeping silent, and avoided getting too close to any of the trees in that area. The beasts tended to live in small groups of three to six. Yet another thing she'd quickly learned after landing on KP.

Thoughts of her sister came, and she smiled. Jessa would be fascinated by the beasts, even if it was only wildlife. Her sister's area of expertise was sentient aliens, but she'd still be keenly interested in any discoveries made on an uncharted planet.

Anabel had so far avoided running into the alien inhabitants, only spying on them from a safe distance. A group of a few dozen had arrived shortly after her pod had landed, probably to investigate what had fallen from the sky. Some sort of reptilian hunters, they wore furs around their waists—indicating they were likely male—and carried sharp-looking spears.

She'd been unable to hide the pod, but they hadn't gained access. Some had poked it with their spears, like it was some strange animal they wanted to kill. They'd touched its sleek surface, hissing words she couldn't understand, before finally leaving.

Anabel had watched them go, tracking them with the vision scope from her pack. Once the aliens were miles away, she'd decided to stay in a tree overnight to make certain more didn't show up.

It had given her a bird's-eye view as other emergency pods streaked down from above hours later. All of them tracking the auto-distress hail she'd purposely left broadcasting, in case more pods were launched from *Soapa Six*. The pod computers were programed to link in an emergency, enabling them to land within a ten-mile radius of each other. Her pod was fully intact with no recorded damage, so the onboard computers in the others would register her location as a safe place to send their occupants.

Nine other pods had made it to the planet's surface. It enraged her that so many of the crew had escaped their fate in space. She'd focused on memorizing where the pods had gone down and plotting the best way to take them out.

The first pod had been easy to spot. Unfortunately, so were the six alien corpses riddled with laser holes. Their spears had been useless against human weapons, and they'd been slaughtered. That had angered her even more.

She'd watched the four crew members who'd made camp next to their pod, following when one of them had gone to take a piss after the sun went down. He hadn't heard her as she slipped behind him.

She'd dragged his body to where the murdered aliens had been dumped. It seemed fitting.

The remaining three had quickly realized the fourth hadn't returned and were brave enough to walk into the dark to search for him, making it easier for her to take them out too. She'd stolen the supplies from their pod before stuffing their bodies inside.

Anabel pushed away the memories when she reached her cliff, putting on her gloves before starting to climb. When she reached a sheer rock ledge, she bent her knees, did a quick calculation of how much strength was required to reach the next ledge ten feet up, and leapt. She grabbed a branch of the small tree that grew there and dropped onto the second ledge.

She entered the small cave opening and dug into her pocket, withdrew a glow stick, and cracked it. Faint blue light emanated after she shook the stick, and she walked around a corner, taking in the welcome sight of the bed she'd made from piled sleeping bags, and the spare supplies stacked next to it.

"Home sweet home," she sighed, removing her gloves.

The cave was safe. At least from humans. They'd need climbing gear to make it to the second ledge. The aliens...she wasn't so sure. They *did* have claw-tipped fingers that might make climbing possible.

It was purely accidental that she'd even found the hidden space. She'd climbed the tallest tree in the vicinity to search for any sign of her fellow crew and instead spotted the hole in the cliff face. She'd deemed it a perfect refuge after scouting it out.

She stripped off her boots, the belt holding her weapons, and jumpsuit, before putting on a clean shirt. She didn't bother with underwear. The two pairs she'd packed in her go-bag were being saved for when her clothing fell apart. They would at some point.

She retrieved the small bag she'd salvaged from the two dead crew members and carefully opened it, peering inside.

"Yes!"

She pulled out a sealed chocolate bar and tore it open, taking a bite. It tasted delicious. A bit melted, but she didn't care. Also inside the bag was a pack of playing cards, a hologram disk cube, and some chewing gum.

She studied the hologram disk cube then tossed it into the corner. The last one she'd found was a vid of a naked woman masturbating. A space guy's version of porn. She wrapped up the rest of the chocolate bar to save for later and took a seat on her bed. Nine stacked sleeping bags made for a surprisingly comfortable place to doze.

She picked up the chalky white stone she kept nearby, making two more marks on the rock wall. "Eleven of you suckers gone now. I only wish I knew how many more of you have to be taken out."

It frustrated her that she hadn't killed them all yet. Her task had been delayed by a series of crappy storms, the dangerous shredder herds that roamed the valley, and nursing a few injuries she'd sustained.

Every day that passed with crew still alive put the aliens in danger. She really wished she had a drone. One equipped to locate human life signs. What she considered her last mission for UE could have been completed within days instead of months.

The blue light began to fade, the shake charge on the glow sticks never lasting more than five minutes or so. She was too tired to activate it again, instead reaching over to grab a nutrient bar from the pile of supplies. They tasted like cardboard but filled her up. Anabel rolled to the side of her makeshift bed and took a sip of water from one of the specially designed filter flasks she'd hoarded.

Exhaustion had her yawning. She stretched out flat on her back, pulled the covers over her, and closed her eyes.

"I'll be the last human standing," she whispered, reciting what had become her mantra before drifting off to sleep.

* * * * *

Raze slowly navigated their ship through the large debris field. Time was of the essence, but destroying *Satrono* with a hull breach wouldn't help them find what they sought any faster.

"No life signs," Bruck stated. "That's a big Earth ship. How many do you believe were on it?"

"Dead is dead," Prasky muttered. "We shouldn't have taken this bounty. Our prey was probably one of the bodies destroyed with the ship."

Raze turned his head to glance at the fourth empty seat on their bridge, grief stabbing at his heart. They all missed Hern. His loss was a bleeding wound that wouldn't heal. "Not prey," he reminded Prasky. "We need this one alive."

"That is your way of saying we won't get paid to bring back a corpse."

The harshness of Prasky's tone had Raze flinching. "A Veslor hired us. And he already paid half up front."

"What's his interest in the prey?"

"*Target*," Raze gritted out. "Not prey. The target is important to Roth. That was the Earth ship she was on."

"*She?*" Prasky leapt to his feet and snarled, rage glittering in his eyes. "You didn't say it was female!"

"This is why." Bruck turned in his seat. "Calm!"

Prasky turned on him. "You knew?"

"Yes. We both believed you would refuse to come if you learned we're here to hunt a female." Bruck blew out a long breath. "You can't hate *all* of them over Hern's death. It makes little sense."

Prasky stormed off the bridge without replying.

"He'll get over it," Raze sighed. "I hope."

"It's been months, with no sign of his rage weakening."

"This is a human female we're hunting. You've seen them. He won't view her as a threat to one of us."

Bruck met his gaze. "I don't agree. Hern wasn't taken from us by battling a female. She lured him into a trap with the promise of becoming his mate. *Any* female could do that, in Prasky's mind. We should keep him onboard after we land."

"I already decided to do so. We'll keep the female secured in my private sleeping place. I've already changed the codes to prevent him from entering."

"Do you believe this female survived that?" Bruck jerked his head toward the screens displaying the destroyed Earth freighter. Parts of the vessel had floated away from the whole, the debris spreading to encompass a large section of space between it and one of the two moons inhabiting the nearby planet's solar system.

"I don't know, but Roth told me to look here. The Earth freighter had life pods. He said her last message stated that she planned to take one to our target planet. It's the only one capable of supporting life near the wreckage."

"How long ago was this?" Bruck glanced at the screen again.

"I'm not certain. Roth wasn't either, but he was told she was shuttled to the Earth vessel over four months ago."

"I have no information on this planet except for what I'm picking up on long-range scanners. Its oxygen-based and can support life. There isn't a warning beacon to mark who it belongs to." He paused. "There are no signals being broadcast from its surface. We'll have to get closer for more detailed scans."

"It's far from any known shipping lanes. Maybe these aliens are reclusive." Raze got more comfortable in his chair, navigating around the damaged freighter, and finally increased speed once they were clear of the debris.

"I'm not picking up any planetary defenses." Bruck scowled. "No traces that the freighter was destroyed by something originating from the planet."

"Keep me updated."

Twenty minutes later, Bruck spoke again. "There are no large cities or signs of any technology. It all points to being a primitive planet."

"Keep scanning. Are you picking up any distress signals? Earth pods normally have those."

"No. They may not have the range to transmit into space."

"Go in closer and keep scanning. It's a big planet. I'd like to sit us down close to our target instead of having to fly from continent to continent, searching."

"I hoped this would be a quick, easy hunt."

Raze snorted. "We rarely get those, Bruck." He glanced at Hern's chair again, his chest aching. That was supposed to be an easy hunt too, finding their missing grouping male when he hadn't returned to their ship on time. They'd believed he'd just lost track of time. Instead, they discovered he'd been murdered.

"I'm running through our database of Earth building materials that shouldn't be found on this planet, focusing our scans on them."

He nodded. Bruck was an excellent hunter. He was also skilled at using technology to assist in finding whatever they were paid to retrieve.

Raze piloted them closer, setting up in orbit low enough to help with the scans but high enough to avoid the pull of gravity created by the planet.

Hours passed before Bruck caught his attention again.

"Reading ten locations with Earth materials." He tapped at his screen. "They're all on one large land mass."

Raze looked up as the view screen zoomed in on one of the continents. The sun didn't currently shine on the surface, but their enhanced scanners still gave them visuals. It was a heavily vegetative area with rolling hills and mountains. Massive rivers snaked along the surface in a few areas. Red dots appeared where the scanner had detected what had to be the emergency pods. They were spaced apart, but the distances weren't too great. "Are you reading distress signals coming from any of them?"

"No. I researched information on Earth pods. Most would run out of power after sixty Earth days." He paused. "That implies they've either been on the planet longer than we suspected, or all the pods were damaged during landing. They're also programmed to lock onto other pod signals and land closely together, if possible. That's probably why they're on the same land mass. I'll focus on life signs in those areas. I need to deploy a robot scout to gain more accurate readings. We'll also be able to get better visuals."

"Do it," Raze ordered. "Deploy the robot scout ahead of us landing." He paused. "But don't program this one to fly over deep water. They are expensive to replace."

Bruck snarled. "It wasn't *my* fault a massive water creature leapt into the air to eat our last bot."

Raze hid a smile at annoying Bruck as he picked up a data pad and turned it on. He scanned over the little information they had on the human female. Anabel Brick. An image had been transmitted, but it wasn't recent; he'd been warned that it had been taken approximately nine years prior.

He stared at the image. Most humans of that sex had long hair, but not this one. The female's shiny black hair had been shorn close to her head. Big green eyes stared back at him. She didn't wear any of the colored paint the few humans he'd met liked to smear on their faces.

He studied her fragile-looking facial bones. Her nose was small, but her lips were slightly puffy. A tiny scar marred her forehead, near her hairline. She appeared young, maybe not fully grown as a female.

"That's the target?"

Raze lifted his gaze to find Bruck had walked over to stand behind him, staring at the pad he held. "Yes."

"She looks helpless. I doubt we'll find her alive."

"She's older than this now. Nine years."

"Roth's grouping didn't have a more recent image?"

"No."

"Why not?"

"Roth is a male of few words. All I know is that this female is important to him. He wants her returned unharmed to his grouping."

A low growl of displeasure came from Bruck. "She's one of their mates? What was she doing so far from her male?"

"No. She's an important family member to a mate."

"That makes sense. Why didn't the humans track this female?"

"They'd have to fly through heavily patrolled Kriror and Elth territories to come this far. Both races would attack a human fleet vessel."

Bruck shook his head. "Neither of those races took out the ship we passed. Both would have completely destroyed it or hauled it away for the scrap."

"I agree."

"So, who attacked the humans? It wasn't the planet. As I said, they have no defenses."

Raze glanced down at the image on the data pad, then held it up. "*She* did."

Bruck snorted in disbelief. "I won't fall for another of your pranks."

"No prank. It is the only detail Roth knew with certainty. The female purposely damaged the freighter and planned to use a life pod to reach the planet below."

"Why would she do that? *How* could she do that? It was a large ship by human standards. And she appears harmless. The other humans would have stopped her."

Raze turned off the data pad and shrugged. "Those are questions you can ask after we have her locked inside my sleeping place and are on our way to deliver her to Roth."

He activated the enhanced controls to land their ship. It could become dicey, entering an unknown planet with possible hidden dangers. The gravity pull wasn't severe as they transitioned from space into the atmosphere, though Bruck braced against the side of Raze's chair during some slight turbulence. Raze activated night vision and the ship's sensors, since the sun currently didn't light up the continent.

"There," Bruck said minutes later, pointing at the view screen.

"I see the clearing. Do you want to fly?"

"No." Bruck strode to his seat and deployed the planetary robot scout.

Raze hovered over the long grass in the clearing, running scans to make certain it would be safe to land *Satrono*. Once assured the ground was solid, he parked and leveled the ship on the slightly uneven surface. "We're down."

"I'm already getting verified readings from the scout. It's confirmed. Ten pods are registering on sensors…unless some broke apart during transition and I'm only reading the largest pieces of the wreckage. I doubt anything from the Earth vessel managed to reach this distance, only to get destroyed in the gravity pull. That will mean more humans than the female down here. What if there are hundreds of survivors? We don't have the capacity to take them all."

"We weren't hired to retrieve other humans. Only the female." Raze knew he sounded cold, but their ship had been built for speed and defensive capabilities. Life support could handle only twenty life forms without strain. They couldn't sustain or house more than that.

"We could pack some humans into the cargo hold and put the bunks from our holding cells in there, for them to sleep in shifts. It would keep them contained. Then drop them at the first space station we reach."

Raze growled. "Do you remember the last humans we helped? They attempted to kill us and steal our ship. Do you really believe it's a good idea to allow that many onboard?"

"They may outnumber us if there are enough survivors, but they're also easy to kill if they attack."

Raze straightened in his seat. "Gather more information from the scout and we'll see how many humans survived. I'll decide then."

Bruck nodded. "The robot scout will have precise information for us after it does a flyover of the region."

"We'll eat, rest, and then begin our hunt when the sun rises. It will give the scout enough time to do a thorough scan."

Chapter Two

Anabel woke early and made her way to the opening of the cave with her view scope. She peered out at the lightening sky. Dawn was her favorite time of day. The planet was beautiful, with a purplish-pink sky that gave the surface a fairytale kind of appearance. She wasn't as fond of the chilly, damp air, though, as she shivered in her shirt.

She lifted the scope to one eye and closed the other, starting her search of the wide valley below. It didn't take long to find a thin stream of smoke rising from the treetops. It was just enough to mark where someone had set up camp. They were a few miles to her right.

The camp was likely where the two crew members who'd nearly captured her the day before had come from, based on where she'd been when they'd spotted her. She didn't like that anyone had moved within visual distance of her cave. She had no way of knowing how many were in the camp, but the smoke told her they were smart enough to have figured out the wildlife avoided fire, and to keep it burning all night.

She returned to her bed and snuggled into the top sleeping bag to get warm again. That was another reason to keep a fire going until morning. She didn't have that luxury. Smoke could be seen for miles, and it was too big of a risk to make a fire for warmth or cooking in her cave.

She blindly slid her hand out from beneath the cover, found an energy bar, and tore it open. "I hate these," she muttered. "But I'm still grateful to have them. Food is food."

The emergency pods each contained a large supply of them. She'd not only taken the stash from hers, but also the pod of the four-man crew she'd killed. Rationing the bars was a must until she'd tracked and killed the rest of the survivors.

At some point, she'd have to figure out what she could eat on the planet without poisoning herself. That was at least a month away, though; maybe more, if she found more pods to steal supplies from. She finished the bar, took a sip of water, then slid out of the bed to quickly dress in her jumpsuit. It still left her a bit cold, but she couldn't stay huddled in bed all day.

"Too many people to kill before they find me or murder more innocent aliens," she muttered.

Boots on, she fastened the belt around her waist last, hooking weapons to it. The two modified ones she'd come with were great, but the ones she'd taken from the first set of men she'd killed had longer shooting ranges. She had a feeling she'd need them. Anabel had no idea how many of the crew had managed to reach those nine life pods, but with six seats each, she could be facing off against about fifty pissed-off ex-cons.

"Bad odds," she muttered. "But it's not like I have a choice."

She walked to the cave entrance and glanced to the right. The smoke still rose. It probably meant they hadn't broken camp yet. At least she *hoped* they were smart enough to put out a fire in a heavily wooded area instead of leaving it unattended. Then again, she didn't have much faith in the intelligence of the *Soapa Six* crew.

She removed the gloves from her pocket and put them on. Getting down from her cave was tougher than getting up. She faced the entrance and slowly backed up, hating the feeling of falling as she stepped off the

38

ledge. She bent her knees a little to cushion the impact as she landed on the ledge ten feet below. Her synthetic legs made it painless. She climbed down the remaining fifty feet to the ground before pocketing her gloves again.

Anabel inhaled fresh air, glad that the planet had an abundance of oxygen. She'd visited others during her career that had been difficult to breath on without a mask. That would have made her job even harder.

She headed toward the smoke, taking her time and avoided getting too close to tree trunks. The tree beasts tended to sleep during the cold night hours, but they stirred early. The last thing she needed was to risk injury again while fleeing an attack. It had happened once already on her second day on the planet. They hadn't caught her, of course, but one of the beasts had thrown a huge rock. They clearly had great aim; it nailed her in the upper back. No bones had been broken, but it was days before she was able to move without pain after the bruising set in.

She'd walked for over a mile when she heard laser fire and quickly ducked down behind a bush. It had been close, but judging exact distances could be difficult in the valley. Sound tended to echo off the surrounding mountains. She cocked her head in the direction that it seemed to have come from, straining to hear voices with her enhanced hearing implant. She wasn't disappointed.

"I hope this meat doesn't poison us." It was a man speaking, and he didn't sound happy.

"Dodge ordered us to find something to cook for breakfast. Something large enough to feed us all," a second man replied. "This thing might even get us through lunch and dinner today."

"Well, I'll let the others take a bite first. Remember that yellow snake we tried the other night? It gave me stomach cramps and a case of diarrhea," whined the first.

Anabel grimaced. This Dodge guy led the men from yesterday, too, if they were taking orders from him. She only wished she could identify the would-be leader. The crew had nicknames that weren't listed in their employee files. She'd avoided talking to most of the men while working. Since there'd only been four women aboard *Soapa Six*, all the men tended to think conversation was a green light to hit on her. No one named Dodge had ever introduced himself. At least she'd confirmed the men who'd chased her were from the same camp.

Also, she'd learned to avoid eating the yellow snakes.

"Let's pick this thing up and carry it back. I don't like being out here. Wayne and Kevin didn't come back last night."

"Maybe they found the cyborg bitch and are holed up somewhere with her."

"They wouldn't dare keep her to themselves. Dodge would kill them. They've seen how good he is with his knives."

Something clicked in Anabel's mind. One of the mechanics had always kept at least half a dozen deadly blades strapped to his hips and thighs on *Soapa Six*. His real name was Herbert Shore. He'd served fifteen years in prison for murdering three bar patrons from a colony planet. He'd slit their throats in cold blood after a dispute over a card game.

He'd then been linked to seven more suspected murders, but there was no proof to charge him. She'd avoided him on the freighter after catching a single glimpse of the man. He'd clearly spent his time behind bars bulking up. She could see how he might easily take control of a group of men. They'd be terrified of the overly muscled brute.

Dread pitted in her stomach. She hoped she didn't have to engage in hand-to-hand combat with Herbert Shore, a.k.a. Dodge. She was skilled, but he'd spent fifteen years surviving Milio Prison. It was well known the guards there turned a blind eye to their charges murdering each other. There had been talk of closing the prison after some vids surfaced of extremely vicious, deadly fights. Few walked out of the place alive. Shore had managed to do it. It meant he must be one tough son of a bitch.

Anabel carefully straightened when she heard the two men grunting a bit, muttering complaints about how heavy the animal was to carry between them. She followed the sound, carefully darting between bushes and trees to keep them from spotting her. When she finally caught sight of movement, she stopped. Both were men she recognized.

Paul was in security. Dirk worked in food prep. It made sense why they'd been teamed together to hunt for food. The creature they carried was an alien version of a wild hog. It probably weighed three hundred pounds. She'd encountered many on the planet. All had run away instead of attacking. They weren't aggressive animals.

"This thing better taste damn good," Paul grunted.

"I'll do my best." Dirk struggled with his side of the animal, weaving on his feet.

Anabel crept closer, aiming for Paul, who had a blaster strapped to his thigh. She deemed him the greater threat. She waited for him to turn her way slightly before she fired.

41

The laser hit him in the chest. He went flying backward, releasing the dead animal.

"Freeze, Dirk," she ordered.

He dropped his end of the alien hog, eyes wide, and threw up his hands. "Don't shoot!"

She darted her gaze between him and the downed security officer. As she drew closer, she realized her shot had been fatal. Paul's eyes were wide open, a hole burned through his uniform shirt where his heart would have been. She gave her full attention to Dirk.

"Don't shoot! Please!"

She stopped five feet away. "Dirk Bee. You served five years for trying to murder your own mother so you could sell her property and get your inheritance early."

He paled.

"That's cold. The woman birthed and raised you on her own. They included her parole statement with your work file. Even after you attempted to kill her, she tried to find excuses for your shitty actions. That's the kind of love you don't deserve. She swore you got in with the wrong crowd...I guess some things never change." She jerked her weapon toward the dead guy. "He served twenty years for murdering two women just because they said no when he wanted sex. He raped them before stabbing them to death."

Dirk's mouth opened but he didn't say a word, just gaped at her.

"Do you want to live? Tell me how many crew members are in your camp. And don't lie to me."

"Um…we were told you were the one who blew up the ship."

"I did."

"Why?"

"Why were you coming to this planet…?"

He paled. "I only cook. What the others do isn't on me."

"You've worked for Gemini for four years. I can tell by the look in your eyes that you knew exactly what those assholes did every time you flew to remote planets. Did you ever contact the fleet to let them know your co-workers and your employers were murdering helpless aliens? That they were causing mass extinctions so your company could claim planets for their extremely profitable survey rights?"

His hands in the air began to tremble.

"I know you didn't. You turned a blind eye. Now—how many are in your camp, Dirk?"

"Eight. Well…seven," he amended, gaze flicking to Paul's body. "And two more who've gone missing. Ten of us piled into an escape pod together." He paused. "Look, it's hard to get a job with my past. Gemini was willing to hire me. I needed the work!"

Anabel felt zero sympathy. "At any cost, apparently. Did you know that there's over ninety thousand aliens on this planet? Think about that for a minute, Dirk. *Ninety thousand.* They're probably the only kind of their species, since they aren't advanced enough for space travel. Your bosses care more about profit than life. Speaking of, Gemini isn't sending another freighter. You're going to die here."

"No. Gemini wants this place bad. A recon team found precious minerals that're in high demand. They'll send another freighter to finish the job, and they'll pick us up when they come."

She snorted and lowered her weapon. "By now, Gemini no longer exists. I not only set bombs on *Soapa Six* to stop the crew from committing mass murder, but I transmitted all the proof to the fleet of what you assholes have been up to." She gave him a cold smile. "No one is coming. Not even the fleet to arrest your sorry ass. Mass murder is an automatic death sentence on United Earth. I should know; that's who I work for. That means it's on *me* to hand out punishment. I'm your judge and executioner."

Anabel saw the second he fully understood the situation. Dirk's eyes turned a bit wild and his breathing sped up.

"I try not to kill unarmed men unless they're absolute garbage." She jerked her head again to the dead security officer. "Like murderers who torture and rape their victims on top of it." She curled her lip. "But I'm still not feeling much empathy for someone shitty enough to try to murder his very loving mom. That's fucked up. Next time we meet, you're dead. Weapon or not. All of you are. Now run."

Dirk didn't hesitate. He spun and sprinted toward the trees. It would have been safer to kill him but it would cause some much-needed distraction in their camp if he returned even half as freaked out as he seemed to be.

Anabel checked her weapons as she jogged behind the fleeing jerk, really wishing she had an armored outfit. The med kits she'd taken from the two pods wouldn't help her much if she took direct laser hits to vital parts of her body.

She smelled the smoke and heard voices. Anabel slowed and changed direction. She could hear Dirk panting hard, trying to tell his fellow crew members what had happened. Anabel stopped well outside of the small clearing where they'd made camp and glanced up at the tree she hid behind. The lowest branch was about nine feet from the ground. No gorilla-like beasts were up there.

She holstered her weapons, took a deep breath, and jumped. Her hands grabbed the limb and she pulled herself up. Then she climbed high enough to get a better view. The men in the clearing were arguing and asking questions.

"The fuck?!" Dodge bellowed.

"It's true," Dirk panted. He was bent forward, hands braced on his knees as he tried to catch his breath. "She confessed it all to me."

"Did you kill her?" That was Ernie. He'd worked in general maintenance with her on *Soapa Six*. He also had a habit of telling disgusting jokes. She'd never liked him.

Dirk shook his head. "She had weird guns with her."

Dodge lunged forward and shoved Dirk. He hit the dirt hard on his ass. "Are you saying she let you go?"

Dirk nodded. "I ran."

"*Fuck!*" Dodge spun, staring in the direction Dirk had come from. "You idiot! She'll trail you right back here. Have you never gone hunting?

You injure a pack animal and it'll lead you right back to the den." Dodge rushed toward the weapons in a jumbled pile on the ground.

Anabel rolled her eyes. Dodge wasn't overly bright. Their campfire still smoldered, not quite burned out all the way yet. She could have found them that way and just outright killed Dirk.

A *smart* person would have realized she wanted them to group together around the freaked-out man...to make them easier to kill.

The second Dodge rose, Anabel took careful aim and fired her weapon. Her other hand was gripped around the branch above her, keeping her steady so she didn't miss her target.

Dodge's big frame jerked and he grabbed for his throat. Then he crashed to his knees, gasping for air that wouldn't come. It was a bad way to die but traumatic enough to do exactly what she needed. Dodge had been her biggest threat, and now he was dying.

The rest of his group stared, frozen, until his big body hit the ground seconds later.

She fired at another armed security officer she recognized, taking a head shot. Kip went down in an instant. That sent the remaining five into absolute panic as they tried to go for their weapons.

Someone got a shot off in Anabel's direction but missed. The laser blast sailed beneath her, hitting a branch somewhere below. She took him out. Two tried to run out of the clearing.

She hated to do it because of her own quirky sense of fair play, but she shot them in the back. Dirk was one of them.

Ninety thousand, she reminded herself. It helped alleviate her guilt to remember the number of aliens they'd come to the planet to slaughter. The crew had neither a sense of fair play nor an ounce of compassion. Two wrongs didn't make a right, she knew, but it sure tipped the odds in her favor. She needed to be the last human alive on the planet. Every single crew member would be a threat to the inhabitants if she let any of them live. That wasn't happening.

One of the bridge crew made it behind a large rock and took a shot. It missed, the laser tearing into a branch nearby. She ducked behind the tree trunk as more shots sailed past.

The tree she was in started to thump, and she clenched her teeth, holstered her weapon, and reached for a branch above her head with both hands.

The telltale noise came next, and she turned her head in the direction of the whistles, lowering herself a little to see past another branch. That's when she spotted the shredders. At least twenty of them rushed toward the clearing.

The bridge officer shot the tree she was in again. It sounded like he'd hit the thick trunk she was using for cover. Another shot. The smell of charred wood filled her nose.

The whistles grew louder, and so did the thumping as the herd of shredders ran closer. Anabel braced her feet, got a better grip on the branch above her, and pressed against the trunk to make herself harder to spot.

The herd ran right at the tree she was in. The entire thing shook. A few of the creatures hit the trunk but the tree remained standing. Then they were rushing past her, right into the clearing.

There was only one scream, maybe from the bridge officer. Only two men had still been alive. She closed her eyes until the screaming stopped. Then she dared to open them and turn, peeking around the trunk.

It was a mistake. The creatures were feasting on the corpses, some of them fighting over limbs. Anabel rested her forehead against the trunk.

Crunch. Crunch. Crunch.

"Fuck," she breathed silently. Shredders ate everything, even bone. She closed her eyes and tried to ignore the sickening sounds. Neither of the remaining men could have gotten away. And at least most had been dead before the shredders reached them. It also helped her feel better about the ones she'd shot in the back. To be eaten alive would have been an even worse way to go. She'd inadvertently given them a quick, painless death.

The bad news was that she probably wouldn't be able to salvage anything from the camp. The shredders would crush everything under their large bodies.

More thumping vibrated the tree and she heard more whistles. Another herd of shredders had arrived. Some of the creatures fought. They weren't aware of her up in the tree. She'd have to remain quiet until they left, then she could sneak away and go back to her cave.

Maybe take a bath, she promised herself. Violence always left her feeling dirty.

United Earth and the fleet had turned her into a killer, but they hadn't been able to remove her conscience. She couldn't kill as many people as she had, even shitty ones, without feeling like a monster. A necessary one, justified even...but it was still hard to digest being a killer.

Ninety thousand, she silently reminded herself. *Those crew members deserved it. Monsters need other monsters to stop them.*

Something thumped hard enough against the tree to jolt her.

Anabel looked down to find two of the shredders using the trunk to scratch an itch. Their big bodies shook the entire tree as they slammed their sides against it, rubbing vigorously. Cracks and pops sounded from the wood.

She silently mouthed a curse and glanced at the nearest tree to the one she hid in. The beasts were large enough to take her tree down—with her in it, if she remained where she was. It was time to leave. She'd have to travel through the trees.

That was something she'd never been trained to do, and the idea of leaping from one tree to another at her current height filled her with rare fear. One screwup and she'd fall, becoming yet another meal for the shredders. There were too many deadly beasts to miss a new meal dropping into their midst. Even if she landed without injury, they could move pretty fast.

"Don't make a mistake," she mouthed aloud. Then she took a few deep breaths before launching out of one tree toward the next.

* * * * *

Raze walked off his ship, taking in the beautiful planet they'd landed on. It reminded him of where he'd grown up...

He quickly pushed that thought away. That was one place he never wanted to return to. His birth grouping wouldn't welcome him, and he had no longing to see them, either. They'd already banished him once.

Bruck stopped beside him. "Are you thinking what I am?"

"Home."

"We're better off without our birth grouping...and all the others who wanted us gone." Bruck lifted a scanner pad. "There are thirty-two human life signs. Some are in small groups but a few are on their own. We can reach them all before the sun goes down if we transform into our battle forms."

"No. We have no idea what kind of life forms we'll be up against. It's best if we use our body shields instead of having to fight any we meet."

"Scans show some large predators that seem to hunt in packs." Bruck paused. Then he snarled.

"What?"

"The robot scout just updated the readings. I have it set to do sweeps every hour in case the humans are traveling, and to know where the largest predators are." He pointed at the pad. "There was a group of nine humans at this location previously. Now all but one is dead." He tapped the pad and snarled again. "Look. There are thirty-four predator animals where they were."

Raze snarled too. He hoped one of the dead humans hadn't been the female they sought.

"She probably wouldn't be with other humans if she's the reason their freighter got destroyed. They would seek revenge," Bruck said, as if reading his thoughts.

Raze met his gaze. "If they are aware she is responsible."

"The closest single life sign is here." Bruck pointed to a red dot. "Shall we hunt together?"

"No. We'll split up. It's faster. Check the single life signs first."

Bruck passed over another pad. "It updates every hour, remember."

Raze accepted the device and studied the readings. Then he lifted his wrist, activating communications to speak to Prasky. "Seal the ship and conceal it. We don't want humans, alien inhabitants, or native animals to attack while we're gone."

The third member of their grouping responded immediately. "Bring back fresh meat."

Raze turned, watching as the large ship disappeared. He could still see where the long grass in the field had been trampled by the weight of *Satrono* but it quickly transformed to match the area. He loved the holographic technology that they'd earned from the Brani.

"I hope the Brani hire us again," Bruck chuckled. "We always get the best technology from them. I want that stun wave weapon we saw protecting one of their transports."

Raze grinned. "We think too much alike at times. It *would* be easier if we could put everything to sleep within a short radius."

"Not everything. Some of our enemies' body shields protect them against it. That's why we traded a job for our own shields. I don't miss our bulky protective suits."

"And it wouldn't be a challenge if everything was stunned. Where is the enjoyment in hunting sleeping prey?"

Bruck laughed. "Agreed. We would grow bored if our prey was too easy to catch."

Raze motioned with his hand. "I'll head this way. We'll meet back here when darkness falls. Good hunting."

"I'm certain one of us will find the female."

Raze wished he could feel the same confidence. A lone human female on an unfamiliar planet didn't have the best chances of survival. He nodded anyway, taking off at a jog and using the pad to guide him toward a single life sign. He left the clearing and entered thick woods. Tall trees shaded him from the planet's sun. He inhaled deeply, picking up an animal. It smelled of fur and mud.

Minutes later, he came across the wildlife. It had a round body on four short legs, and two tusks growing from the frontal region of the head. It spotted him and fled.

Part of Raze was tempted to chase it down for fun. He resisted. It was nice reprieve, being on a planet instead of his ship, but he was there to locate a female. Maybe he'd go hunting for that fresh meat Prasky demanded once he had the target secured on *Satrono*.

Twenty minutes later he slowed, checking the scan results. The life form dot was directly ahead. It was possible they might no longer be there, since the scans only updated hourly, but he proceeded with caution all the same.

He heard the human male before he spotted him. The male spoke loudly, the sound of snapping twigs accompanying the verbal barrage. Raze crept forward, remaining hidden.

The trees parted to reveal a very small wedge of ground bathed in sunlight. A human male seemed to be attempting to build a shelter with broken branches. It had to be the sorriest shelter Raze had ever seen. The location was equally bad.

"I want a fucking steak and a comfortable bunk. And a woman. Gemini better pay me for being stuck out here. Loads of fucking overtime!"

Raze backed away, not wanting the male to become aware of his presence. Once he put some distance between them, he looked at the scanner again. It hadn't updated yet, but the next nearest single life sign in the direction he'd chosen was in the vicinity of the eight dead humans.

Bruck was probably right; he doubted the female would travel with males if she'd destroyed their ship, but it was possible she'd been captured. He needed to view the bodies. He would have to be careful of the large pack of wildlife in that same area.

He was almost to the location when the stink had him halting again. Whistles also sounded. He put the pad away and freed his hands, unleashing his claws. Then he leapt at a thick tree trunk, climbing it easily.

A smile curved his lips. He did miss living on a planet. His childhood memories were good. Until the day came when everything had gone bad.

He returned his focus to the task at hand, climbing higher until he spotted a nearby clearing.

The dozens of creatures were large and eating human bodies. Not that much of them remained. A soft growl rumbled from him. He narrowed his eyes, scanning what was left of the dead. None of the bodies appeared to be that of a female, but it was difficult to tell.

He began to strip out of his clothing, carefully securing each piece on the tree limbs. His boots and the pad were left wedged between a branch and the trunk. He climbed down to a lower branch, flexed his body, and intentionally remembered the day he'd been banished from his planet.

Rage had him seeing red, his bones cracking.

He shifted into his battle form, leapt from the branch to the ground, and roared. He surged forward, attacking the creature closest to him. He landed on its furry back, using his claws to rip into the animal. It screeched in agony.

He roared louder.

The other creatures panicked at his sudden appearance. He wasn't anything they'd ever seen before. They ran, scattering, and their big bodies were heavy enough to make the ground thump and vibrate.

He finished off the creature he'd attacked, withdrew his claws from its still warm flesh, and padded toward the human remains. Most were missing large pieces but a couple had enough left to identify them as males. The few he couldn't be certain of, he sniffed. They scented male. At least to him. He wasn't an expert on humans.

The faint sounds of the creatures retreating faded and Raze cocked his head, listening. Where was the surviving human?

He glanced around, not hearing or seeing any movement. Then he lifted his head to the trees. It was possible that one of them had been smart enough to climb above the large animals in hopes of staying safe.

He checked each tree around the clearing, not spotting anyone. The sight of damage on one, however, caught his attention. He walked to the base of the tree and climbed. Laser fire had scarred the trunk in several places on one side, and a lower branch also sagged from damage. He adjusted his big body, using his claws to circle the trunk to the other side.

The faint scent had him growling as he sniffed. *Female.* He was certain. A human had been in this tree, and someone had tried to shoot her out of it. He inhaled her scent again, memorizing it. It was faintly on the bark, as if she'd rubbed against the trunk just enough to leave a trace of herself behind.

He turned his head, looking for a way the female could have escaped if she'd needed to. There were more trees nearby, but the branches appeared too thin to hold much weight, even a small human. He walked along a thick branch and leapt into the nearest tree with a sturdy limb.

A soft gasp of surprise left him as he picked up her scent there.

He turned his head, staring at the tree he'd jumped from. It was a good ten-foot distance, at least. He wasn't aware that humans had such abilities.

Clever and talented human. Or desperate.

Either way, Raze was intrigued and impressed. He tried to follow her scent but lost it two trees later. He jumped down and used vegetation to scrub away the blood of the animal he'd killed from his body before it dried. Then Raze retrieved his belongs before shifting back to his relaxed form on two legs. He put on his boots and pants, not wanting to stain one of his favorite shirts with the blood he hadn't been able to remove.

He checked the pad, and it had updated. The single life form had moved a great distance from the area. He grinned.

"You are fast too, female." He felt a sudden surge of excitement. His hunt might soon be over...but it wouldn't be an easy one.

Chapter Three

Anabel climbed out of the water, shaking her head vigorously since she didn't have a towel to dry her hair. She visually scanned the area, not liking how many trees surrounded her. Danger could easily remain hidden until it was too late. But this was the only part of the creek deep enough to submerge her body when she sat on the bottom, and it had been nice to get clean.

There was a wide river not too far away, but she hadn't scoped out the dangers of whatever alien creatures might live in the deeper water. With her luck, it would be killer fish the size of Earth whales or something like a crocodile. She stuck to the creeks for bathing, since they were shallow and clear enough to see all the way to the bottom, enabling her to spot anything that might swim her way.

Now that she'd gotten clean, her mind switched back to earlier. An entire camp had been wiped out. That called for taking the rest of the day off. She'd had her fill of killing. She picked up her jumpsuit, which she'd left to warm in the sun, and put it on, not caring how damp it would become from her body. Her only plans were to return to her cave, climb into bed, and spend the evening daydreaming.

She did that a lot to pass the time. Not that she had much to fantasize about. Her life would end on this planet at some point. It would also be lonely, since she didn't see the local aliens becoming her friends. It was against fleet regulations, anyway. The reptilian race wasn't advanced in any way, and therefore she couldn't risk influencing their culture.

Once the human threat was over, she should probably figure out a way to disassemble each pod enough to be able to drag the parts into one of the rivers. That would be the responsible thing to do, to keep future generations of aliens from having any proof of otherworld visitors. That was in the handbook, too. Destroy or hide any evidence of an intrusion on a primitive planet.

"I hate that fucking handbook and their stupid rules. I should be able to at least *try* to make alien friends," she muttered, bending over to pick up her belt. She'd strap her weapons on first, before donning her boots.

Someone grabbed her arm near the elbow and jerked her upright. Shocked, Anabel gasped and spun, blindly punching with her free hand.

Her fist made contact with a solid mass of hot flesh. Her hit didn't even make the firm body stumble back. She dropped the belt to free her other hand. She'd need both for this fight.

Anabel glanced up. Then adjusted her chin even more.

It was a tall male alien, not a reptilian native, and certainly not one of the crew of the *Soapa Six*. They'd all been human.

"Female," he said in a deep, growly voice. "I have captured you."

Anabel heard his words, realized he spoke in perfect English, and instinct took over. She yanked her arm free of his grasp and threw her body against his much bigger one. It knocked him off balance enough to force him back a step, and she threw another punch, going for his throat to take him down.

He dropped a wrapped bundle of material he carried in his other arm as he flinched away. She missed his throat. The alien had quick reflexes.

She jumped back and kicked out, targeting the kneecap area of his humanoid body.

He avoided the blow with a twist of his leg, then *she* was the one who had to retreat. The bastard was nimble for six-and-a-half feet of bulky male who had to weigh close to three hundred pounds, if she had to guess at a glance. He only wore pants and boots. She assessed every inch of him as they circled each other.

His race looked familiar but she couldn't place it, too busy trying to find a weak point to attack on his muscled body. His skin was dark, with a soft fuzzy texture. The alien possessed a broad chest and massive biceps. Well...every inch of him seemed packed with muscle, actually.

He had pointed ears, a mass of curly black hair on the top of his head only, but it could flow down his back. From her frontal view, she couldn't tell for sure. The sides of his head appeared to be shaved, or perhaps he couldn't grow hair there.

His eyes were a pale blue and feline-looking, the pupils vertical slits instead of round. Something about that trait clicked in her brain, but she didn't have time to follow the thought. The big bastard had snuck up on her—something not easy to do—and grabbed her.

That screamed "hostile intent" to Anabel.

She wasn't about to be captured by some alien. That rarely ended well for humans. Especially women. She'd gone undercover a few times in the past when women had disappeared from colonies, and even from a few space stations. Not all of them had been taken by asshole humans forcing them into the sex trade. Some alien races wanted human women for sex slaves, too. That wouldn't become her future.

She fisted her hands tighter and lunged again, trying to land punches on his body that she hoped would take him down and give her a shot at escape. He used his big open hands to deflect the blows, easily taking the rapid punches against his palms. The sight of sharp claws growing from his fingertips alarmed her, but she'd been trained too well to let anything thwart her attempt to incapacitate him.

The alien bastard had the nerve to laugh.

Anabel switched tactics, leaping at him bodily. His eyes widened and his massive hands gripped her hips. She felt the tips of those sharp claws along her butt but ignored them, since there wasn't any pain.

She'd hit him chest to chest when she'd jumped, making him stagger, the weight of her body heavier than anyone would guess by appearances, thanks to her synthetic legs. With his hands occupied, she finally landed a blow to his face. The force of the punch made his entire head snap back, and he grunted.

They hit the ground, Anabel sprawled on top of him. She adjusted her position fast, straddling his waist and squeezing her knees against his ribs as she punched at his throat and face, landing more blows.

His hold on her waist tightened before she was suddenly thrown. Shock jolted through her—the bastard had just proven he was super strong. No human guy could have torn her off him once she got a grip with her knees. She landed in the creek, hitting the water and going under.

She surfaced as he was getting to his feet. Red showed on his full bottom lip that she'd smashed with her fist. He reached up and swiped at it, gazing at the blood on the back of his hand, then his gaze locked with hers.

Anabel climbed out of the creek on the other side and thought about making a run for it, but her weapons were across the water. She wasn't about to abandon them, or her boots. The only other footwear she had were the ruined work shoes she'd worn the day she'd sabotaged *Soapa Six*.

"Who in the hell are you?" she shouted at the alien.

He lowered his hand and wiped the blood on his black pants. "I'm a bounty hunter. Stop fighting me, female. I'm taking you back to my ship and plan to hand you over to the male who paid me to find you."

Surprised at his answer, Anabel gaped at him as she pushed her wet hair off her face. "There's a bounty on me?"

That was bad news. Somehow, Gemini still existed.

Kurt must not have gotten her message—or the proof she'd transmitted. That wasn't supposed to happen. One rocket may have been lost, but surely not two.

Kurt had been aboard the *Russel*, a stealth fleet ship waiting at the edge of safe space travel lanes. The navigation system on all the rockets were programed to fly directly to the *Russel*.

"Yes. Come with me peacefully, female. You will not be harmed. I give you my oath."

His deep voice didn't convince her one tiny bit that he wasn't a liar. "Right. Sure." Anabel really needed to get to her weapons and boots. Especially her boots. She could abandon them but her feet would have no protection. That sounded hellish. Her legs might be synthetic, but the skin and nerves weren't. She still felt pain.

"How much are you being paid? I'll double it if you walk away. I can give you an account access code useable on any space station or colony where humans are located." It was worth a shot. Not that the emergency funds she had access to would be near enough to buy her freedom, but he wouldn't realize that until he was far from her.

His black eyebrows arched. "I gave my oath to my client to retrieve you. This isn't a negotiation."

He was smart. Anabel would give him that. "I have a million Earth creds in there," she lied. "Don't be hasty. Gemini won't pay that." She figured they actually would, if it meant saving their asses, but the alien bounty hunter didn't need to know that, either.

He stepped closer to the creek. "Who?"

She huffed in frustration. "The man who hired you, whoever he was, works for Gemini. It's a corrupt company based on Earth. They hate aliens, lie about virtually everything, and will screw you on this deal. You can't trust them. They'll kill you before they actually pay what they said they would."

"That is not my client."

That had her scowling. "Who is?"

"A Veslor male."

The news stunned her—but something suddenly clicked. *"You're* a Veslor, aren't you?"

"Yes."

She shivered as the wind blew over her. It was a little chilly, what with her being soaking wet from the cold creek. "Your people once helped a fleet vessel in distress."

He inhaled deeply, his muscular chest expanding. He was a good-looking alien. There was no denying that. She'd even admit that he was damn sexy. That was rare, in her experience. She'd had to deal with all manner of aliens races in her career. Most grossed her out or left her feeling deeply disturbed by their appearance.

Ke'ters came to mind. She'd helped get revenge against them for an incident on the *Gorison Traveler*. The fleet had sent four stealth ships to take out a couple Ke'ter vessels as payback and a "don't fuck with humans ever again" message. Not that she could share that. It was classified.

"I'm impressed by you, female."

She walked closer to the edge of the creek, moved down a little, and then jumped over the narrowest part. It was only about five feet across. He watched her closely but didn't move. She slowly approached her weapons and boots.

"Why is that? I'm going to put on my boots."

"Don't go for your weapons."

"I wouldn't dream of it," she lied again.

He suddenly lunged toward her and Anabel stumbled back, fists up, prepared to fight. He didn't come at her, though. Instead, he crouched near her belongings, lifted her weapons, and tossed them into the creek.

Disbelief filled her as she watched them sink below the water's surface.

He stood and backed off, leaving her belt and boots.

She glared at him "That wasn't nice."

"I don't feel like being shot."

"Back off more. I don't trust you."

He did as she demanded, which surprised her, but she took a seat, yanking on her boots and sealing them around her ankles. Part of her expected him to attack while she was down but he remained still.

She stood, happy to have her boots on. They'd be impossible to replace. She had small feet. None of the crew she had yet to kill would wear her size.

"We will return to my ship now." He gave her his back, walking toward the bundled cloth he'd dropped.

Anabel was in motion as soon as he turned. She spun, taking off. She leapt over the wider part of the creek, moving as fast as possible. A roar that sounded like a lion came from behind her. She assumed he must have some type of alien cat in his DNA to have those eyes and make that noise.

She picked up her speed, dodging trees. No human could catch her once she got going. As she ran, she almost smiled. The weapons could be replaced when she tracked down more crew members; she was certain some had to be armed. She just needed to lose the alien bounty hunter first.

Her confidence disappeared fast when she heard something heavy gaining on her.

She glanced back—and the alien ran right behind her. It almost made her stumble but she faced forward, nearly tripping on a bush. A rumble of a snarl came from her pursuer.

That was her only warning before two large arms wrapped her around her middle.

She was too out of breath to even curse. She tensed, expecting a hell of a lot of pain when she hit the ground with him on top of her. It didn't happen. She went down, alright—but on top of his large, solid body. His arms tightened around her as she opened her eyes, staring at the treetops and sky above, her back to his chest.

The alien had obviously twisted them in the air when he'd tackled her to take the brunt of their landing, surprising her yet again. It would have been to his advantage to crush her beneath him. She grabbed his wrists, trying to open his arms to free her middle.

He suddenly rolled them, and his weight was enough to knock the oxygen from her lungs. He grabbed her wrists and yanked them to her sides. He pinned her flat, even using his feet to spread her legs enough that she couldn't get purchase to try to roll him off her.

"Cease, female," he panted next to her ear. "You are captured."

She threw her head back. Pain exploded in her skull as she made contact, probably with his chin. He grunted but his hold on her wrists didn't go lax for even a split second. He just shoved his head to the side of hers, forcing her cheek into the dirt.

"Enough!" he snarled.

"Fuck you." She shoved her ass up against his front, trying to wiggle out from under him.

The feel of something hard pressed against her had Anabel going still when he drove his hips forward to force her flat. He not only looked humanoid...but seemed to have every *other* part associated with a male body. She'd trained with enough guys to know exactly what was pressing between her butt cheeks.

"You're turned-on? You sick bastard!"

"That is *your* fault."

She panted, not happy to have her face pressed against the dirt or his dick against her ass. "Right. Sure it is. All men are pigs. I'm fighting for my freedom while you're thinking about sex. Give me a break—and the answer is *hell no*. Get off me!"

"You engaged me in battle." He slowly lifted his head enough that she could move hers.

She twisted her neck, their faces close together. They locked gazes.

"You appear confused. Our females engage us in battle as foreplay."

She studied him. She hadn't hit his chin with the back of her head, like she'd thought. The skin on his cheekbone had been split a tiny bit, some blood smeared on his face from the cut. She didn't feel an ounce of guilt. Especially since what felt like a large, hard penis was still wedged between her butt cheeks. Her jumpsuit remained soaked and plastered to her skin. She guessed the cold wetness didn't bother his libido.

"You've got a twisted culture then."

"Stop fighting me, female. You can't win. I respect you for your attempt and you've impressed me with your bravery, but enough. We are returning to my ship."

"I can't let that happen. Gemini will kill me."

"I do not work for the company you mentioned. My client is another Veslor."

That still didn't make any sense to her, no matter how many times he said it. She'd never pissed off one of those aliens before, as far as she knew. "Why would a Veslor put a bounty on me?"

"You are a relative to his grouping."

"Um...no. I'm not."

"You are."

Anabel chewed on her bottom lip, a bad habit of hers when she mulled things over, but then she spat when dirt ended up on her tongue.

It was also distracting that the alien remained hard. His dick felt like a metal pipe between her cheeks. *Doesn't that thing ever soften?*

"Let me up and I won't run. At least until after we talk. I give my word."

He didn't move his big body off her or ease his hold on her wrists. "I do not trust you, female."

She couldn't really blame him after she'd already tried to ditch him once. He had adjusted his oversized body until she wasn't in any danger of being crushed by his weight, and he'd made sure she could breathe fine. It wasn't exactly comfortable, though, being pinned against the ground.

"Maybe you're after another woman who was on *Soapa Six*. I admit there were very few of us, but I wasn't the only one. I've never been to Veslor space, if this woman screwed over one of your people. You're the first one I've ever met. Swear. I never joined a grouping. Is that like a gang? You've got the wrong woman."

"You are Anabel Brick. I was given an image of you but warned it is outdated. Your hair is longer now but you *are* the female I seek. You even have the mar on your forehead."

Her heart pounded in her chest as she stared into his eyes. He knew her real name. Not the one she'd been assigned to go undercover on *Soapa Six*. The crew knew her as Annie Spindle.

The Veslor had her full attention now.

"A grouping is not a gang," he continued, appearing insulted. "It is family made of the heart."

"Okay. Well, I didn't join a family of the heart, either. Again, you're the first Veslor I've ever met. Who told you that name?"

"Roth. He is the grouping leader who hired me to hunt you. Your relative is mated to a male in his grouping."

Anabel was stumped. She took a deep breath and coughed, obviously too close to the dirt, since she inhaled a little of it.

The big alien on top of her adjusted their arms, bringing them closer to her body. "You may lift up a little but do not ram me with your head again. You won't like the consequences." He raised his upper body to give her a little room to do just that.

She put weight on her forearms and pulled her face and upper chest a little off the ground. "I'm getting a kink in my neck from twisting to see your face."

His eyes narrowed with suspicion but he leaned a little to the side, putting his face closer. He glanced at her mouth. "Do not bite." He flashed some scary fangs. "I will bite back."

"Got it. No biting." She didn't want to experience his version of payback. His fangs looked like they would cause way more damage than her own teeth. "Deal. So this Roth told you my name? Did you get my image from him too? You implied that you did."

"Yes. The mate gave it to him to make certain I brought the right female to his grouping."

It had to be an old enemy she'd made. Shock and anger filled her. As an operative, she was deeply classified. Whoever betrayed her had to be one of her direct bosses. "Where are you supposed to take me?" Their destination might help her discover who had it out for her.

"Roth is currently living aboard *Defcon Red* with his grouping. Our king asked them to assist the humans."

Astonishment ripped through her. She knew that name well. Her sister had been assigned to the fleet battle vessel. "Are you fucking kidding me right now?"

He scowled. "No prank."

She broke her gaze and stared at the ground, mind racing. Her baby sister was an alien research specialist. As if being a medical doctor for humans hadn't been enough for the little overachiever.

Tears filled her eyes, blinding her.

How would Jessa know to send someone after her? Kurt would never be allowed to tell her sister the truth about her mission, or the outcome.

Then again, if anyone could make friends with an alien race and send them to rescue her ass from an out-of-bounds planet, it would be an alien research specialist.

"Female, you are in distress. There is no need. You will be taken to Roth's grouping and returned to your female relative unharmed."

"That little idiot must have hacked into fleet records to learn the truth. I'm going to wring her neck if the fleet doesn't arrest Jessa before I see her!"

"You will not harm a mate." He pressed against her back tighter. "That is a killing offense. Her mate and his grouping would seek vengeance for even attempting it. All Veslors would. It is an unforgivable crime to our people."

She blinked her tears away and twisted to glare at him. "Not *literally*. Jessa is my baby sister. I'd never actually hurt her. I might spank her ass, though. Damn it! She swore she'd never mess with fleet databases when it came to me, but if anyone could hack that deep, it would be Jessa. Her and that damn brain implant they shoved into her head. They'll have her arrested for treason and I won't be able to save her! She probably broke her promise after being told I'd died, wanting the details of exactly how it happened. Instead, she must've seen the last transmission I sent to my handler...

"*Fuck!*" She started to struggle. "Let me go!"

"No." He yanked her arms farther from her body and pinned her tight to the ground again. It also pressed his large, still-hard penis tighter against her ass.

"Watch that thing! You'll crush my tailbone."

He lifted his hips a little but the weight of his alien penis remained. Anabel lay there, helpless, fuming. The fleet would arrest her sister if they ever discovered what Jessa had done.

Anabel being returned alive to a fleet vessel would be all the proof they needed.

"Damn it!" She wanted to scream.

"I will return you to Roth's grouping and your sister."

"You can't."

"I will."

"Fuck!" Anabel pushed her ass against him in frustration, since she didn't want to risk another blow to the back of the head again by his rock-hard face.

"Are you attempting foreplay?"

She snorted. "I need to hit something!"

He surprised her again when he suddenly released her, removing his weight from her back. She rolled, staring up at him. He retreated a few steps and opened his arms in a taunting gesture, inviting her to attack him. "Foreplay it is. This time, don't run."

She sat up, her gaze going to the front of his black pants. The outline of his cock was clear. There was no missing the sight of a turned-on Veslor. *Everything* on this guy was oversized. "You can't return me to the fleet. They'll figure out what my sister did. They'll arrest Jessa. Treason is a death sentence if she's convicted, and she *will be* eventually, after they've used her until her contract is up. Death is the only retirement she'll ever see. The fleet doesn't fuck around about highly classified missions being hacked. The shit I do...my bosses will do *anything* to prevent the details from being leaked. There's no other way she would have known where I was, or that I'm not really dead, unless she obtained that information illegally."

"Her mate won't allow anyone to take her from him."

She snorted. The Veslor was clueless if he thought the fleet would care about pissing off an alien. Hell, the big bosses wouldn't even count the alien as her sister's...husband? She figured that was the closest term to use for what a mate might be considered.

She and her sister didn't have the right to get married until their fleet contracts ended.

"Oh, they'll arrest Jessa, alright. She's too valuable to execute for treason immediately, but they'll stash her somewhere remote where they can keep a close eye on her until she's worked off her debt. Hell, they'll probably use what she did as an excuse to extend her contract for life, to make sure she can never tell what she's learned after reading my real file."

"Her mate and their grouping will take her to Veslor-controlled space before he allows anyone to take her from him. Our king would refuse to hand a mate over to your Earth."

"And they'd just send someone like me to go in and bring her back to Earth."

His eyebrows rose.

"Never mind... I'm sure you're right and her mate will totally protect her." Anabel resisted rolling her eyes. There was no reason to argue with him anymore. She wasn't allowing him to take her off the planet. It was the only way her sister would be safe from any blowback her rescue caused. She just needed to find an opportunity to escape the bounty hunter. And she would.

"I am taking you to my ship and we are leaving. Get up. And don't fight me unless you want to test a mating." His gaze ran over her body, and he shook his head. "That would be a bad outcome for both of us."

"We can't leave now."

"The female mate will be safe from your fleet."

"There's that...but I also have a job to finish here first. I can't leave yet."

"We *are* leaving." He took a step closer.

"What's your name?"

"Raze."

She lifted her hands, showing her palms. "Okay. Cool name. How much did Roth and my sister tell you about how I ended up on this planet?"

"You blew up the Earth ship you were traveling on. We passed it coming here."

"Did they tell you why?"

He shook his head. "It doesn't matter."

"Oh, but it does. Do you have any morals, Veslor?"

He cocked his head.

"The human crew of *Soapa Six* came here to exterminate every sentient alien living on this planet. They're reptilian people who are extremely primitive. We're talking fur clothing and spears. The aliens are

73

helpless against modern weapons. The crew was paid to carry out a mass extinction of their entire race."

He gaped at her. "Why?"

Anabel hesitated, needing to be careful of what she said. It was highly doubtful bounty hunters would speak with others. They tended to be loners. Then again, they were also known to sell information if they felt it was juicy enough. "I'm a police officer. Do you know what that is?" That was close enough to the truth. She did hunt and take out bad guys.

"Law-seeker."

"Yes. I was sent undercover on the freighter to find out why they were traveling to such dangerous areas of space. It was suspicious, to say the least. Their company seems law-abiding, but my bosses suspected otherwise. It was *my* job to find out either way and get proof so they could be arrested if they've been committing crimes. I found the opportunity to break into the captain's cabin and gained access to his files. I learned that everyone on that freighter is an ex-convict. It turns out that Gemini—that's the company that employs them—purposely picked that crew to come here and murder all the aliens on this planet."

He growled, looking pissed.

"Do you know what ex-convict means?"

"It sounds bad."

"They served time in prison for committing horrible crimes like murder. Gemini obviously hired them because they wanted people who wouldn't hesitate to kill. I blew up the freighter to prevent them from hurting any aliens. But some managed to escape in pods and reached the surface. I've been hunting the survivors and taking them out. The aliens living here have no chance against laser rifles."

The Veslor snarled.

Anabel slowly got to her feet. "Those criminals have already killed some aliens. I found the bodies. You were able to locate me, so I take it you have some tracking ability or drones to scan for life signs. Will you help me take out the threat to the aliens here? I can prove everything that I've said, if you think I'm lying. I downloaded all the employee files from the captain's personal computer. I can even show you the order from the company telling the crew what to do here. They *will* keep killing if I don't stop them."

He studied her with his strangely appealing blue gaze. "That's why you caused all that damage to the Earth ship?"

She nodded. "I had to take out the threat to the aliens living here before the crew set up in orbit. At that point, they would have started sending teams in shuttles to locate alien communities and wipe them out to steal ownership of this planet."

"I will see your proof, and if they are bad humans, we will hunt them."

She relaxed. "Thank you."

"Then I will take you to Roth and his grouping."

Anabel sighed. She'd have to change his mind to protect Jessa, but for now, she'd won half the battle. Raze wasn't going to try to force her off the planet while some of the crew remained alive.

Chapter Four

Raze tended to believe the female. He'd dealt with other aliens slaughtering each other to steal natural resources and to claim a new world to call home. It wasn't noble. "What happened with the beasts?"

Anabel cocked her head. "What beasts?"

"I tracked life signs to a group of humans. I found bodies instead, being eaten by beasts, but you survived. I also saw where the humans must have fired on you in the trees."

"Ah. The shredders. It's what I call the...beasts. Nasty creatures. Noises like laser fire draw their attention. That's why I was up in a tree, where the shredders couldn't reach me. I'd tracked that group of humans to the clearing, killing most of them before the beasts arrived. There are at least six herds of shredders that I've seen in this valley." She glanced at Raze. "But you ran into shredders and survived? Impressive."

"I'm Veslor. Beasts fear *me*."

She remembered reading a report of what had happened on the *Gorison Traveler*. "You're not wearing body armor, unless you ditched it."

"I don't need it."

Anabel suddenly noticed that his claws had retracted into his fingertips. "Neat trick with your hands." She raised hers and pointed to her fingernails. "Do you flash those sharp weapons hidden under your skin and roar to make them afraid?"

"I transformed into my battle form."

That's when she remembered hearing a rumor about Veslors being shapeshifters. "That's true then? You...um...go from this shape into something else?"

He nodded.

"Let me guess. It's something feline?"

"I know that word. We're more dangerous than your Earth versions."

"I believe that. You don't appear cuddly or cute. You're too big and fierce looking. How did you learn Earth standard so well? You speak it perfectly."

"All Veslors who travel in space receive implants. I accessed your language when Roth hired me. He said it's what you spoke. I wanted us to be able to communicate well."

"When did you take the job?"

"It's been six solar cycles."

She knew that equated to days. "Damn. That's fast to learn a language."

"It is a rapid process. We keep data on all known races. I downloaded your language in minutes."

"I'd love one of those implants."

"You are not a Veslor."

"Right. You probably don't share your tech with us. You said that my sister is a mate to a Veslor?"

"Is she your relative living on *Defcon Red*?"

"Jessa is the *only* relative I have. Period. Our parents died when we were young kids. We had an uncle and aunt living on Earth but neither of them wanted the burden of raising us. I'm not even sure if they're still alive or not. We grew up as orphans on Mars, raised by the fleet."

Fury gripped Raze. "Your family turned their backs on you while you were cubs?"

"Yes. We came with some heavy medical bills, if they'd taken responsibility for us. That doesn't make me forgive them, though. Jessa, my sister, is my only family. I never bothered to look up our aunt or uncle to find out what happened to them once I was able to. I didn't care. But we're getting off the topic. My sister is mates with a Veslor?"

"That is what Roth said. You are the relative to one of their mates."

"What do you know about this Roth?"

"We can discuss that once we reach my ship."

The female shook her head. "No way. I'm not going anywhere until I've taken out every other human on this planet."

"I agree that they need to die if they're planning to kill the inhabitants of this world."

"You could lie, take me to your ship, and fly us away. I'm not going to your ship until my work here is done. I've already come across dead aliens that the crew murdered. That was too many."

Raze growled, frustrated. "I would not do that. You told me why we need to stay a little longer. I wish to gather my males. My grouping can track the other humans faster than you can on your own. I give you my oath."

"I don't trust you."

He growled. "You should. I have honor."

"You admitted that you're a bounty hunter. I've come across others in your line of work plenty of times. They would turn in their own beloved mothers if the price was right."

The female insulted him greatly. "I am a Veslor. Our oath is always kept when given. It is a matter of honor."

The frustrating female frowned at him.

He tried to assure her. "Roth would not have entrusted my grouping to retrieve the female relative of a mate if my honor wasn't in good standing. He would only send someone he trusted to bring you back safe and unharmed."

She stared at him for long seconds. "If he was a good guy. I know nothing about this Roth."

"Our king sent Roth's grouping to aid the humans. Those males are highly revered as fighters." It was possible the female didn't understand. "They are the best of our people to represent Veslors to your fleet. Do not insult Roth or his grouping males. Your sister is mated to one of our most respected fighters."

The human finally inhaled deeply and blew it out. "Fine. I'll have to take your word on that. I am *not* going to your ship, though. You can go back to it and get your men to help us hunt the remaining crew members. I'll meet you here in the morning. Say an hour after the sun rises? Does that work for you?"

He was stunned. "You expect me to leave you here?"

"I do."

His gaze ran over her quickly. "I am not leaving you unprotected."

She rolled her eyes. "Trust me. I'll be fine."

"I captured you. So could the humans."

"You're an alien. The remaining crew can't run as fast as you did to catch me."

He cocked his head, confused. "You're also human."

"I am. But I'm also a little more. I take it that Jessa didn't tell you I'm modified. I lost both of my feet when I was a kid."

Shocked, Raze stared down at her boots. He'd seen her bare feet before she'd put them on. They were dainty but appeared to be flesh.

She sighed. "You can't tell by looking, or hell, even by feeling them. Medical scans won't reveal the truth, either. They'll only see real legs because of a nifty transmitter device imbedded in each one." She reached down, touching her fingertips to the area above one of her knees. "Everything from this point down is mostly synthetic on both of my legs." She straightened. "I can outrun humans easily."

"Your entire lower legs are robotic?"

"You could say that."

"I saw flesh."

"My lower legs have real cloned flesh to cover my...robotics."

He shook his head. "I am still not leaving you." He lifted his wrist, pressed a finger to a black band. He switched to his own language, knowing the female wouldn't understand Veslor. "I have located our target."

Bruck responded immediately. "Is the female alive?"

"Yes. She is unharmed." Raze noticed the frown return to Anabel's face. She didn't like not knowing what he was saying.

Prasky snarled, his anger clear. "Females are trouble."

Raze sighed. "Enough," he ordered the male. "She is human, not Delorian. This female is harmless to us."

Silence came over the communications.

"We have a problem. The female claims the other humans on this planet wish to kill all the inhabitants to steal their planet."

"Humans," Prasky spat. "Always trouble."

Their interactions with some humans on space stations over the years had left them tending to distrust the race. Raze couldn't deny that. "Have you come across other humans in your hunt today, Bruck?"

"Two, but both were male. I concealed myself from them."

"Head back to *Satrono*. I'm bringing the female in but we aren't leaving the planet yet. The female says she has proof of her claims. If true, we need to hunt and kill the other humans before we go."

"We're killing them?" For the first time, Prasky's tone was more shocked than angry.

"We are protectors," Raze reminded them. "We will review her proof before we take action."

"I am heading back to our ship now," Bruck informed him.

"See you both soon. The female will fight. She doesn't want to come to *Satrono*. Ready soft restraints, Prasky."

"You stated she couldn't harm us. Which is it?" he snarled.

"Do it," Raze snarled back, ending the communications.

Anabel stood a few feet away, watching him warily. "What was all that about? I don't know growl. I caught a few words though, like 'humans.'"

Raze knew she'd fight him rather than willingly going to his ship. He withdrew a small patch he kept trapped between his wrist and communicator, careful not to touch the center as he activated it by breaking the seal with his claw. "I will meet you here tomorrow after sunrise."

She appeared relieved. He hated deceit, but he also didn't want to harm the female. She'd already proven that she'd fight him to the exclusion of her own safety. He held out his hand. "Shake on it. That's what you humans do, correct?"

"Words are fine."

He lunged, surprising her, and slapped the patch on the side of her neck. She threw a punch at his chest but it didn't hurt. The drug worked fast, and he saw her eyes roll back, her body going lax.

He caught the female, and lifted her into his arms, carefully placing her over one of his shoulders. It was time to go back to his ship and share what proof she had with his grouping. It was already clear that she'd lie to him if necessary, and he refused to murder humans unless it truly was to protect a helpless primitive race from being slaughtered.

He picked up his discarded belongings and walked fast toward *Satrono*. The use of the scanner helped him avoid other humans and the pack animals on the planet. The last thing he needed was to come across what Anabel called shredders with her unconscious. He wouldn't be able to effectively fight them with the female draped over his shoulder. His shield had been designed for one body. Not two. It was currently off since it would shock anything touching him. That would be the female he carried.

He wished he could run. It would be much faster, but he didn't want to jostle her. Human females weren't as sturdy as Veslors. Although Anabel had fought much better than he'd imagined a female of her species could...

A grin spread across Raze's face at the thought. The female had even put up a better fight than what he'd experienced with her male counterparts in the past. She *did* impress him...even stirred his lust when they'd been sparring.

He picked up the pace and was nearly back to *Satrono* when Bruck met up with him. The male openly studied the female slung over his shoulder. "Did she pass out from fear?"

"No. I had to drug her."

"Why? She appears little and weak."

"Anabel is a surprisingly good fighter."

Bruck chuckled. "You and your pranks."

Raze reached up and pointed to his face where she'd damaged his cheek and mouth. "She did this."

"I do not believe you."

"I wouldn't lie." He smiled. "She's a fighter." Then his amusement faded. "I drugged her to avoid another sparring session. I didn't want to have to hurt her."

They reached the ship and Prasky disengaged the cloak, extending the ramp. Raze carried the female inside and walked directly to his sleeping area. Prasky met him at the doors, his features showing his displeasure as he held out the soft restraints.

"She's not a big alien."

"No, she's not," Raze agreed.

"What happened to your face?"

Raze wasn't about to tell Prasky the truth. "I leapt into a clearing with a pack of beasts and took one of them out. They were eating humans, and I wanted to make sure this female wasn't one of the dead." He'd let the male assume that's when he'd been injured.

"Keep her away from me." Prasky spun away, stomping off.

Raze opened his doors and strode in, taking the female to where he slept. He dropped the restraints and carefully lay Anabel on the soft mattress. He removed her boots to reveal small feet. He studied them, even ran his fingertip over one of her tiny toes. They appeared flesh and blood. He wondered again if she'd been telling the truth.

He secured her wrists to the headboard before leaving her alone. She was safe on his ship. He paused at the doors, turning on a motion sensor. If she moved around on the mattress, he'd be notified.

His two grouping males waited in the kitchen, both already eating.

Prasky grunted. "Are we really going to kill humans?"

"Anabel said the other humans will continue with their plan to annihilate the aliens living here to steal their planet if we leave any of them alive," Raze shared.

"Humans lie," Prasky hissed.

"Not all are dishonorable. Some Veslors have mated to their females." Bruck suddenly stared at Raze. "Did she arouse your sexual interest?"

Raze sat at the table, digging into the meal Prasky had prepared. He ignored the question.

"That is insulting," Prasky snarled. "Raze would never test a mating with a weak female."

"He said she was a good fighter."

Raze shot Bruck a warning look, before glancing at Prasky. The male scowled.

"You *did* say that," Bruck reminded him. "Other Veslors have mated to human females. I read the updates our people send out. A human mate named Vivian writes about being mated to one of our trader males, and her stories are widely shared. The pair have had at least one cub."

Prasky made a rude snort. "Prank."

"Not a prank. There was an image of the cub. Our king even made an announcement that human mates would be welcomed on our planets, and that they are compatible to have our cubs. It is truth."

Raze swallowed his food, contemplating what Bruck had shared. The male did like to know what was going on with their people. "Truth?"

"Truth." Bruck reiterated.

"We are undesirable," Prasky reminded him. "Stop speaking of taking mates. We will never have those. No cubs. We will hunt prey until death." He suddenly got up and left the room.

Raze looked at Prasky's mostly uneaten meal and sighed. He locked gazes with Bruck. "You know better than to speak of such things near him."

"He can't feel rage over Hern forever."

"We lost Hern because he wanted a mate. The subject is a bad one to speak of."

"The Delorian female set a trap and caused Hern's death."

"Prasky is always going to associate mates with death after what happened."

"*I* want a mate." Bruck sighed, his shoulders slumping. "Not a human though. They are frail-looking. I studied the one you captured while you carried her. I'd be afraid of causing her pain if I got her under me. I need a larger female. One tough, like our females."

It was Raze's turn to sigh. "No Veslor female will ever consider us."

"We have honor and are in good standing with our king."

"We were banished from the world on which we were born and the lies told about us were spread to others. None of our females would have wanted us, even if we'd taken our king's offer to resettle in new territory. We were already considered undesirable before we took to space. *Satrono* is our only home, where we will be fully accepted." It was a sore spot for everyone in their grouping, but it was Raze's duty to always be honest.

Bruck lowered his gaze, sadness reflected on his features. He took a few slow, steady breaths before he spoke, changing the subject. "It may cause problems later if we kill the surviving humans on this planet. Our king has signed alliances with their people. Prasky does have a point. Humans do lie. We've dealt with enough of them to realize it seems a universal problem with their race." Bruck returned his gaze to Raze. "I don't feel comfortable killing them unless I'm certain it must be done to save alien lives."

Raze nodded. "Agreed. I'll ask to see the female's proof and share it with you and Prasky. We'll decide what to do with the other humans then. I don't want to anger our king, either. I am certain that he would sanction us doing whatever it took to protect primitives from aggressive invaders. That's what those humans are, if they came here to steal this planet."

Bruck nodded. "I believe that is what the king would order, too."

Raze returned to his sleeping place and sat facing the bed. It gave him ample time to watch Anabel while she slept.

She wasn't what he'd expected.

His gaze kept going to her lower legs and bare feet. If they weren't real, he wondered who had hurt her enough to cause their replacement. The thought stirred his rage. The human looked so fragile...

Chapter Five

Anabel woke, instantly alert. The damn Veslor had drugged her. She opened her eyes to evaluate whatever situation she found herself in.

The room wasn't a holding cell. It appeared to be a large bedroom, where she lay on a massive bed. Her hands were restrained to a metal headboard but there were a few feet of thin material that allowed her to move enough to sit up.

The reason for her anger sat on a long, padded, backless couch a few feet from the end of the bed. "Asshole," she muttered to Raze, tugging on the restraints.

"Apologies. I knew you wouldn't return to my ship without another fight. I didn't want to risk hurting you."

"Tell me that you didn't leave the planet."

"We haven't. I spoke to my grouping. They aren't willing to hunt and kill the remaining humans without seeing proof that they are here to cause harm." He paused. "I tend to believe you, but the other males aren't as trusting. Our past experiences with humans weren't good examples of your race."

Anabel scowled, watching him as she got more comfortable on the bed. She used the headboard to lean against.

"We've had small groups of your race attempt to rob us on space stations."

"Were those stations normally visited by our fleet ships?"

"We avoid your fleet. The stations didn't have military."

That told Anabel everything. She'd bet the Veslors had come across some really shitty humans on stations owned by private companies. "Got it. Most humans living on outlying space stations do so because they're wanted criminals with bounties on their heads. Those are the only humans you've met?"

He nodded.

"What about my sister, when this Roth hired you? How did she look? Tell me everything."

"I didn't see your sister. Roth contacted me via communications."

That made her frown.

"You don't look pleased with that answer. Roth is a good male."

"How would you know that if you've never actually met him?"

"I've met with Roth many times in the past. His grouping are fighters. We've joined our groupings to handle some aggressive situations to protect innocents."

"I'm not sure what that means," she admitted.

"The last time our groupings fought together was against the Elth. They attacked Morna. It is the home world of the Kluza. They are a nonaggressive race who trade their art for supplies. The Elth were kidnapping their people and the Kluza rulers hired Veslors to help. Roth's grouping remained on the planet to stop the Elth from snatching more citizens. We went after the ships with captives already taken, to return them to their home."

Anabel chewed that information over in her mind. "Did you get them back?"

Raze scoffed. "Yes. The Elth are no match for Veslors. Once we got involved, they left Morna alone. The Elth have lost too many ships and people battling us."

"How many men do you have on your ship?"

"Three now. There used to be four in our grouping."

Anabel could tell by the flash of pain in his eyes that he'd probably lost a crew member to death. The idea filled her with sympathy; she'd lost a few of her own comrades in battle. "Fighting the Elth? I'm sorry."

He suddenly stood. "Hern wasn't killed by the Elth. Do we need to fly to the destroyed Earth ship to retrieve your evidence? I would like this hunt to be over soon. That means showing my males your proof if you wish for us to kill the remaining humans before we leave this system."

Anabel noted his abrupt change in demeanor. "I hope your computer systems can read Earth files. That's my proof. I have them on me."

He scowled as he stepped closer to the bed. "No lies, female. I searched for weapons and didn't find anything in your pockets but hand coverings."

"They're called gloves. And the proof is inside me, actually."

His eyes widened.

"Synthetic legs, remember? Let me go and I'll show you my proof. I'm going to trust you, since I know my sister is a genius. Jessa wouldn't send someone after me unless she thought you were trustworthy. I'm also willing to accept that if any human married an alien, it would be her. She's *Defcon Red's* A.R.S."

"What is an A.R.S?"

90

"Alien Research Specialist. Jessa was trained to be a doctor and received her license. She absorbs information easily and retains it like a sponge, so she graduated early. She had some time to kill before she was old enough to be assigned to her first post for the fleet. They enrolled her in alien studies. Jessa's brilliant at dealing with alien medical issues when shit goes down."

He hesitated next to the bed. "What shit?"

"Like if the fleet sends people to an alien planet and they're exposed to some strange alien infection. My sister's the one who figures out what caused it, how to cure it, and she'll do it faster than any other doctor, because she's that damn smart."

"She sounds like a fine female. Do not fight with me when I release you. Your vow."

"I won't give you any trouble if we take out the remaining crew of the *Soapa Six* before we leave this planet. They really will keep killing innocents if we leave them here alive. I already mentioned they work for Gemini. It's a corrupt company that buys rights to planets that aren't classified as alien owned.

"I was sent undercover on their freighter after someone attempted to murder an entire survey team from a competing company, on another planet. Things weren't adding up to one of the lead investigators and the case got kicked back to the United Earth ruling committee. I was ordered to take a closer look at why the company was sending freighters into deep space that smart people would otherwise avoid."

Raze released her wrists from the restraints. "I was surprised to hear that an Earth vessel was in this sector of space."

"So you understand why it was suspicious. That's why I was aboard that freighter. To learn the truth." She scooted off the large bed and stood.

Raze stared back at her, a few feet separating them. "They shouldn't have sent a female."

"And you shouldn't scowl like that or your face will stick," she smirked. "I'm highly qualified and not easy to kill. The fleet knew I could do the job, and I was perfect for it *because* I'm a woman. It instantly made Gemini less suspicious about my motives when they hired me. I was set up with a false history that implied I'd be desperate for a job. Any job."

"What false history?"

"My documents make me look like an ex-convict who was recently released from prison." She shrugged. "Bad enough crimes that it would make jerks think twice about attacking me, since they think I like to kill men."

His gaze raked her from head to toe. "You don't appear dangerous. Humans are stupid."

It was her turn to scowl. "In reality, I have an even higher body count than my fake file does, Raze. Don't let my looks or size fool you. It's just that when I've killed, it was my job. I take out bad guys. And I'm damn good at it."

He didn't appear happy with that news. "I will take you to the bridge and you will give me your proof. I'll show it to my grouping." He turned away and stalked toward the doors.

Anabel followed. The ship wasn't like any she'd ever been on before. Probably built by the Veslors. She glimpsed some writing on one of the walls, but she couldn't read the foreign symbols. They ended up on a large bridge with a viewing screen that took up the entire front wall. Two other Veslors were already there.

They looked like Raze, with their dark skin, pointed ears, and the bald sides of their heads. One had paler blue eyes. The other one had golden. Both of them were tall, muscular...and they stared at her with an intensity that made Anabel feel a bit unwelcome. She didn't get creepy vibes off them, necessarily. Neither man leered at her. They just felt...dangerous.

"This is Bruck," Raze pointed at the blue-eyed Veslor. Then to the other one. "That is Prasky."

The male with golden eyes flashed his fangs at her, obviously in warning. He didn't appear friendly. Anabel nodded at both. "Anabel."

"You say we must kill the other humans who crashed here from your ship. Tell me why," Bruck demanded.

"They came here to murder every alien native." She quickly explained. "The company they work for would make a lot of money if they could take ownership of this planet. That can only happen if no sentient alien life exists." She walked over to a chair and took a seat, lifting her leg. "Look away if any of you are squeamish."

She shoved up the jumper material and exposed her ankle, pressing her fingers into the right spots on her leg to trigger the release. She felt her skin split. It always hurt.

One of the Veslors snarled loudly. She peered up at them.

The one named Prasky looked horrified. Raze seemed shocked. Bruck actually stepped closer, his eyes wide. None of them seemed freaked out, though. That was a relief.

She paid attention to her leg, removing the chip she'd stored there, then releasing the pressure points in her skin to allow it to close. She wiped the blood off the chip and stood, holding it out to Raze.

"Do you have anything that can read Earth language? There's a lot of information on this chip, since I copied everything on the captain's private computer, but I'll show you the orders from Gemini to the crew to wipe out all the aliens on this planet.

"I'll also pull up their old flight logs from other planets they've been to, including the one where Gemini murdered almost everyone on a survey team, starting the investigation that put me on that freighter. One of Gemini's employees failed to secure the rights and another company won the bid. Gemini had to be terrified the other company's survey team would discover what they'd done. Maybe the crew of *Soapa Six* did a sloppy job of making sure there were no bodies or other signs of a recent civilization. Bottom line—they attempted to murder that survey team."

Raze came forward, but he ignored the chip she held out to him. He crouched instead, hesitating for a moment before yanking up the pant leg of her jumpsuit to expose her ankle. He inhaled deeply before his head jerked up, his eyes narrowed.

He ran his fingers gently over her leg, where there was still a trace of blood, but her skin had resealed. He sniffed his finger, where her blood had transferred. "This smells real."

Anabel sighed, knowing he was probably shocked by what she'd just done. Only a few of her co-workers were aware of her body modifications. "It *is* real blood."

"You said your legs were artificial." Raze shot her a skeptical glance.

"They are. That's why I'm able to store the chip inside my leg. Part of it opens to reveal that hidden compartment. I also told you that my lower legs and feet look so real because they're wrapped in cloned flesh. It's actually enhanced lab-grown skin from my own DNA. It heals way faster than the flesh I was born with. The rest of me isn't like that." She took a deep breath. "Can we focus on the important thing now?" She waved the chip in her hand.

Raze slowly stood.

She tipped her head back, staring into his eyes. They really were striking. "Most people never know I work for the fleet. I only told you because of the situation we're in. I really do need your help to take out the rest of the crew of *Soapa Six*." She glanced at the other two Veslors. "The inhabitants here wear furs and their only weapons are spears, for fuck's sake. They don't stand a chance of surviving a fight against men with laser rifles. The assholes from the freighter will slaughter them if we don't help."

The Veslor with the lighter blue eyes approached her and held out his hand. "We can view anything on our ship and translate it. Tell me what to look for."

Anabel passed him the chip, giving him the name of a file. "That's the transmission you want to read. It's orders from Gemini to annihilate every alien on the planet. It even mentions there's over ninety thousand lives they're required to snuff out."

A snarl tore from Bruck as he stalked to one of the consoles. "Ninety thousand aliens?"

"Yes. I'm just as furious," she admitted. "That's why I sabotaged the freighter before it reached the planet. There were chemical bombs stored on *Soapa Six* that would have murdered the inhabitants in a matter of seconds once deployed. The crew was ordered to use the shuttles to drop bombs straight onto villages, then dump all the bodies directly into a few active volcanos afterward. Lava would have burned up all the evidence. They were also supposed to clear any signs of the villages by burning them down and making it appear as if lightning strikes had caused wildfires."

Bruck snarled louder, viciously punching the console.

"Calm, Bruck," Raze ordered. "We will stop them." He looked at Anabel. "I believe you."

His men didn't. That was Anabel's take. Then again, she wouldn't blindly kill people without proof they needed to die, either.

It took a few moments before Bruck motioned her forward. He'd managed to open the files on a smaller screen built into the console. He indicated for her to pull up the one she wanted them to see.

It was all touch controls. The files were in English. She found the order sent by Gemini and opened it, stepping back. She wondered briefly if they could read her birth language but needn't have worried; Bruck did something that changed the English to alien symbols. She backed up farther as Raze and the third Veslor crowded around the console.

Once they were done, a hologram screen appeared over the console, filled with symbols. Bruck was doing something, the images changing quickly. Raze turned away and walked to stand in front of her. "He's verifying as best as he can that the message was sent from Earth."

"It was. He can also go back in the freighter's flight logs to other planets they visited to find more evidence of the mass murders they've committed." She could wait, as long as the Veslors ultimately decided to remain on the planet and help her take out the rest of the crew. "I don't enjoy killing," she confessed softly. "But I don't hesitate when innocent lives are on the line. I wouldn't have blown up my only way to get back to Earth unless I was absolutely certain every single asshole on the *Soapa Six* needed to die. You have no idea how painful it was to do the right thing. I resigned myself to dying alone on this planet with no chance of the fleet sending someone to retrieve me."

Raze didn't seem to like what she'd said, based on his low snarl. "You said you work for them. That they put you on that Earth ship."

"They did. But the fleet tries hard not to start wars with other alien races. One life isn't worth risking a ship full of people flying into a dangerous sector of space to retrieve me. It's how it is in my line of work. I understood the consequences and knew there would be no rescue."

"I don't like your fleet."

She shrugged. "Sometimes I don't like the way they do things, either, but I understand why they have certain rules."

"You should quit. Find a better job with humans who care about you."

Anabel met his gaze. "I don't have that option."

"Earth forces all humans to do jobs they hate?"

"Not all people. Just a small handful. It's complicated."

He glanced briefly at her chest before meeting her gaze again. "Because you are female? Do they abuse your females?"

"I mentioned before that I'm an orphan raised by the fleet. It means I owe them years of service. They fed, clothed, housed, and educated us. In my case and Jessa's, they also paid for extensive medical bills. It's not an order to work for the fleet, so much as an obligation to pay them back."

Raze curled his upper lip, flashing fangs. "That is wrong. You were a cub! Someone should have done all those things for you because it was *right*."

She shrugged. "Life isn't always perfect or fair. I'm twenty-eight years old. The fleet owns me until I turn thirty-five. The same goes for my sister." It was a good time to talk about his plan of returning her to Jessa. "My sister won't be safe like you implied earlier, simply because she's with a Veslor. Their marriage can't be a legal one, not on Earth. People like Jessa and I aren't allowed to get married until after our contracts end. The fleet literally *owns* us right now. She won't be allowed to flee to Veslor-controlled space to avoid being arrested for hacking into secured databases. The fleet is *not* going to let her go. Hell, she's on a fleet ship right now. And if she somehow escapes, they'll send people after her until she's returned."

"Your fleet condones slavery?" Anger hardened his alien features.

"No." She sighed. "But I can see where you'd get that idea. I told you, they raised us and paid our medical bills. They don't see it as slavery, but rather as repaying a debt. I won't lie. It sucks. But that's how it is. And none of that even matters. Jessa obviously did some hacking in order to learn about my mission and send you after me. The people I work for will assume she's a threat who may share information about what I've been doing. The missions I'm sent on are highly classified for a reason."

Raze stepped closer. "Are you a criminal for your fleet? Do they commit crimes?"

"No. But some missions I've been on would cause problems if anyone learns about them." It was Anabel's turn to move closer, and she lowered her voice. "Take what happened here on this planet, for example. Gemini is a really horrible company based on Earth that's been committing mass murder. Most of Earth's citizens would be horrified if they found out. Gemini doesn't represent *all* humans. They're a very small portion of bad ones. But other alien races may blame every human for what almost happened here. It's best if no details get out. What Jessa did puts that secrecy at risk. She could cause all kinds of damage if she shares anything she's learned by looking at my file."

He frowned.

"Do you understand what I'm saying, Raze? The fleet is going to want everything I've uncovered to remain buried, out of fear of it causing other aliens to think we're all a bunch of murdering assholes, willing to take out entire worlds for profit. That's not true. We *stop* them. That's the important part. We take on missions like this to uncover bad humans and prevent them from doing something that could hurt our species as a whole, and to keep the peace."

He gave a small nod.

"Please help me take out the humans stranded here...but you *have* to leave me behind once we're done. There's no way possible for you to return me to the fleet without them wondering how I survived. They'll suspect my sister immediately. She's the only one motivated to save me. The fleet knows what she can do. They *gave* her all her abilities when they fucked with her brain."

"Fucked with her brain?" He appeared confused by the description.

"I got new lower legs and increased hearing abilities in one ear, but Jessa suffered a brain injury. She also lost an eye. They gave her implants. Not only is her eye synthetic, but a small part of her brain is, too. She can hack *anything*...along with a few other useful talents. I love my sister, Raze. I'd rather remain here on this planet, for the rest of my short life, than put Jessa at risk of being arrested. Some of my bosses are serious assholes who would probably lock her up somewhere, find something she could do that doesn't expose her to civilians because she'll have lost their trust, and keep her there until she dies. Please believe what I'm saying."

"Who hurt you and your sister to cause your injuries?"

"No one. It was an accident. We lived underground on Mars. That's a planet near Earth. It doesn't have breathable air, so there are domes over cities that are buried under the surface. My parents had jobs there. We were sleeping when an accidental explosion happened. It caused the floors above us to collapse on top of our apartment. I was later assured that my parents died instantly, but Jessa and I were trapped under tons of debris. It took the rescue teams a few days to reach us. My feet were crushed under a beam, and part of the debris that fell on Jessa impaled her head. It took her eye, damaged an area of her brain, and the medical team working on her had to reconstruct part of her face."

Raze appeared too stunned for words.

Anabel reached up and touched her own face, tracing a path from the middle of her eye to one ear. "This entire section of her had to be rebuilt. I was sure she was going to die when they pulled us out, and I saw her. They had to cut the rod to free her, then leave part of it in to get her to a trauma team. It was imbedded through her skull. I'm so grateful that the fleet medical teams saved her. But there was a cost though. Time owed to the fleet."

"You said your feet were crushed, but you lost more than that from what you've pointed out to me."

"The rescuers had to amputate at my ankles to get me free. There was additional damage above that, though, from the injury and because it took them a few days to reach me. My lower legs couldn't be salvaged. The surgeons decided to take my legs from just above the knee to make my synthetic ones more efficient. I couldn't run as fast as I can or leap as high as I do if I had my original knees. There was even talk at one point of completely taking both legs from the hip joints down, and even replacing parts of my hips. I fought that, though. I'd have been even more useful as an operative...but they were *my* legs. I wanted to save as much of them as possible."

Raze still looked appalled by everything she was describing. "Operative?" he asked finally.

"Police officer, or as you called it, a law-seeker. I know how bad all of this sounds. Believe me, I've had a lot of years to come to terms with it, including the other modifications my medical team *wanted* to do to me. The knees made sense, since there was so much tissue damage below them that they had to cut out anyway. The rest of it was bullshit that would just make me feel less and less human.

"We compromised, with them tweaking one of my ears. It was always about making deals with them. I agreed to become an operative if they honored my wishes about what was done to my body and my sister's."

"Why would you make such a deal?"

"So they didn't keep experimenting on us."

"I don't like your fleet—and I am not leaving you here on this planet."

Anabel opened her mouth to argue but one of the other Veslors joined them, drawing her full attention. He faced Raze.

"Prasky and I have gone through a lot of information. The Earth ship *was* sent to this planet to eliminate the inhabitants. I also found the cargo manifest, verifying they had the means to do massive harm." He snarled. "The female speaks the truth. I came across a reference in another file to the poison they would have used to kill the primitives. It verified the deaths of aliens from another world from two years prior. They've done this before."

"There were also vids of their murdered victims," Prasky added.

The golden-eyed Veslor startled Anabel. She hadn't even heard him approach. He was a big guy but he moved silently. It was something that she'd have to remember about their race. Never underestimate Veslors. She twisted her head to peer up at him.

102

Prasky looked furious as he glanced at her. "We hunt to the death. Your stolen files have convinced me of what needs to be done. It is our duty to protect innocent lives from hostile invaders."

Raze nodded. "We hunt the humans and end this."

Anabel was relieved that she'd be able to complete her mission. The aliens on KP would be safe once the remaining crew of *Soapa Six* were wiped out of existence.

Chapter Six

Anabel ate cooked meat and some alien vegetables, appreciating the dinner that Prasky had served. The Veslors were eating something different. She'd asked about it, and Raze had informed her that their information on humans stated they didn't like what the Veslors were having. The food would be too spicy for her to eat without injury. Prasky had made a meal for her milder tastes.

"Thank you." She flashed a smile at the golden-eyed Veslor. "This is delicious. And I'm not just saying that because I've spent three months eating tasteless ration bars, either. One of my few pleasures in life is treating myself to great food. This is one of the best meals I've ever had."

Prasky grumbled under his breath and lowered his chin, eating a chunk of meat that resembled a roast. There were no veggies on the Veslor plates. It was possible they didn't eat them, but she figured they must, since they had them onboard. Their meat also seemed real instead of artificial. The fleet and United Earth headquarters served artificial meat actually made from plant-based products most of the time, so she was an expert on it.

"There are twenty-three remaining humans alive on the planet," Bruck stated. "Anabel isn't included in that number. We should hunt during the night while they sleep. It would be kinder. They won't see death coming."

Anabel shook her head. "Bad idea. No offense. I've spent months here learning all the dangers, or at least most of them. A good portion of the animals hunt at night. And I've dubbed this place KP—it stands for killer plants. I'm talking vines that suddenly drop on you from above and tear you apart, and huge plants that will grab and crush you to death. Laser fire has no effect on them. At night, these ground rodents come out, too. Vicious little things. It's why I chose to sleep in a cave. No way was I going to end up with dozens of them making me their dinner."

All three Veslors stared at her in what she guessed was disbelief.

She sighed. "We're going to have to trust each other, guys. We're a team on this. I know I'm a human, and Raze explained you've met the worst of my kind, but I'm not a criminal. I work for the fleet and United Earth. We're allies. It's best if we track down the crew right after dawn. Most of the plants sleep when the sun comes up, unless you literally run into them and wake them up. I've never seen the flesh-eating rodents out and about when the sun is up. I don't know if they're light sensitive or maybe the sun hurts them.

"The deadliest daytime threat seems to be the shredders. They hunt in packs and are attracted by sound. Day or night." She quickly described them and what they could do. "I get off the ground when I run into any of them or hear their whistles. They can take down trees, though. Scratching their sides against bark seems to be something they like to do, and I've seen them snap trunks before. That just means making sure they aren't aware of where you are while they pass by."

"You survived here," Prasky sneered. "The planet must not be too dangerous."

Anabel resisted rolling her eyes, even though she wanted to. "I'm a well-trained operative and have skills most humans don't. A typical human would be out of luck if they had to jump ten feet to reach a branch to get out of the path of danger. It's not an ability they have. They also can't run as fast as I do."

"She *is* fast," Raze admitted. "I barely caught her."

That had her smiling slightly. "Synthetic legs. They've got some get-up-and-go to them."

"We will hunt at first light," Raze stated, glancing at his grouping.

Both males nodded, to her relief. She had already realized that Raze was in charge of his crew. She'd also noticed they were all on a first-name basis, instead of using titles. Every indication she'd learned so far implied they worked more like siblings than crewmates.

"Are the three of you blood brothers?"

All three males stared at her again. Raze shook his head. "We are brothers but not by blood. We grew up together in the same large grouping. It consisted of many families. We are close in age and played together as cubs to form a bond."

Anabel tucked that information away. "You're the oldest, I take it?"

"I am," Bruck said. "By nearly one of your Earth years."

"So you don't pick leadership by age?"

Bruck chuckled. "No. Raze is the youngest, but he was the most assertive of our grouping."

"Why are we sharing this with the human?" Prasky huffed. "She has no reason to know anything."

"Stop," Raze ordered, shooting him a glare. "She is not our enemy. Get over your aversion to females."

The golden-eyed Veslor lifted his plate and drink, stood from the table, and stormed out of the cooking and eating area of their ship. The door sealed behind him.

"I'm sorry. I didn't mean to upset him," Anabel said quietly, knowing she'd somehow stepped in something with her questions.

"It is not your fault. It is his." Bruck stood, taking his plate and drink. "I will go calm him." He left them alone.

Anabel still felt bad. "I really am sorry."

"Listen to Bruck." Raze ripped off a chunk of meat and ate it. "Prasky has a problem with all females right now. We lost Hern because of one."

"Was she a human?"

"No. That female was Delorian."

"I'm not familiar with them."

"You wouldn't be. They live far from anywhere your fleet would travel."

Anabel visually appraised him. "They must be a tough alien to kill one of your men. I'm very sorry for your loss."

He snorted and wiped his hands on a cloth napkin, taking a sip of his drink. "Delorians are not a tough race. They are larger than your kind but not by much. She lured Hern into the mating ritual of her people, but instead of forming a bond, she drugged him and sold him into slavery. He should have returned to our ship from the planet's surface with his mate in two days...but he didn't. We went hunting for him." He stared at his plate.

"I'm so sorry." Anabel was horrified. "I take it the slavers got him off planet before you were able to retrieve him?"

Raze continued staring at his plate. "He was dead. We found what was left of his clothing and his broken communicator band after his body had been burned with that of other slave fighters. That's why they wanted him. To fight to the death to earn them money."

"I hope you killed the bitch who did that to him."

That got him to look up at her, and he appeared surprised.

"That's reprehensible, to promise to mate a guy, only to betray him like that. I'd have killed her." She shrugged and looked away. "Just being honest."

"She is dead. Prasky was enraged when she admitted to what she'd done, and we tracked the fighting ring where Hern had been taken. We kept her with us." He took another sip of his drink and stared at his food again. "He snapped her neck and ripped her throat out on the spot when we found what was left of Hern in the burn pit."

"Understandable."

His blue gaze locked with hers. "We don't kill females."

"There should be exceptions. That's one of them. You said you're like brothers. Did he torture her and make her suffer first?"

Raze shook his head. "The female was dead before she realized what happened."

"Well, I have a sister...and I'd have made that bitch scream, bleed, and beg for death before ending her suffering if she'd betrayed Jessa like that." She shook her head. "We all have emotions, no matter what species we are. The bitch deserved to die."

He inhaled deeply and blew it out. "That is what our king said. We had to send a report to him. He didn't order us to take Prasky home to be punished."

"Would you have taken him if he had?"

Raze remained silent.

She smiled. "I wouldn't have, either. Sometimes the ones in charge have no understanding of how shitty people can be. They sit safely behind a desk with no clue how things really are."

"Our king isn't soft. He's battled in many wars. He was glad the female had been put down and no longer remained a threat to other Veslor males, desperate for a female to mate with."

"Smart guy." Raze's words prompted other questions. "Are Veslor males normally desperate for mates? I don't know much about your culture. I've never had to deal with Veslors."

"Not most, but some who travel in ships are." He began to eat again. "Our females would never agree to do that. It is an instinctual need to have and raise cubs on our home planets. Males who travel for work are undesirable to them, so the few of us who mate are always to aliens."

"Like Vivian Goss. She mated a Veslor she met when a ship of them docked with the *Gorison Traveler* and saved the crew from Ke'ters. I'm very familiar with that incident."

"I was recently made aware that one of our males mated to a human. They have a cub."

That was news to her. Then again, unless she was preparing for a mission, her handler didn't give her unnecessary intel. She'd learned about *Gorison Traveler* when Kurt had sent her after Ke'ters as payback, with a small team. She frequently missed seeing Earth news, too. A lot could happen that she wasn't aware of because of her long stints being out of contact on an assignment.

"That's...surprising," she finally said. "I didn't think different kinds of aliens could breed together, or assumed it was very rare that they could."

"Our species must be compatible." He met her gaze. "That's why it would be a bad idea for you to test a mating with me by engaging in a fight. A ship is no place to raise cubs. They deserve fresh air and space to roam."

"I still don't get how fighting with you was considered foreplay."

He turned away and sighed. "Our females must be assured that we are strong fighters and able to defend them and their cubs after a mating takes place. It is instinctual. No female wants a male she can beat in battle." He looked up at her, his gaze quickly scanning her upper body, before meeting her eyes again. "How do humans test a mating?"

"We don't. Not really. We get to know someone, and if we believe they're a good fit, humans marry if they fall in love. Sometimes it's done out of loneliness or sharing the same career goals. At least it is for people who choose to have full careers with the fleet. Those are mostly the ones I know. My parents were a love match; they met working together on Mars. Both were engineers who kept the air systems for the domes functioning. Mars doesn't produce natural oxygen, so the cities there needed people like them to survive."

"It is sad that they died."

It was her turn to look away. "Yeah. It sucked big time. They were good people. Especially my mother. She always made time for Jessa and me. Dad was busier, since he managed all the engineering teams. He also had to travel a lot to other dome cities. Not that he was a bad dad. He wasn't. When he had time off, he would spend every minute with his family. We'd play old-fashioned board games from Earth and he'd take us out for nice dinners. He said he wanted to show his girls off so everyone would envy him. Then he'd laugh." She paused, feeling a little choked up. "He had a great sense of humor."

"I miss my parents sometimes."

She had the urge to reach across the table to take his hand as she met his gaze. The sadness she saw couldn't be missed. "I'm sorry. You lost them, too?"

His features hardened. "They remain alive and well. We no longer speak or visit them."

That surprised her. "Because work keeps you away so much?"

"No." His voice deepened. "They sided against us and voted to banish us from our home planet."

Anabel gasped. "Why?"

He remained quiet for so long, she assumed he wouldn't answer...but then he did.

"Veslor groupings combine with others when matings happen. It can mean a dozen or more groupings being led by one leader. The couples start to have cubs. Those cubs grow close and can form their own groupings." He paused. "Not from blood relations, but by age and closeness...what you would call friendship. Once that grouping reaches adulthood, some leave if they aren't able to remain submissive to their leader, but live close to their original grouping. It happens with males like me. I knew my grouping would follow me, and they did. We claimed a territory nearby. It was going well...until it wasn't."

She hesitated only a moment. "Do you mind me asking what happened?"

He slumped slightly in his seat. "There was a second grouping that had left our original one two years before us, that had also claimed territory nearby. Yebi was the first son of our birth grouping leader, Yendo, a male who was very powerful on our planet. Other grouping leaders often came to him seeking advice, and he was the one who approached our king on their behalf. We were on what you'd call a growing planet. There are a few in our system. The king lives on our original home world, where we all lived before we had the ability to move to others."

She nodded. It was known that the Veslors had a vast solar system, unlike Earth's. They had at least four known planets that were able to sustain life without domes. Anabel was pretty sure they had four moons, too, and a couple of suns.

"Yebi showed interest in a female for his mate, but she ignored him. It is forbidden to approach a female not interested in a male. Trilla was raised in our birth grouping. She was very beautiful but extremely timid. Her parents were as well." Raze growled. "Some felt Trilla should be grateful that a strong male like Yebi wanted her, but she avoided him. So he took her by force. She escaped and ran to our territory, severely injured. That's when we learned what had happened."

Anabel had a sick feeling in her gut. She could guess how that ended, if Raze was anything like the good guy she suspected he was.

"He'd abused her badly to force her shift, to mount and get her pregnant. She resisted, and her wounds were bad enough to enrage us. She would be heavily scarred for life. We took her home to her parents, believing she'd be safe and protected." Claws suddenly shot out of his fingertips. He retracted them just as fast, then balled his hands into fists. "Her parents came to us in grief the next day and begged our help. Their grouping had returned Trilla to Yebi. Of course we went after her. It was too late...Yebi had killed her in a fit of rage."

"*Fuck,*" she muttered.

"We slaughtered Yebi and his entire grouping. His males had allowed that abuse to happen to a female...witnessed it and did *nothing*. They should have battled him to protect her. Yendo shouldn't have allowed his son to take her by force in the first place, or ignored that she'd been injured. Instead, he handed her right back over to his son. We lost all respect for our birth grouping leader.

"He raged over us killing his son and his grouping." He paused. "He sent some of his own grouping to kill us. We battled them and won. Some were allowed to return home, but several refused to yield."

"You had to kill them?"

He nodded. "We were banished. Yendo used his influence to make us appear dishonorable to other groupings across our planet. He told falsehoods, which is..." He snarled loudly. "That is not our way. He claimed

113

one of us wanted Trilla, and murdered her mate and his grouping to take her. That she died defending them against us."

Anabel's heart bled for him.

"Yendo contacted our king, demanding he send fighters to punish us. Instead, the fighter grouping asked us to go with them under orders from our king. The four of us went without a fight and were asked what happened. Our king believed us. He confronted Yendo and our birthing grouping. He ended up killing Yendo and six others he found guilty. Our king refused to allow dishonorable Veslors to influence so many of our people. A dishonest Veslor is a sickness that no one wants to spread. It is an unforgivable abuse of power."

"I'm glad your king believed you."

Raze nodded. "My parents refused to see Yendo's sickness and blamed my grouping for the death of their leader. Our king relocated Trilla's parents and younger cub siblings to another growing planet, with a kind grouping who welcomed them happily. But he didn't feel it was safe to order our planet to take us back, and we had no desire to return. As retribution for the wrong done to us by our entire planet, we were given the means to buy this ship and became bounty hunters. Our king made it possible. We are in good standing with him, and take jobs from him often."

"Was it not safe for you to return because some of the other groupings might try to murder yours?"

Raze sighed. "Yes. Veslors trust their instincts...but they were wrong to trust Yendo so deeply. But we understood their refusal to believe he

114

could do something so terrible, that the males closest to him would allow it without challenging him for leadership. It came as a shock to us as well."

"Does that happen much? Challenges?"

"Only if a Veslor grows sick in his mind. It is rare, but when it happens, it is the grouping's duty to end their lives before others are hurt by that male or female, and to do so painlessly and fast." He paused. "It is heartbreaking, but the only option. A Veslor who has lost all honor is too dangerous to allow to roam free. It is for the good of all, especially cubs. Protecting them is always the greatest priority over everything else. Trilla was timid enough to be counted as a cub. She was meek and defenseless."

"I'm sorry that happened to your grouping. Then losing Hern the way you did..."

He finished his meal and stood. "We seem destined to feel pain, but we are strong."

She admired him for that. "I can relate. Life has screwed me plenty of times."

He returned to the table after disposing of his empty plate and cup. "Are you mated?"

"No." She took her last bite and drank the rest of the fruit juice they'd given her. "I have no right to get married until my contract ends. Not that I could ever see anyone signing up to take me on."

Raze appeared confused. "Signing up?"

She smiled. "That's just an expression, but marriage contracts *do* require signatures. First off, I could beat up most guys with one hand tied behind my back, with the kind of training I have. That tends to put men off. I've had other operatives interested in me over the years, but that changed after we trained together. Their egos couldn't take it.

"Second, I could never share most of my history with anyone who wasn't in my line of work, since most of it is deeply classified. No one wants a secretive partner.

"Then there's the fact I can only rely on myself most of the time. It's nearly impossible for me to let anyone get close. It's pointless, since attachments aren't allowed for people like me. I've learned it only hurts when you start to feel something for someone, only to have to give them up. Most of the time, I'm flat-out ordered to never see or speak to them again when I'm sent on a new mission. I'm sure it wasn't any easier on the few guys I've tried to have relationships with. I was there one day and gone the next, without a goodbye or explanation. It's fucked-up all around."

"I know things about you."

"I'm aware." Anabel didn't bother telling him that what he knew was inconsequential, since she planned to die on the planet. She stood and took her plate to the counter, setting her dishes next to Raze's discarded ones. "Should we wash these?"

"Prasky will. It's his kitchen duty rotation."

She faced him. "You take turns?"

He nodded. "We should rest. The sun's rising won't be far off."

"I appreciate you letting me finish my mission." There was still the matter of talking him into leaving her on the killer plant planet. No way could she be returned to Jessa without her baby sister facing treason charges. Maybe she'd be able to escape and avoid whatever sensors they had to track people, once she learned how they worked. The Veslors couldn't take her back if they couldn't find her.

"I'll take the sitting place and you will have my sleeping place."

"Is that what you call a couch and bed?" She followed him as he led her out of the ship's kitchen.

"Yes. Some of our words are different than yours. I'll make a mental note."

"No need. I could guess the meaning. You're not the only aliens I've been around. Just the first of your kind. I'm a quick learner."

It didn't take long to reach his cabin. He took a seat on the weird backless couch, which left her with the bed. He crossed his arms over his chest. "Would you like to shower?" He jerked his head. "We have a private bathing room."

"I got a bath in the creek. Do I stink after our fight?"

"You smell pleasant."

"Good. I was happy to find deodorant was part of the emergency kits on the pods. They include the kind that saturates your skin and lasts about a week every time it's applied. Otherwise, you sure wouldn't describe me as 'pleasant.' Humans stink when they sweat. Most people think men are worse, but not true. We're equally stinky after a fight."

"Never challenge any Veslors males in the future. They will believe you wish to test a mating."

"I was just trying not to be caught."

"Our cultures are very different."

"Apparently. I'll take you up on that shower in the morning. I don't suppose you have a way of making me clothing that would fit?" She fingered her jumpsuit. "This outfit has about had it."

"I can try." He stood. "You are locked in. No offense, but it's for the best. Prasky doesn't trust females. He wouldn't hurt you, but he'd see it as a sign of aggression if you roamed the ship without me or Bruck. He'd probably put you in a cell. You'll be much more comfortable here." He paused for effect. "He'd assume you were trying to entice him if you fought him."

She sighed. "So you've said. I won't try to break out of your cabin."

"Good. I'll be back soon with something you can wear. The bathing room is right there and will handle all your needs. It should be easy to figure out how things work. Our bodies' functions aren't too different. I researched humans after you became our target."

Anabel watched him leave, thinking she probably *should* take a shower. Raze had her pinned in the dirt earlier. The more she thought about it, the idea of possible hot water was too much to resist. Especially since she'd been positive she'd never see or experience such technology again after marooning herself on the planet.

She got off the bed and the door to the bathroom activated on a motion trigger, opening automatically. The bathroom had a toilet, a weird sink, and a tube-shaped space that appeared to be a shower. She stripped fast and figured out the alien tech without any problems.

There *was* hot water. She enjoyed every minute she spent beneath it, getting cleaner than she'd been in months.

It sucked to put her jumpsuit back on, but she had little choice. Then she climbed into his huge, comfortable bed. It had to be eight by ten feet, she guessed, the mattress like an oversized fluffy pillow.

A yawn broke from her lips. She was comfortable, had a full belly of good food, and didn't have to worry about some reptilian alien discovering her cave while she slept.

She trusted Raze enough to know he wasn't the type to do her any harm while she slept. He'd have already done something if he were.

Chapter Seven

A groan woke Anabel the next morning. For a split second she was confused, until memory hit. She sat up, shoving off a blanket that had been draped over her, probably by Raze, and stared around the dim room.

A huge shape suddenly lifted from the floor to her right.

Her mouth opened but she didn't make sound. A normal person probably would have screamed. Training had beaten that kind of response from her. Instead, she tensed, prepared to fight as she balled her hands into fists.

The shape was a massive beast. As her eyes adjusted, she saw hair on top of its head, a long, thick body, and skin that appeared to be the texture of dark leather or something equally as tough. It stretched, its back to her, one massive paw lifted. Vicious-looking claws flashed before it settled that paw back down on the floor.

She remained frozen, wondering how in the hell something like that could have breached the Veslors' ship. Or the cabin. It seemed unaware of her presence, and she wanted to keep it that way. The bathroom was close but the door automatically opened. It wouldn't be safe to run in there.

She needed to find a weapon to defend herself with. Anabel highly doubted her fists, even if she used her fingernails, would do much damage. Her gaze darted around Raze's room. Nothing seemed useful in a fight against something so obviously lethal. The only objects she could toss at the beast were books on a shelf near the bed. It seemed Raze liked to collect dozens of them.

The beast groaned again and drew her attention. It moved its massive head as if it were stretching its neck muscles. Then it lowered— and she watched in utter shock as it began to make disturbing noises.

Bones popped and its shape suddenly changed. The legs elongated, the neck seemed to shorten—and within less than a minute, a totally nude Raze crouched on the floor. He rose up, showing off his muscled bare body. He had a great one, too. The shock of seeing it had Anabel sucking air into her lungs.

He jerked his head her way. The room was dimly lit, but she saw his features clearly. He frowned. "I thought you were sleeping. Apologies." He kept his back to her. "I didn't sleep well on the sitting place, so I used the floor. It's more comfortable when I'm in my battle form." Then he sniffed the air. "I'm not picking up fear. I'm glad."

Anabel cleared her throat and found her voice. "I was too surprised to be afraid. More like wondering how in the hell something like you got in here."

He smiled. "I warned you that Veslors have two forms. Now you've seen them both."

"Yes, I have." She wasn't certain what else to say.

"I will shower and we'll start our day after first meal." He pointed to a small table by the cabin doors. "Clothing for you." Then he sauntered to the bathroom and stepped inside, the door closing behind him.

Anabel smiled. "Smug son of a bitch with zero body shame. Great damn bod, though, so he's earned that attitude." She climbed out of his bed and went to the neatly folded fabric. There was a shirt with short sleeves and a set of pants with a stretchy waist. That killed her good mood. They were more like pajamas than actual clothes. The legs had been trimmed, probably so they weren't way too long for her to wear. "I'm expected to go hunting in this?"

At least they were clean. Anabel stripped quickly.

The shirt was too big, the bottom hem falling to her thighs. The trimmed pants fit, thanks to the elastic waist, but the legs were still a little long. She rolled the bottoms twice before tucking them into her boots. Part of her missed having undies, since she had left both pairs in her cave. Especially around aliens who seemed to have a heightened sense of smell.

Bras were another thing she missed, but she luckily wasn't top heavy. She could go without them easily. The one she'd been wearing the day she'd destroyed *Soapa Six* had been lost after she washed it. One second it had been drying in the sun. The next...the damn bush she'd hung it from had shredded it.

Anabel hadn't packed any spares in her go-bag. That was only for necessary items. Her small boobs weren't a priority. The medical team hadn't enlarged her breasts to make them more appealing, like they did for operatives assigned as sex bait on most of their missions.

A shudder ran down her at the thought of that kind of duty. Thankfully, her handler had learned fast that she was more likely to beat the shit out of a target than try to seduce them. Kurt had done his best to make that clear to the big bosses.

That was one thing the fleet and United Earth ruling committee could never make her do. She flat-out refused to fuck an assignment. The one time they'd attempted to make her, she'd killed the bastard on sight. Mission over. It didn't matter that the big bosses wanted the human trafficker brought in alive.

That hadn't been an option since, he liked to fuck women with a bunch of his criminal buddies watching. She'd have had to endure that horror until she could find an opportunity to get him alone. Shooting the bastard dead before he could touch her and fleeing during the ensuing confused panic had sounded like a better plan. One she'd implemented.

She smirked, remembering the white-haired general who'd yelled at her when she'd been ordered to go before him. Kurt, her handler, had been at her side. He'd gotten his ass chewed, too.

Anabel had taken the verbal abuse without comment. The gasbag who'd been pissed had even threatened to kick her out of the fleet. It quickly told her that he didn't have high enough clearance to see her full file. He wouldn't have dared raise his voice if he had.

The general would have known she was too dangerous to treat that way...without fear of Anabel killing him, too.

Kurt had chuckled as they left. "Thanks for putting up with his bullshit and not decking him. It makes them feel better if they believe they have control over people like you. He can't have you tossed."

"I wish he could. Then I'd be free. It wasn't worth the pay suspension to punch him in the mouth. I've had more idiots insult me worse. I *did* want to suggest he bend over and let you fuck him, when he said sex was 'no big deal' and I should have just taken it. He'd have changed his tune if *his* ass was on the line."

123

"Don't ever offer up my dick for something like that. I've never pissed you off that much, have I? No one wants to fuck that guy. Especially me. I like men, but hot ones. He was old and gross."

She'd laughed at that. "That's why I kept my mouth shut. You haven't ever done me wrong."

The memory made Anabel miss Kurt badly. He'd been with her from the first mission she'd been assigned. Some handlers didn't give two shits about their operatives. He was different. She knew Kurt cared enough to fudge some reports of her missions to keep her from getting into trouble. He'd give her a copy first, wink, and walk away. That way, their stories always lined up if there were questions from the big bosses.

She trusted Kurt. That was everything in her line of work. Also very rare. He would have done everything possible to follow her last request by getting her death vid to her sister.

That thought angered her. Jessa had no right to hack into fleet databases to find out how she'd supposedly died. It was reckless and foolish, a mistake that was compounded when she'd sent Veslors to retrieve her. She understood *why* her sister did it. If she had the skills, she'd probably hack every database in the universe to learn how Jessa was killed. But that wasn't the point.

"She fucking *promised* me, damn it," she muttered.

The bathroom door opened, and Anabel turned. A surprising wave of disappointment hit when a fully dressed Raze stepped out. She'd been wondering what he looked like naked from the front. That would have to remain a mystery.

He wore a black short-sleeved shirt that showed off his impressive biceps and wide shoulders, form-fitting black pants that enhanced his slim hips and muscular thighs, and the same black ass-kicker boots.

"The bathing room is yours." His blue gaze tracked down her. "They fit. Good. I had to guess at your size."

"This is what your people wear while hunting?"

"No. You are too small to wear our clothing. We keep a supply of outfits for bounties we go after. Those have never been worn, if humans are offended by being given discards."

"Why do you keep clothing for your bounties?"

He smiled. "We find a lot of them in pleasure houses. They rarely come without a fight or take the time to put on clothing. Some species are highly uncomfortable being bare in a cell for days or weeks. It also tends to offend the ones who placed the bounty when we hand them over bare. We don't have a clothing fabricator onboard."

"Do you go after prostitutes often? What are their crimes? Do they steal from customers?"

His smile faded. "We go after the customers, as you call them. It is a common place to find them; most males enjoy copulating. We rarely accept jobs when the prey is female, unless she's a deadly threat to many."

"You came after *me*. I'm a female."

"At the request of Roth."

"Right. You said you've worked with him in the past and he's a good male."

He nodded. "You are the relative of a mate in his grouping. Veslors help each other. I gave him a big discount."

"So I'm a bargain bounty. Great."

"I would have done it for cost. Mates are precious, and so are the family of mates. Especially females. Someone should protect you, Anabel. Roth told me a little about your situation of being stranded in a section of dangerous space, and I couldn't say no." Then he smiled. "I like that. Bargain bounty."

She shook her head, amused. "Never call me that again, or I'll send a message to this Roth to tell him you said you'd do it solely for gas money on this boat. Then you wouldn't get paid."

"He would pay me more than I requested if he knew I'd given him a discount. Veslors are honorable. Are you hungry? Prasky will have first meal ready for us."

"I could eat. I've missed real food. Those ration bars suck."

"You say that often. I take it that 'suck' means bad?" He led the way out of his cabin, the doors opening for him. They returned to the kitchen, where both Veslors were already seated at the table and eating.

"Suck does mean bad." She took the seat with different food on the plate from the others, figuring that had to be hers. They were eating fruits and veggies for breakfast. She received what looked like cooked meat and chunks of bite-sized bread. There were once again no forks or silverware, so she used her fingers. The bread was soft, flavored like pancakes with something sweet, but not syrup, and it was good. The meat kind of tasted like bacon. "Yummy." She winked at Prasky. "Thank you."

He grunted at her and turned his gaze away.

"We made sure there were human-friendly ingredients onboard before we came after you." Raze dug into his fruits first. "We tend to do that with all of our prey, if the bounty is to bring them back alive."

She caught his word usage but didn't ask questions. She didn't feel like prey. The Veslors had treated her extremely well, and she wasn't afraid of them. "Well, I appreciate it."

"One human didn't survive the night," Bruck announced.

"And then there were twenty-two," she said after swallowing and taking a sip of juice. It was the same kind from the night before. "They probably pissed off one of the gorilla-like beasts by setting up a camp under one of their trees and not lighting a fire. Or maybe they had to piss and decided to do it on a killer plant. That makes one less for us to find."

All three Veslors stared at her with stunned expressions.

"Sorry if that sounded harsh, but these aren't exactly nice people out there. Would it make you feel better if I pretended to be sad that the planet took out one of them for us? That's not going to happen. I'll remind you that those assholes came here to cause mass extinction. They *deserve* to die for that."

Bruck suddenly laughed. "I like you, female."

"We were startled by your words." Raze smiled at her. "Most females we know wouldn't describe how they believed someone might have died."

"I'm not most females. All I hope for is that none of the natives were murdered by the crew. That would upset me. I've buried six, and that was six too many. They'd be alive if I'd done my job better on *Soapa Six* by taking out the crew in space. I tried my best to lock them out of the pods, but I couldn't blow them all up. I didn't have enough bombs or the materials to make more." She looked down at her plate, adding quietly, "Those deaths are on me."

"You didn't kill the inhabitants." Raze leaned closer. "The other humans did. You are trying to stop them. How many of your people have you killed so far that escaped your ship?"

"A bunch."

His eyes widened.

"You said she wasn't dangerous," Prasky snarled.

She looked away from Raze to meet the other Veslor's angry glare. "I'm only deadly to really bad guys. You're safe from me."

Prasky stood.

Raze did, too, and snarled at him. "*Sit*. You won't stalk out again. Deal with your grief and stop placing the blame where it doesn't belong. She is human, and not our enemy. You've sulked long enough."

"What he said," Bruck growled. "We all saw the proof yesterday. She hunts dangerous prey, just as we do. Hern wouldn't want you to be bitter."

Both males sat, and for long minutes, the only sounds were their chewing.

Anabel quickly finished everything on her plate and downed the juice. "I'm sorry to all of you that I've caused tension on your ship."

Then she stared at Prasky until he met her gaze. "I'm not like the bitch who tricked your brother. That was really fucked up. I'm also sorry you lost him. I can't help that I have breasts and a vagina, but I also have

128

honor. It's my job to right wrongs. Sometimes that means going undercover to catch criminals, find proof of what they've done, and bring them in to face justice. Sometimes, it means taking out threats with deadly force. It's an automatic death sentence by United Earth to murder aliens and steal their planet. I'm the only one who can hand out justice here, so far away from the fleet. These assholes are from my planet. It's *my* responsibility to stop them."

Prasky blinked finally and gave a single nod of his head. "I hear you."

"Good." She used a cloth napkin to clean her fingers and wipe her mouth. "That being said, I don't want any of you to get into trouble, since I don't know Veslor laws. I would appreciate your help tracking down the surviving crew members, but you don't have to kill them. It's probably best if I do that alone. That way, there's no blowback that can touch you."

Raze finished his meal and stood. "You gave us your proof of what those humans have done and planned to do. Our king would not punish us for ending the threat to this planet. It is our duty to protect aliens who are being invaded by a more powerful species. This is considered a hostile situation. We will help you kill them."

Dread hit as something occurred to her. "You can't share those files I showed you with your king. I told you what would happen. Those assholes from Gemini and *Soapa Six* don't represent all of Earth or the human race, but other aliens may blame all of us anyway." She rose to her feet. "It could start a war."

His lips pressed together as he watched her, but remained silent.

"We have an alliance between our people," she argued further. "That information could sever it if your king believes all humans are like the assholes who came here. I'll say it again—it's one really shitty company compared to millions of good ones that follow the law. It would be like someone hearing about that dickhead Yendo, and assuming all Veslors were like him. But that's not true. He was a lying asshole who didn't protect someone he should have, then fucked you over while trying to save his own ass after allowing that shitshow to go down. I believe everything you told me wholeheartedly, but some humans would assume the worst.

"Every race has people who love to blow things out of proportion and hate out of fear. I can't risk my planet being seen as the enemy to all aliens until someone decides to blow it to hell and back. Billions of humans live on Earth. At last count, Mars has nearly a million residents. A good portion of them are children and people who have never hurt anyone in their lives. They're just civilians. I think you'd call them timid."

"Calm," Raze stood from the table and moved toward her, stopping a foot away.

"What if your king thinks humans are all murderers? I can't risk that, Raze. It's why I made the choice to blow up *Soapa Six* and maroon myself on this planet to begin with! One death—*my death*—is worth it to avoid a war United Earth couldn't win against aliens banding together against us."

Raze reached out and gently gripped her upper arms. Anabel didn't jerk away. His features softened, and so did the look in his eyes.

"We won't share the files with our king. I hear you and understand your fears. They are valid. I don't believe our king would break the treaty, because he is wise, but I still give you my oath."

Prasky stood, drawing both of their attention. He met her gaze. "We aren't obligated to share every job or the details with our king. No one likes wars, and I can see now that not all humans are bad. You are the first good one I've met...but I am willing to believe there are others like you." He fisted his hand and pressed it to his chest, before turning to clean empty plates off the table.

Bruck rose next and smiled at her. "That means you have his respect." He fisted his hand and touched it to his chest. "And mine. I never saw those files and will delete them from our records." He left the kitchen.

Raze gently squeezed her arms, and Anabel peered up at him. He released her and took a step back, fisted one hand and touched it to his chest. Then he grinned.

"We will help you end the threat to this planet. It is our duty. No one needs to know what happened here. You can tell your humans you did all the killing. We are fine with that." He paused. "None of us saw any files. We just picked you up and left."

A gamut of emotions almost overwhelmed her, mostly gratitude. "You'd lie for me?"

"Omitting details isn't a lie. It is not speaking about things that could cause trouble or harm. It is important that our alliances with other planets remain in good standing. You are proving humans are worthy of being on good terms with. My grouping is in agreement. You have our oath of silence."

"Thank you."

"Let me show you some of our weapons. You'll need at least one to hunt armed prey."

"Lead me to your armory," she said after a moment. "I bet you have all kinds of neat stuff."

He chuckled and turned away. "Yes. We do."

Anabel couldn't say more. She was too busy wrestling with her emotions. She was finding herself wanting to stay close to Raze. He was a really good guy, honorable, and so were his grouping brothers, even the one who was leery of her.

Her gaze repeatedly dropped to Raze's ass in those tight pants.

Nope, she told herself. Her heart couldn't afford another hit by letting her attraction override her common sense. It never ended well when she attempted a relationship. She'd done so just twice in her life. Both had ended in heartbreak. The fleet and United Earth always made sure of that by separating her from whoever she got too close to. They didn't care what she wanted or if she suffered.

It also wasn't fair to Raze, either. Sooner or later, she'd just disappear from his life...as if she'd never existed in the first place.

Chapter Eight

Raze took charge of their hunting party. He'd decided they'd stay together. He also didn't want his males to have to kill anyone; he'd do it himself. They were there to help protect Anabel, if the need arose. He wished he had a body shield for her, but they'd acquired the tech after they'd lost Hern. There were only three.

Anabel swore she could handle the laser rifle she'd chosen. She had been carrying two weapons similar when he'd first located her. He regretted tossing hers into the water, but at the time, he hadn't known she'd need them again.

Their first prey was easy to find. It was the male he'd seen the day before, building a sad shelter. The male slept on the ground under branches he'd bundled together. It wouldn't protect him from weather or any animals that saw him as food. They walked right up to the human before he even opened his eyes.

To his surprise, the human grinned and sat up. "It's about damn time! Gemini sent you, right? I want food first and then—" He abruptly stopped when his gaze landed on Anabel. The human's smile faded and his face reddened. He quickly jumped to his feet. "An hour alone with *that* bitch! I'm glad you caught her. She fucking blew up our freighter! You cunt!" He lunged toward her.

Raze snarled and blocked his path.

The human halted, fear flashed across his face. "I'm serious! That cunt blew up our freighter! There was an announcement from the head of security and her face came up on all the screens with the abandon-ship notice. We've all been stuck on this shithole because of *her*." He tried to charge around Raze. "I owe that bitch some pain!"

Raze swiftly unleashed his claws and sliced them down the male's arm before he could take more than a step. The human screamed and fell to the ground, clutching his bleeding limb. "That fucking *hurt*. You could have just told me you want her all to yourselves! Fuck, man. Not cool. I'm one of the bridge crew. First Mate Brandson. I'm important!"

Anabel tried to walk around Raze, but he held out his arm to stop her. She shot him a glare but held still.

Raze stared down at the male. "We were not hired by Gemini. This female works for your fleet—and they know why you came to this planet."

The male on the ground made a choking noise. "No shit?" He stared at Anabel.

"No shit," she told him wryly. "Do you know the penalty for what you and the crew planned to do to the natives of this planet?"

The human on the ground seemed to turn whiter. "I didn't have nothing to do with that. I'm pleading not guilty." He released his bleeding arm and held up both arms, hands together. "Take me before a judge. I'll turn evidence. I'm willing to make a deal for a lighter sentence."

"Idiot," Anabel muttered. Then louder, "There is no lighter sentence or plea bargains for mass murder. I've already submitted the proof to the fleet. There's also no courtroom here. I'm your judge and jury—and I find you guilty of the deaths of harmless aliens you slaughtered on other planets, and for what you planned to do here. Your punishment is death.

Take a minute if you need it to say a prayer. Then close your eyes. I'll make it painless. It's far kinder than you deserve."

"I said I'm giving up! I demand to be returned to Earth to see a real judge. I've worked for Gemini for six years. I have a lot of dirt on them!"

Anabel sighed loudly. "Which is it? You had nothing to do with it, or you know so much that you believe you can bury the company that you worked for to save your own ass?"

The male on the ground hesitated. "Both?" He rapidly continued. "I'm surrendering and I'm unarmed. Nobody would give me their weapon on the pod. Then the assholes kicked me out of their camp because they said I was pissing them off. You need to arrest me and take me back to where I can get an attorney. He'll get me a good deal."

"We're far from fleet jurisdiction. They can't send a fleet ship here to pick up prisoners, and you damn well know it. You also know what that means. By the authority of United Earth, I find you guilty of committing heinous crimes against alien races. Now close your eyes and let's end this." Anabel pointed her weapon at the male's face. "I would recommend thinking about something good."

Raze quickly grabbed the barrel of her weapon.

Anabel frowned at him. "I know it sounds cold, but remember what he came here to do. What he's done before. You heard him. He's worked for Gemini for six years. You saw the files. He showed no mercy to the aliens they've slaughtered. It's my duty to sentence him to death." Her voice softened. "He won't get any deals, Raze. He can die here quickly, or back on Earth by lethal injection. And I have no way to haul his ass back there."

Raze sighed. "I do. We have cells. My grouping can turn him over to your fleet. It's wrong to kill a male who refuses to fight."

She closed her eyes and sighed. Then she opened them. "You swear you'll tell the fleet that he was on *Soapa Six*? They'll know what his crimes are and take him into custody."

"My oath," Raze swore.

"Fine." She gently tugged on the weapon he still held, and he released it. She lowered it to her side. "It's your lucky day, asshole. Get up. I hope you put up a fight or try to flee. I'll kill you in an instant. You got me?"

The human rose to his feet and whimpered, gripping his still bleeding arm. "I surrender. I want off this shithole planet."

Raze turned to Prasky. "Take him and lock him up."

Prasky nodded. "I'll do that and return in case more humans...surrender." He said the last word with disgust.

Raze smiled. "We can easily accommodate some of the humans in our holding cells."

"Not all of them are going to give up that easy," Anabel warned. "The only Brandson I remember from reading the employee files was convicted of trying to murder his pregnant girlfriend. He didn't want to pay child support. Luckily, he had shitty aim. He shot her twice, but she and the baby both survived."

Horror washed through Raze as he stared after the human male walking away with Prasky. "He tried to kill his mate *and* their cub?"

"They weren't mated, but yes. She was his female, and she was pregnant. His plan to fix that was getting on the roof of another building and attempting to shoot her inside her home. All because he didn't want to be financially responsible for his own child. He served just two years for that. *None* of the crew are decent humans, Raze. And I wouldn't have minded shooting him. That's why I read the files and memorized their crimes. It helps me feel no guilt for ending their lives."

Bruck snarled. "It's not too late. He's still in firing range."

Anabel started to lift her weapon.

Raze moved between her and the retreating males. "No." He glared at Bruck.

The male frowned. "Anyone who could do something like that is extremely dishonorable and should be put down. We shouldn't waste time taking him back to a holding cell. Prasky and I could hunt together while you remain with Anabel. We'd be able to find the humans faster."

"I agree with that plan," Anabel said, giving her vote. "I feel no guilt for killing these assholes, even if they aren't armed or trying to kill me at the time. They've killed plenty, and will do so again if given the chance. Gemini didn't hire petty thieves. I'm guessing the company only wanted the vilest assholes who wouldn't flinch over doing the despicable jobs they're given."

"We will put any of the humans who surrender in our cells and turn them over to your fleet." Raze held her gaze. "It is the honorable choice."

She did something strange by rolling her eyes. "Fine. I respect that, but they're only going to die when you take them to *Defcon Red* or any other fleet base. They aren't even worth sending back to Earth to face

137

trials there. I'll also warn you to expect them to try to escape. Most of them are undernourished and weak right now. Once you have them on your ship, feeding them regular meals, they're going to be highly motivated to kill your crew and steal your ship. This is your heads up."

Bruck lifted a pad. "The next life sign is close. We should go."

"One of your prisoners will fake being sick or even injure themselves," Anabel continued, following Bruck. "They'll want to fool you into thinking they need medical help, just so they can attack you if you open their cell. It's a common tactic used by prisoners. They also might beat or critically injure the weakest in the group in hopes you'll try to rescue that person, then all turn on you when you attempt it. Another common ploy. Never trust criminals. They won't care who they have to kill to escape, even if it's their friends."

"This is what we do. None of our prey have ever escaped our cells." Raze scowled, not liking that the female believed they were so naïve.

"Humans like these ones are liars and devious as fuck. I'm only making sure you know what to expect." Anabel sighed again as they walked. "You're honorable, as you said, so I'm worried that you won't realize just how horrible these assholes can be. It wouldn't cross your mind to turn one of your friends into bait, especially if it meant killing him in the process."

"I hear your warnings." Raze took a deep breath and blew it out. "They are absolutely corrupt."

"Nailed it."

He glanced at her with a look of confusion.

She laughed. "That means you're right. Dead-on right. Nailed it."

"These humans we are hunting suck."

"Exactly. I'm going to teach you very bad English, Raze," she predicted. "But that's okay. It will help you interact with humans easier in the future."

"We tend to avoid them," Bruck muttered. "The few times we've encountered them, it wasn't pleasant."

Anabel glanced at him. "I'd like to hear those stories in detail sometime."

"They attempted to kill us and steal our ship. We've encountered two human groupings on stations," Raze shared.

"Gangs," she muttered. "That's what humans are called when they band together to commit crimes. Gangs are bad."

"I will remember." Raze glanced at Bruck. "How far?"

"This one seems to be in a small cave system near the hill." Bruck pointed.

They were walking through a thickly treed area when Anabel suddenly grabbed Raze by his arm and came to a halt. She released him and made a strange hand motion to Bruck. Both stopped walking to watch her. She pointed up and shook her head, then started moving sideways.

"Gorilla-like beasties. They live in the trees and get quite violent if they happen to have any babies up there. We need to go around," she whispered. "I don't think they're hostile otherwise. I spotted one, which means there will be more."

"We don't fear beasts," Bruck looked up, seeking the threat.

"We don't provoke, either," Raze reminded him, also glancing up at the trees. He spotted a large dark creature peeking around a thick trunk about nine trees away, forty feet up. "Follow Anabel's lead. She's survived on this planet." He lowered his voice. "She seems to respect them. We will as well."

Bruck gave a sharp nod. They circled around. It took more time, but Raze didn't want to have to fight creatures who may be able to harm Anabel if it could be avoided. He wished that she'd remained aboard *Satrono*. She'd be safe on his ship.

They came to the bottom of a hill and spotted several small cave openings behind a series of large bushes. Bruck withdrew his pad and studied it, pointing to a certain location. "There," he said. "Unless the human has moved since the scan."

Anabel stepped forward. "Let me go first. I'll make some noise to draw him out. Then we'll see what we're dealing with. Why don't the two of you get behind some trees so you're not spotted?"

Raze didn't like that plan. "You can do that, but I'm getting above the cave to drop on the human if he's got a weapon. Wait for me to get into position."

He gave a sharp look at Bruck, knowing the male would protect Anabel, before he took off running. He kept behind the bushes until he passed the caves, then began to climb the rock, using his claws. He climbed higher than the largest opening, then made his way back to where he could see Anabel and Bruck. Both had remained where he'd told them. He nodded and braced his body, prepared to pounce.

Anabel hid the weapon behind her back and moved forward. "Help! Anyone?" She started to limp, dragging a leg as if injured. "I was attacked! Anyone? I need help."

Raze picked up a sound below him to the left. He adjusted his body, waiting. A human male came crawling out of a cave on his hands and knees. He held a weapon in one of his hands. The male stayed low enough under the bushes that he doubted either Anabel or Bruck saw him.

He pointed and held up one finger.

Then another human male crawled out, this one on his belly. He also carried a weapon.

Raze bit back a snarl and gestured again, showing two fingers.

Bruck nodded and his mouth moved, probably warning Anabel. She dragged her leg forward, hunching a little. "Shit. I think my ankle is broken. Anyone? I need help!"

Fury filled Raze. She shouldn't still be advancing toward the two humans. They were too close to the rock for him to land on them. They needed to move farther away from the opening.

One of the males suddenly rose, pointing his weapon at Anabel. "It's you!" The male sounded enraged.

Anabel lifted her head. "Emery!" She flashed him a smile. "You survived. I did *not* see that coming. You're kind of an idiot. I take it someone grabbed you and got you to a pod?"

Raze nearly gasped at Anabel's taunts and insults. The human had a weapon pointed right at her. It was as if she *wanted* to be shot.

"I'm going to fucking kill you, Annie. You blew up the freighter."

141

"I did." She kept advancing. "But it would be really stupid if you kill me. I'm the only woman on this entire planet, and Gemini isn't coming for a really long time. They'll probably wait at least another six months to avoid suspicion before sending another freighter out this way. Do you know what the other crew members would do to you if they found out you shot the only woman available to fuck? It'll be ugly, Emery. How do you feel about giving blow jobs? That's going to be your future if you don't get out here and see to my leg before I die of shock or something."

The male cursed loudly but lowered the weapon slightly. "What do you have behind your back?"

"I'm keeping pressure on a wound on my ass. I fell onto a stick and it punctured me. Do you happen to have a med kit? I need a patch fast or I'm going to bleed out."

The lies the female told so easily stunned Raze a little. She looked so sincere, and even grimaced as if she were in severe pain as she limped closer to the bush separating her and the male.

The male lowered the weapon farther. "I have a med kit from the pod. I'll patch you, then I'm gonna fuck you—hard." Lust had the male's voice pitching in a bad way. "I'll turn you over to the other men when I'm done with you. Not that there'll be much left."

Anabel came to a stop and shrugged. "I figured you'd have a med kit. You *do* love to drug and rape women." She suddenly dropped to her knees and swung her weapon forward. Falling to her side and aiming, even as the male lifted his own weapon.

She fired first. Her aim was true, catching the male in the face. He was thrown back.

The other male rose to fire at her, and that was when Raze snarled. The male twisted, looked up, and his eyes widened. He lifted the weapon to shoot as Raze jumped. Before he could land on the human, laser fire sounded and the male crumpled.

Raze landed and went for the weapon, ripping it out of the male's hand. It wasn't needed. There was a burn mark high on his chest, right under his neck. The male wasn't breathing. Anabel had shot them both.

He stalked into the cave, having to crouch to enter. It wasn't a deep space, and two thick mats had been laid out. A few bags sat between them. No other humans hid inside. He stormed out and checked on both humans again. Definitely dead.

Anabel walked closer and paused, weapon aimed at the two downed humans. She crouched, feeling the neck of one male, then the other. She lifted her face to Raze. "Serial rapist." She put the weapon down and turned the other male over. "Ah. This one is also a rapist. Not a shocker that the two of them banded together."

"We might have taken them alive." Raze didn't know if he should feel impressed at her skills with shooting or angry that she'd put herself in danger to kill both males.

"They were armed. I would have been wishing for death if they'd captured me. Not fun times for me, but I'm sure they would have enjoyed the hell out of raping me over and over. Emery here used to try to bring me drinks and food. We were on the same maintenance team. I'm sure he drugged it all so he could get his sick hands on me. Not that I was ever stupid enough to take anything he offered. I'm feeling no guilt."

Raze just scowled at her.

143

She sighed. "Emery had his weapon pointed at me. I took out Sharp when he popped up and tried to get a bead on you. He could have gotten off a lucky shot as you dropped on him. I wasn't risking your life for his." She paused. "You're asking too much of me if that's what you expect."

Bruck quietly came up behind her, glancing at the dead humans. "I agree with her. They also didn't surrender. He threatened to hurt the female." Anger flashed in the male's eyes.

Raze looked down at the humans. "We need to take the bodies to our ship."

Anabel cocked her head. "No need. I hear shredders coming. I knew any in the area would hear that. Laser fire seems to be their new dinner bell." She glanced up at the rock wall. "We need to climb now, guys." She hooked the weapon strap over her shoulder and backed up a few feet, crouched, then shocked them both when she jumped.

He watched her land roughly on the rocky hill about twelve feet up, then she began to climb. He heard strange sharp noises, the same ones from the beasts he'd encountered before, and unleashed his claws.

"Climb," he ordered Bruck. "The creatures are unpleasant." Raze picked up the slight thumps on the ground. They were also heavy and large in size.

He leapt and hooked his claws in the rock, following Anabel. She didn't have the advantage he did but she seemed to easily find handholds for her fragile fingers.

Bruck landed near him and turned his head. A low snarl came from him.

Raze twisted his head and saw what Bruck did. The large creatures were rushing through the thick trees, some of them slamming into smaller ones and nearly taking them down. Small rocks on the hillside began to fall from the vibrations the heavy creatures created.

"Climb," Anabel hissed from above. "I've seen them slam their bodies into shit to knock stuff down. I'd really like to not be here if they cause a mini landslide."

Raze jerked his head around and started to climb. He put his body under Anabel's in case she slipped. The hillside was rocky, and he had to avoid small stones from hitting his face as the creatures got closer.

Bruck climbed to Anabel's side, staying close. They must have climbed a few hundred feet before they reached an area where the rocks were covered in thin grass and flattened near the top of the hill.

Anabel took a seat, breathing heavily, and checked her fingers. Raze sat next to her and sheathed his claws, taking both of her hands in his. He snarled when he saw blood.

"Easy," she panted. "It's just a few scratches. I should have brought my gloves."

"You're going back to *Satrono*."

Her big green eyes met his. "Don't growl at me. I've had far worse injuries. This is nothing. Remind me to tell you about the time I had to get forty-two stitches. That was a wound to worry about."

Raze felt rage just imagining her so hurt. He wanted to ask how it had happened and if the persons responsible had died. He couldn't imagine anyone harming a female. Even a tough one like Anabel. For all her strength, she still appeared delicate to him.

"They are eating the bodies." Bruck sounded disgusted. "Including the clothing and bones. Those are some impressive jaws and teeth they must have to do that."

Raze glanced at him, seeing the male standing near the edge, looking below. "Come over here where they can't glimpse you. We need to get Anabel back to our ship."

Bruck stalked over and crouched, studying her hands, which Raze still held. He made a low, displeased noise.

Raze could relate.

Anabel shook her head and sighed. "It's going to take forever to find all the missing crew if both of you react this bad to every little scratch."

Chapter Nine

Raze finished applying the healing cream to Anabel's fingers. She knew he was upset. The sight of a little blood really seemed to disturb Veslors. She wasn't certain if it was because she was a woman, or if they believed humans were so fragile that scratches were deadly. Either way, they'd made her come back to their ship for medical treatment.

"There are more of them out there," she reminded him.

He met her gaze. "Prasky and Bruck are hunting them."

"Those criminals are *my* responsibility."

"Now they are ours as well. You got hurt."

"It's only a few scratches to my fingers from climbing. That's *nothing*. Have you forgotten that I killed two of them? I'm not some delicate woman that you need to coddle and protect, damn it!" She tried to slide off the wide, tall bed they had in their version of a Med Bay.

Raze moved quickly, blocking her with his big body. He lowered his face, putting it inches from her own. His blue eyes once again captivated her momentarily with their vivid color and those slitted pupils. A low growl came from his throat.

She reached up and pressed her hands to his firm chest. "You're very intimidating, but I'm not afraid of you. This is my job, Raze. You're not stopping me from going after the remaining crew. *Move.*"

He suddenly had his hands on her. One of them cupped her ass where it met the mattress, the other speared into her hair, where he grabbed a thick fistful at the base of her skull. It didn't hurt...but he had a good grip.

"I am keeping you *safe*," he stated, his voice raspy.

"I'm trying to do my job!"

"I am as well."

His alpha side was *so* damn sexy. She glanced from his eyes to his mouth. He had a *great* mouth. His lips were full, and she wondered if they'd feel as soft as they looked. The lower one was a tiny bit fuller than the top. The urge to nibble on it struck her hard. Which just pissed her off more. She had no time to feel attraction to a man, even if he was the most tempting one she'd ever met.

It had to be the reason she wasn't trying to hurt him. Anyone else who'd pinned her in place, put a hand on her ass, or dared to grab her hair would already be bleeding. Possibly unconscious...or just wishing they were, after having their nuts smashed.

Raze was just too damn hot. She even admitted part of it was because he was an alien. He wasn't like anyone she'd ever had to deal with before, and there was a thrilling unknown factor, made more so by how strong he was. He wouldn't be easy to take down; she doubted that she'd win if she tried.

Those two facts happened to really turn her on.

"Female," he growled.

She looked back into his eyes. "Male?"

"You're testing me."

"I haven't hit you. Isn't that what you're into?" she couldn't resist saying.

A low groan came from him, and he inched so close, his hot breath fanned her lips. She saw his eyes narrow a little and the blue seemed to darken. *Definitely hot.*

His fist tightened in her hair as he very gently forced her head back a little, and to the side. His gaze darted down to her throat. She didn't feel any fear. The very idea of him biting her made Anabel so wet, she even shocked herself. She didn't think he'd hurt her, but Raze's fangs would probably damn good. Just the idea of them made her nipples bead.

It was a reminder that it had been way too long since she'd had sex. Years. Not since Don. She'd discovered that he'd taken her leaving hard enough to fuck up his career, and the fleet had forced him into rehabilitation. He'd gone from being a respected top chef on a fleet vessel to being busted down to some shit cook job at a fleet-run prison.

It had all been *her* fault. She'd turned a funny, sweet, kind man into a bitter drunk just because he'd fallen in love with her. Sex wasn't worth the price he'd paid, or the guilt she still felt.

"Female," Raze rumbled again, the growl back in his voice.

Raze wasn't some sweet guy who would get super attached if they had sex. She'd bet lots of women had graced his bed without him giving them a second thought afterward. Not that she was ever willing to gamble on something like that again. She was more afraid that *she'd* be the one left unable to forget him until she turned to a bottle to find solace.

"I'm toxic," she whispered, trying to remind *herself* as much as him.

149

His nostrils flared. "You're the sweetest poison I have ever scented, if that is true."

The fact he could smell her, and his words, only made the need worse. She wanted him bad. The urge to close that inch between their lips to get a taste of him was almost unbearable as they stared at each other silently.

He very slowly tilted his head, his breath moving across her skin, then he closed the gap himself.

The feel of the tip of his tongue brushing her throat, right under her ear, had her heart racing. His lips whispered across the spot next. Then he opened his mouth, his fangs lightly raking her skin.

Anabel curled her fingers, grabbing hold of his shirt. She knew she should shove him back but she didn't, instead trying to pull him closer.

"So sweet," he rasped, lifting his head and meeting her gaze. He inhaled deeply—then his gaze flew down between them.

A snarl flew from Raze as his hand tightened on her ass. He jerked her closer to the edge of the bed. At the same time, he tugged on her hair. His unexpected moves forced her to fall back on the wide, padded medical bed.

Anabel gasped to find herself staring at the ceiling. Raze yanked his hand from her ass and shoved up the shirt to expose her stomach, even as he stepped closer to the bed, using his hips to part her thighs. With his other hand, he gripped the front of the stretchy pants she wore. Anabel felt a tug, her body jerking, then heard material rip.

The cool air of the room hit her bare skin.

The reality of what he'd done finally snapped her out her stupor, and she tensed, trying to assess where to hit him first to get him to slow down.

"Kuzuno," he snarled. Or something that sounded like it. Whatever it was, the word didn't translate into Earth English standard. He was staring at her now-exposed pussy, since he'd literally ripped her pants open with his claws and her legs were still spread.

When she looked at his face—Raze appeared utterly enraged. His lips were pulled back, fangs bared, and his breathing had sped, as if he were about to hyperventilate.

Unfortunately, nudity wasn't anything new to Anabel. The fleet had stripped her of any bashfulness. Orphans were placed in dorms with bunkbeds three and four rows high, all sharing a communal bathroom. At first it had only been girls. Once she began her military training, it had been unisex. She'd been forced to shower, pee, and dress with boys just feet away. Some of them checking her out wasn't anything new.

Raze's reaction was.

"Let me go if what you see offends you," she managed to say, her own temper flared hot. His reaction hurt her feelings. Something she wasn't very used to...and she didn't like it. "Back the fuck off me."

He snapped his head up, his gaze locking with hers. "I'm not offended. I'm frustrated. You're so small."

She tried to sit up, still furious and confused over her hurt feelings. He stopped her by pressing a large hand between her breasts and shoving her back down flat on the medical bed. She swiftly grabbed his thumb, ready to break the damn thing, but he jerked his hand away. His reflexes were faster than hers.

He grabbed her behind her knees and yanked her legs up high, spreading them wide. Then the bastard dropped to his knees and his mouth fastened over her pussy.

Anabel gasped, shocked by his actions yet again. His tongue pressed tight against her clit, and he licked. The texture of his tongue was... A moan tore from her. And he didn't just lick. He *sucked*. Literally.

Another snarl came from Raze—and then it was an all-out attack, as if his life depended on tasting and teasing her.

She clawed at the mattress and threw her head back. The sensations of ecstasy shot straight to her brain and all she could do was writhe and moan. Her climax was fast, brutal and vicious. It ripped through her entire body. Not that it stopped Raze. He just moved his mouth from her clit to her slit, lapping at her juices. He growled, and the vibrations he caused were so strong, she whimpered. It was too much, too intense, too...*everything*.

Raze tore his mouth off her and she watched him rise. He licked his lips, his blue eyes definitely much darker as their gazes locked. He reached for the front of his pants.

She knew what was coming. He was going to fuck her. Her legs felt like jelly now that he'd released them, but she managed to lift and spread her thighs herself this time. She wanted him.

He opened the front of his pants and shoved them down. She lifted her head to get a look at whatever he'd revealed. She already knew it would be big and hard, since she'd already felt it a few times pressed between her butt cheeks when he'd had her pinned the first time they'd met.

She didn't get a glimpse before he gripped her calves again and closed her legs. It confused her, and she opened her mouth to ask him what he was doing, but he suddenly used his hold to flip her. He had her on her stomach in a heartbeat, pulling her back and repositioned her until she was bent over the side of the bed. Raze fisted her hair again, exposing her neck, then his mouth was on her flesh.

She moaned as he licked and nipped the delicate skin. He pressed up against her, pinning her against the bed. Anabel never let a guy control her, but she felt no urge to change her current situation. She'd lost control the moment he'd put his hands on her.

"Spread," he demanded gruffly.

She parted her legs again, and he put a little space between their bodies. He positioned himself to line them up. The feel of something thick and very hard rubbed against her slit...and then he pushed forward.

Her body resisted for a second before giving way to the intrusion. He was so big. She'd expected that. What surprised her was how slow he went, careful to enter her only a little. He froze like that, before settling his body more heavily on hers.

"Tell me if it hurts. You're too small..."

"I can take you."

His mouth returned to her neck, and he slowly pushed in deeper. Anabel moaned. He felt too good. Large, almost alarmingly so, but she was taking him as promised. Raze was giving her body plenty of time to adjust to his size. He released her hair and slid his hand under her, getting a firm grip on her breast. She moaned louder as he lightly pinched her nipple.

He growled against her throat and pushed deeper.

"Oh fuck!" she panted. He felt extraordinary, but she wasn't sure if she hadn't lied; maybe she *couldn't* take all of him. Her inner walls felt stretched to the limit.

He froze again. His mouth left her skin and a low groan came from behind her. "Pain?"

She shook her head. "Just keep going slow. Please. I'll adjust."

"Torture," he growled. "So good..."

He slowly pumped his hips, taking her with slow, shallow strokes. He went even deeper and hit a spot inside her that jolted her entire body with extreme pleasure. She moaned loudly and tried to move with him, but he had her pinned too tightly in place.

"Pain?"

"No! Pleasure."

He started to move again, going deeper still. Something hot, wet and hard pressed up against her clit. Her eyes widened and she clawed at the medical bed. Whatever the hell it was, it rubbed against her clit just right. There were bumps on it, too. It damn near had her climaxing again already.

"Oh fuck me," she panted. "Faster!" It was hard to even think.

Raze took orders well, apparently, while they were having sex. He increased the pace and strength of his thrusts. His hips rode her ass, and

154

Anabel could only moan, feel, and come even harder when the second climax hit. She was pretty sure she cried out his name.

He drove in deep, and she felt wet heat blast her from inside. His large, heavy body shuddered hard, and he snarled loud enough that it probably would have made her wince if she hadn't turned into a boneless, highly sated blob beneath him.

She'd never come that hard before in her life, nor twice in a row so quickly. The massively hot alien had super-sex skills. Anabel didn't even care that she couldn't breathe well from him crushing her.

Raze must have realized, since he lifted his chest off her back slightly. She sucked in more air but had zero ability to move. Anabel was just happy to lie there limp and feeling really good. Mellow. Hell, she realized that if he tried to kill her, she'd probably let him.

"Anabel…" He adjusted again, his hands stroking her arms.

She closed her eyes. "Give me a minute to recover."

He snarled and slowly withdrew his cock. "I hurt you."

"No." The worry in his tone forced her to find the strength to open her eyes, lift her head, and twist it to look at him over her shoulder.

Raze seemed to be staring at her ass. He inhaled deeply before meeting her gaze. "You're not bleeding."

"You're big, but you didn't break me." A laugh escaped her. "No complaints, Raze. Promise."

He opened his mouth to respond, but a loud beeping sounded. He lifted his arm and touched his wristband, snarling repeatedly.

155

More snarls sounded, but not from Raze. She realized his chunky black band must be a communicator. His features hardened and he snarled again, tapped the band, and then reached down to close his pants.

"I need to go. Six humans have a hostage. They are threatening to kill the female." He spun away, rushing out the door.

Anabel shoved up hard and slipped off the edge of the higher-than-normal surface of the medical bed. Her boots hit the floor and she felt the pants slipping down her hips when she turned to go after him.

She looked down to see the damage to her pants. Raze had literally torn out the entire crotch area with his claws. She cursed, grabbing hold of the sagging material and rushing after him. "Wait up! I'm coming with." She headed toward the armory. It had to be where he'd go before leaving the ship.

She was right. Raze had a previous locked storage locker open and was yanking out a bag. "Give me two minutes and another pair of pants. I'm coming with you."

"No. Stay." He tried to get past her.

Anabel released her pants and grabbed hold of part of the bag he carried. She also stepped in his path. "I'm going with you, damn it!"

"We have shields. You don't. The males can't harm us."

"Give me a shield."

"There are no extra. We traded for them after losing Hern. Go to my sleeping place to wait for me."

"How am I supposed to get in there?"

He growled, tore the bag out of her hand, and stepped around her. She kept hold of the waist of her pants as she jogged after the long-legged Veslor. He could move fast when he was motivated. They reached his cabin and he pressed his palm on the pad next to the doorway. It opened. She stepped in the doorway, hoping that would keep it from closing.

"Stay inside. We'll be back soon." He spun, quickly storming down the narrow hallway and out of sight.

She turned, seeing a table within reach, and she dragged it toward her. It would prevent the doors from closing. Then she entered the cabin and rushed into his bathroom. There were storage drawers in there. She assumed it was where he kept his spare clothing, since he'd showered and been able to dress inside the room.

She heard a thump and looked back. The doors had tried to close despite the table in the way. They didn't auto-open again, just remained pressed against the sides of the table. It didn't close all the way though. That was good enough. She rushed into his bathroom and started opening the storage cabinets. Raze was big, but something would have to do.

She found what probably amounted to a pair of Veslor underwear. The waist was stretchy and there was definitely a pouch in the front to house his huge alien dick. She removed the destroyed pants and put on the black underwear. They almost reached her knees. The waist still had to be rolled twice, but they didn't slip down her hips. Anabel put her boots back on and then rushed out of the bathroom.

The doors wouldn't budge, even when she waved her hand over the table, hoping a sensor would read something living and open them. She cursed, dropped to her knees, and crawled under the damn table. It was a tight fit, but she got back into the hallway. That time she avoided the armory. Everything in there was locked up tight.

The kitchen was another matter, though. It took her only a minute to get there and find weapons.

Raze wasn't within sight when she stepped out of the ship, everything quiet in the grassy field. Frustrated, she walked down the ramp. She'd been hoping to catch a glimpse of him so she could follow. She took a few steps into the field—and felt the hair on her arms rise. It brought her to an abrupt stop.

She looked back and gasped.

The ramp and ship weren't there. Just the field of grass.

That wasn't possible. She backed up, and the hairs on her arms rose again just as she stepped onto the ramp, now visible again. The ship was there; it had somehow cloaked itself.

She walked forward, ready for the weird sensation that time. One look back showed no ship.

"Damn. The U.E. and fleet would kill for that kind of tech."

She studied the field, looking closely at the grass. "Old school," she muttered, seeing where some of it had recently been trampled by Raze, not yet having time to recover. "Got you!"

She rushed forward. The path got easier to follow, and she wondered if Raze had transformed into his other form, which would account for the wider path in the grass. It would also explain losing sight of him so fast. He was fast as a male, and she guessed he was even faster as a beast.

She picked up her speed until she left the field and entered the trees. Big paw marks had torn into the ground. They weren't like anything she'd seen before on KP. The size of them reminded her of molds she'd seen of Earth bear tracks, while taking a tracking course.

From the length of spacing between the strides, Raze had to be running. Which made sense; he'd want to get to his men quickly. That also meant taking the most direct route. She gripped the weapons she'd stolen from the kitchen and took off after him.

He might be an alien shifter, but she wasn't an average human.

Anabel gave it everything she had to gain speed. Every time her foot touched the ground, she elongated her pace. The resulting bounce took her higher and higher into the air with each step. Soon, she spotted a dark shape streaking into the distance.

A grin split her face. It had to be Raze. She wouldn't catch him, but she'd be able to follow if she kept him in view.

But her delight was liberally spiked with anger at the thought of a potential female hostage. *That* was the emotion required to find the strength and willpower to keep going. Running so fast would also cause her legs to dose her with a proprietary fleet drug cocktail that would keep her from tiring.

That was, if any remained. It wasn't like she had an expert medical team to resupply her anymore.

Chapter Ten

Raze reached his grouping where they were waiting behind a few large boulders near a vast mountainside. He noticed scorch marks on other nearby rocks. He came to a stop and shifted, dropping the bag strap from his mouth as he did so.

Bruck turned, appearing furious. "They have a female alien. Six human males. They are threatening to kill her if we approach."

"Did you see this female? They could be lying."

"We saw her," Prasky snarled. "She's a Cobona."

That surprised Raze. "A Cobona is working with humans?"

"Doubtful," Prasky shook his head. "She's wearing furs."

"Definitely a Cobona," Bruck confirmed. "She screamed for help in their language. It's why we rushed to this location too quickly and the humans saw us. We had already tracked the six humans in this direction."

"They are armed," Prasky added. "Cobona scales will not protect her from their laser weapons." He motioned to the singed rocks nearby.

Raze studied the damage, silently agreeing. It also confused him that a Cobona was on the planet, and wearing furs. He remembered what Anabel had said about the inhabitants. They were supposed to be a primitive race. That was not the Cobona.

He'd figure it out later, after they safely got the female away from the humans. "I'll activate my shield and transform back into my battle form. The humans will only see a beast. They'll attack me instead of the female. Use the distraction to stalk them." He motioned to the bag. "I brought stunner devices. You just need to get close enough to toss them within range."

"That Brani stun weapon would be good to have right now."

Raze nodded at Bruck. "We'll trade for one soon. But only to use in a hostage situation to protect a captive. There's no honor or excitement in easy prey."

Both males nodded in agreement.

Raze activated the shield built into his Veslor communicator, which the Brani had added to the device for the Veslors. The odd sensation of a light electrical current ran through his entire body, assuring him that it worked as it should.

He dropped to his hands and knees, allowing his rage to flow, and succumbed to the shift. It was more painful than normal, since he was shifting for the third time within about fifteen minutes. It left him feeling sore and tired, but he stomped his paws on the ground and shook off the pain.

Bruck crouched in front of him, studying his face. "Are you strong enough?"

Raze gave a nod to assure him all was well. Transforming often was a strength he possessed. It just came at a cost. He rushed off, using the large rocks to keep low to the ground, and ran a distance farther down before he headed toward the mountains. He noted various cave entrances, some low to the ground, some higher.

His senses were sharper in his battle form. The wind blew and brought him the stink of human males. They hadn't bathed recently, from the smell. It helped him locate them; he instinctively knew they weren't in a ground-level cave. Smart.

He ran toward the mountain and pounced, his claws digging into dirt to climb. The vantage point would be helpful, and humans wouldn't expect a predator to come from above.

He made it about forty feet above the ground, then moved in the direction he knew the humans were. It took longer that he'd like, since he didn't want them to hear his approach. Every paw placement was calculated.

"We want a ship," a human male bellowed. "Or the alien cunt dies!"

Raze's anger deepened. Humans, at least the ones on the planet that weren't Anabel, had no honor. It was unthinkable to murder a female. Anabel's warnings replayed in his mind. She'd insisted the males were killers who wouldn't hesitate to take innocent lives.

His males didn't respond. Raze was glad. Let the humans worry and wonder. He moved closer and heard more male voices, now lowered.

"Maybe we killed whatever the fuck they were," one whispered from below.

Raze inched toward a row of jagged rocks that formed a natural ledge, and stopped.

"Or they ran. They didn't look like this cunt. Maybe the assholes who spotted this planet and reported it to Gemini didn't survey it long enough. What if there're more aliens living on this shithole than we thought?"

"Shut up, Wade," another one snapped. "It's more likely aliens picked up a distress hail from *Soapa Six*. I'm sure the captain sent one. It's probably still transmitting. Or they picked up signals from our pods."

"He didn't," another male voice hissed. "Do you know where the fuck we are? No way did Captain Mase want any aliens finding us. It's fucking hostile space! Any responding aliens would have just killed us. And long-range pod transmitters were shut down two solar systems ago. Only the captain could override to turn them back on."

"Maybe he did. The pod *had* to be sending out signals. We landed close to each other but we launched from different parts of the freighter."

"The pods' computers link together. It's a whole different system from the distress hails. Once we launched, each pod's computer would have autopiloted themselves to be near the others."

"Then how the fuck did we end up on this shithole?"

"Fuck if I know! They probably seek out the nearest planet. I think pods are only good for about twenty days in space. One of them obviously made it here and signaled the others that it had safely landed, and the atmosphere was livable. Or someone could have hacked the onboard system to intentionally come here."

Raze flattened his body and peeked over the edge. He couldn't see the humans but their stench was strong. Definitely in an elevated cave, but still a good twenty feet below Raze.

"Please let me go," a soft female voice pleaded.

His males had been correct. Her language was Cobona.

"Shut up, you ugly bitch. I'd slap you again but your damn scales tore up my skin," one of the males yelled.

The humans would die, Raze silently promised himself. The male had just admitted to abusing the Cobona female. They were all born extremely docile. To strike one was the act of a coward. Their males were aggressive, but never to the females.

Time was up. He couldn't risk one of them hurting her. He'd leap down to show himself, and hope the males attempted to kill *him* instead of harming the female. He lifted his body, tensed, and looked for the best spot to land. He'd have the element of surprise, but even if the humans fired immediately, with his shield on, their blasts would just bounce off him, thankfully.

"I hate this goddamn planet!" a familiar female voice suddenly yelled. "Fucking bugs the size of my fists. Ouch! If I had my weapon, you'd be a dead motherfucker. Get away from me, bug jerk!"

Raze's head snapped up right as Anabel stumbled out from behind a boulder near the lower cave opening. Shock had his jaw dropping open. She wore the long shirt he'd given her, her boots, and...his urga covering her female sex.

She should have been locked in his sleeping place!

"It's the bitch that blew up our ship!" one of the males whispered, just as surprised.

"Let's get her," another hissed.

"Finally, something we can fuck. I get her first."

"Don't shoot. I wanna fuck her while she's breathing."

A fog of rage surged through Raze's body. He was about to roar out his fury at their words—when Anabel suddenly looked up, their gazes meeting.

She flashed him a smile.

That stunned him enough to go utterly still.

Anabel made a lot of noise, stomping her boots on the ground and turned, giving the mountain her back. "Fucking bugs. Fucking planet. Ugggg! I hate this place!"

She started to back up, blindly getting closer to the danger below. A loud sniffle came from her, as if she were in distress.

Small rocks skittered below, drawing Raze's focus. Three males rushed down the gentle decline to the ground, straight toward Anabel.

She spun, smile still on her face despite her sniffles. She whipped up the front of her shirt and reached into his urga, withdrawing two thin metal spikes Raze recognized from their kitchen.

"Hello, boys." Her smile dropped. "Were you looking for me? It's your lucky day. Here I am."

The three males all tried to grab her.

Anabel dodged their hands, twisted and bent to one side, slashing out with the spikes. One of the tips pierced a male through the meaty part of his forearm, between his wrist and elbow. The second one sliced open the cheek of another male's face.

"I've got these assholes," Anabel yelled.

Raze was furious, but he'd deal with Anabel soon enough. He leapt down. His paws hurt when he landed but he spun, staring into the cave.

Three more males were there, and he spotted the female Cobona sitting on the ground behind them.

He lunged, a roar blasting out of his throat.

Where were his grouping? They should have seen Anabel's approach, and stopped her. He'd have to trust them to help her defeat the three males while he handled the ones in the cave. He took down the closest one quickly, his claws tearing into the male. The human screamed in pain.

Another managed to get off a shot. The laser fire hit Raze in the side of the head but felt like a tiny tap. The shield absorbed the impact. He leapt off the downed human to go after the one holding the weapon. He slashed out his left paw and hit the male hard. The human went flying into a wall, blood spraying everywhere. His claw had penetrated the prey's skull and ripped open his face.

The third male had grabbed the Cobona, yanking the female to her feet and hiding behind her. The male assumed he was a mindless animal, willing to attack anyone in his path. Most aliens did, when they saw a Veslor in their battle form and were unfamiliar with his race. The male was hoping he'd attack the female to save his own life.

Raze snarled, showing his fangs. The female cringed, her arms coming up to protect her throat, and started to whimper. It was apparent she also believed he'd attack her.

Raze prowled forward. The cave wasn't deep. Suddenly, the human shoved the female toward him. Raze had to jump to the side to avoid the female falling against him. His anger surged again when she hit the rocky floor with a pained cry. But he had no choice. Touching his shield would have zapped her with an electrical shock. The burns caused by coming into significant contact with his shield would have been worse.

He leapt at the male, now that nothing was between them, and went for the human's throat. He swiped the male so hard with his paw that it tore the human's head off.

Another whimper came from behind him and rocks skittered. Raze turned his head to see the Cobona scrambling away from him on her back, her dark eyes filled with terror. He closed his mouth and sat on his hind legs, hoping she'd understand he wouldn't attack.

He glanced out of the cave opening but didn't see Anabel or the other three humans. He didn't hear sounds of a fight, either. It was too quiet. He wanted to move closer to the opening to check on her but the Cobona whimpered again. It would only terrify her more if he moved.

Raze closed his eyes, locking all his emotions down. It wasn't easy to do. He needed to find calm and peace. His body wouldn't transform without control.

The first memory he latched onto was Anabel under him while they copulated. Her need for him had been the most incredible scent he'd ever inhaled. The feel of her tight body accepting his rod, pure bliss.

His bones began to reshape as he transformed. The Cobona cried out in fear and he opened his eyes to watch her. She'd backed up until she'd trapped herself against the side of the cave, her body crouched into a ball and pressed to the rock wall.

He finished the shift but stayed on his hands and knees. "You are safe," he told her in her own language. The words didn't come easy for him; Cobona vocal chords allowed for a hissing language not normal for a Veslor, but he knew she'd understand regardless.

Her eyes widened and her lips parted. She was a younger female, adult, but barely. Now that he studied her, he noticed something startling—she wasn't implanted with one of their transmission nodes on her forehead. Nor did she wear any tribal jewelry to indicate which she belonged to. The only clothing she wore was fur that encircled her from under her arms to just above her knees.

"You speak to me," she hissed. "You know our words. How?"

Raze cocked his head, still not hearing anything outside. It worried him greatly. His males should have taken out the humans with ease and rushed inside to help him...but they hadn't.

"I am Veslor. Our races are allies," he reminded her.

She appeared confused, then her black eyes flashed red. A sign of strong emotion. "Your people are from before?"

Her question didn't make sense to him. "Before what?"

She lifted her clawed hand upward and made a fist, then dropped it. "When we fell."

"I don't understand."

"My people fell into an ocean. From the great black. No one came for them. There was no way to contact our race. We had to make life here, and gave up our dreams of any others coming. You know our before people?"

Raze took in her words. The story made sense, explaining why she was on the planet. A ship of Cobona had crashed here, stranding them. It must have been a horrific adjustment. Their race was highly advanced.

"Do you know what caused the crash?"

She shook her head but appeared baffled.

"Do you know what caused you to fall from the black?"

"No. Our lisssa too sad to share many stories of before. There is no reason to speak of it. This is the now."

Her lack of a transmission node implant also made sense. The female in front of him must have been born after they'd lost their ship in the ocean. He remembered Anabel mentioning spears. The Cobona had clearly lost all their technology, surviving only on what they could find on the planet. He couldn't imagine the hardship that must have caused.

"I know your before people," he told her, using her own terms to help her understand. "I can contact them, and they will come."

Her eyes widened in shock. "I must tell my lisssa! We are now people." Fear tinged her words.

"I will speak to your lisssa before I do anything. Are you hurt?" He noticed some of the scales on her cheek appeared shiny. It might be where one of the humans had struck her. The damage was only superficial.

"I will go to my lisssa. You stay. I get. Not far." The female tried to rise but she was trembling.

Raze slowly got to his feet and offered his hand. "I am a Veslor," he reminded her. "Our races are allies. We will not harm you. You are safe."

She hesitated, but took his hand.

He respected her for being so brave. Raze helped her to her feet. "Is it safe for you to travel to your lisssa alone?" He couldn't believe a female roamed unescorted. It wasn't done for their race, but stranded on a strange planet, it was possible the males had to learn to quiet their protective instincts.

She released him fast. "Safe. Stay. I get lisssa." Then the female fled.

Raze followed her out of the cave, watching her scale the mountain once she was outside. Her short claws tore into the dirt and rock, her toe claws as well, as she scrambled upward. He paused there to make certain she wouldn't fall, but the Cobona seemed to be excellent climbers. She moved fast, disappearing over the ledge.

He turned then, surveying the situation below—and fear instantly struck.

Prasky stood over three unmoving human males, but Bruck crouched over a smaller figure. It was Anabel.

He ran.

Prasky turned, his arms opening to stop him as he stepped in Raze's path.

"The female is injured but alive," he quickly told him. "Calm!"

Raze shoved him to the side and rounded on Bruck. Blood was smeared on Anabel's mouth and some of it ran down her face, where she lay sprawled on her back in the dirt. Blood also covered her hands and part of one arm. He saw and heard her breathing, a small relief.

"She took a hit to the face when one of the males kicked her. She went down but is breathing," Bruck assured him. "It knocked her out."

A snarl tore from Raze as he gently reached out for Anabel. He needed to hold her. The sight of his extended claws made him hesitate. He was too angry to touch her without possibly scratching her delicate skin.

Bruck gripped his wrist. "She breathes, and I checked her neck. I don't believe it is broken."

The very thought enraged and terrified Raze at the same time. A broken neck could kill her. Probably would, since she was a human. "Shift and run to get a medical bag. Now! Not the aliens' med kit. Ours."

"I'll go." Prasky didn't bother to remove his clothing. He just transformed, shaking off the material, and took off toward their ship.

Raze was able to calm enough to withdraw his claws and he crouched closer to Anabel, watching her chest rise and fall. She breathed. Her heart beat. The blood disturbed him, as did the damage to her lips. It appeared as if the male had smashed both with a kick to the face. He saw a partial imprint on her face from the human's foot covering.

"How did you let this happen?" Raze glared at Bruck.

The male snarled. "We didn't. She snuck by us while we waited for you to attack the humans. The moment we heard her voice, we started to advance. She killed two of the males before we even reached her, but the third kicked her." Bruck lifted his bloody hands. "I ripped out the heart of that male when I saw Anabel go down. I punched my claws through his chest to avenge her."

Avenge. "You believed he'd killed her?" he rasped. "Why?"

171

"Her neck is not broken. I am almost certain..."

But what Bruck *didn't* say gave Raze his answer. He must have heard the familiar crunch of bones breaking when the male had struck Anabel.

Raze's hands trembled as he gently stroked her face, careful to not touch her injured mouth. "I am here, Anabel. You will be fine. I won't allow you to die. Prasky will return with medicine that will fix everything. Even if the male broke your bones. Just breathe for me."

Anabel didn't stir, but she did continue to breathe. He remained crouched over her, not able to move away, needing to touch her.

"You copulated with her," Bruck said quietly. "I can smell you on her. I am sorry that she refused to bond with you. She's human. Perhaps they need more time to decide. I see how much you feel for her. Do not give up hope of her changing her mind."

Raze didn't take his eyes off Anabel in case she stopped breathing. "She doesn't understand our ways, and I didn't explain."

Bruck sucked in a sharp breath. "You must tell her once she is healed and test a mating again, so she can give you an answer. She might accept you."

Raze didn't want to discuss it. "Now isn't the time."

"Don't allow Prasky's distrust of females to darken your view of mating. She is your chance. Even if she is human."

A threatening growl rumbled from Raze.

"That is not an insult to the female. Anabel is just of a fragile race. Perhaps you want to test with a stronger female?"

Raze ignored him. He wished Anabel would open her beautiful green eyes to say something. Anything.

"You've always been the strongest," Bruck went on. "I am actually surprised you copulated with her. I don't even understand how it is possible. They don't appear hardy enough to take on one of us."

"Silence!" Raze ordered. He lowered his face closer to Anabel's until her breath brushed across his lips. The scent of her blood made him want to roar in rage. She'd been hurt.

All thoughts of capturing the remaining humans alive ceased. He'd kill them all.

Time seemed to stand still until he heard Prasky's return. The male rushed from the thick trees, a medical bag hanging from his mouth. He'd run fast and gotten what was needed to heal Anabel. Raze reached out and took it. Appreciation and gratitude filled him.

"My thanks, brother." He ignored Prasky's heavy breathing and tore open the bag, grabbing the injector he needed and lowering the dose by a third. Then he gently injected Anabel in the side of her neck. He sent hopes to his ancestors that it would work on a human.

Every second seemed like forever...then he saw the damage to her lips begin to rapidly heal. Anabel's breathing increased and her body tensed.

Her eyes opened, meeting his.

"I am going to punish you for escaping my sleeping place," he softly snarled. "You could have died." Then he slid his hands under her, ignoring her gasp, and lifted her into his arms. He clutched her against his chest as he fell back on his ass...just holding her.

173

Chapter Eleven

Anabel was being crushed by a very naked Raze. She suddenly understood what a child's stuffed animal felt like when clutched by an upset kid. He held her on his bare lap, both of his arms wrapped tightly around her. It smashed her face against his hot skin, trapping her arms so she couldn't move them.

"Um, Raze? What happened?"

"You almost died," he snarled close to her ear.

She'd followed him from the Veslor ship. At least for the most part. She'd lost sight of him and had activated her hearing implant. She'd heard human voices finally. They'd echoed slightly, telling her they had to be in a cave or near a rock surface. That had brought her toward the mountain, where their voices had grown louder.

Then she'd heard where the bastards were hiding. She knew the Veslors had to be nearby; that's why she'd felt secure enough to try to draw out some of the crew. They were holding one of the primitive aliens captive. The longer they had the poor woman, the bigger the risk that they'd try something stupid. Like attempting to rape a reptilian. Gemini hired a lot of assholes who wouldn't hesitate to do just that.

Three of the crew had rushed at her. The sharp, pointy skewers she'd stolen from the kitchen weren't the best, but they were about eighteen inches long with sharp points at the end. Good enough, since she figured the jerks would want her alive.

She'd taken out two of the men by shoving the metal rods into their necks, and had turned to take out the third when pain exploded in her face, snapping her head back. Then...nothing.

Until she woke to Raze clutching her tight. She focused on trying to assess her injuries. Nothing hurt. Not even where she'd taken the hit.

"Punish me how? I don't do spankings. That's not my thing," she murmured against his skin.

A low growl rumbled from Raze, and it caused his chest to vibrate. It tickled her lips. Part of them felt oversensitive for some reason.

"Raze? I can barely breathe."

His hold on her loosened enough for her to lift her head and see his face. He looked pissed. Not that she hadn't expected it. He'd ordered her to stay behind.

Anabel wasn't known to apologize, since she was rarely sorry. But she didn't want to fight with him, either. "I'm sorry. But you know it's my job to take out those assholes. I couldn't just stay behind."

"You could have died," he snarled.

She was grateful that she'd turned off her hearing implant or that would have hurt. "I'm fine."

He moved one arm and suddenly dangled something close enough that it banged into her shoulder. She turned her head to see a ripped bag about the size of a kid's backpack. It was black with no markings. Anabel looked to Raze for an explanation.

"I had to inject you with..." He snarled something that didn't translate. "I broke our laws to save you."

"We all did," Bruck sighed. "I didn't stop you, and Prasky went to get it. The female is the relative to a mate. The rightness overrules the law."

Anabel turned her head and found Bruck crouching just feet away. A large, terrifying beast also sat close to him. One look at the golden eyes and she knew it was Prasky. Seeing a Veslor shifted in full daylight, up close, was something she couldn't look away from. They were big bulks of terrifying menace.

"Anabel." Raze's hand suddenly gripped her chin gently and turned her head back to him. He'd dropped the bag.

She stared into his eyes. "I said I was sorry. Especially if you had to break a law. I have no idea what you gave me, though."

"We gave you a Veslor medication that we're not allowed to use on aliens unless given prior permission from our king," Bruck explained. "It is rarely given. We once had an ally turn on us after we shared it with them. They attacked our home world, attempting to kill the king to take control of our race."

"We keep your secret about the bad company killing aliens to steal worlds, and now you will keep ours," Raze growled.

She saw worry flash in his eyes and reached up to cup his jaw. "I give you my word that I won't tell. Why did those other aliens try to start a war?"

He hesitated. "It heals most injuries very fast."

"Within minutes," Bruck whispered. "Including broken bones. We don't risk others attacking us to learn how it's made. They would kill for it if they could. We learned that over a thousand years ago. Sharing wasn't enough. They wanted to possess the drug for themselves. Only one of our planets is capable of creating it."

Raze added, "We wish it were as simple as a plant we could give to others to grow. That, we *would* share. It only grows under limited conditions that our scientists haven't been able to artificially recreate. The only way for others to get it is to take over that planet."

"Shit," Anabel muttered. "I can see how that would make you a target." She saw worry flash in Raze's eyes again. "I swear on my life that I won't ever tell." Then it sank in that they must have used that miracle drug to save her life. "What happened to me?"

Raze just growled.

Bruck answered. "One of the males kicked you in the face, and I heard bones break as your head snapped back. I believed it was your neck, but you still breathed. Just not well."

"We will need to run scans when we return." Raze remained furious. "Broken bones can mend wrong if they aren't set before giving the..." He snarled the untranslatable word. "We might have to realign them and heal you again. No more fighting."

Fear hit Anabel so hard, she couldn't even argue. Had her neck been broken? Anabel wiggled her toes in her boots. Her fingers weren't numb, either. She'd seen a lot of injuries in her line of work. Not all people instantly died with a broken neck. Some survived, but dealt with severe and long-lasting damage that couldn't be healed.

A low snarl came from Prasky, and he stood, his body tense, as he stared at the mountain behind Raze. Anabel tried to wiggle out of Raze's lap to get a look around him, since he blocked her view.

"The Cobona come," Bruck whispered, getting to his feet.

"The who?" Anabel wondered how long she'd been out and what else she'd missed.

"The aliens you told us about. We know their race," Raze informed her as he gently lifted her off his lap and helped her to her feet. "They are Veslor allies. I learned from the female that one of their ships crashed here, and I believe they were unable to save their ship. The female said it went into the ocean."

A low grunt came from Bruck. "They lost everything?"

"I believe so." Raze pulled Anabel to his side and put his arm around her. "Do not move, female."

It was an order—and a threat, based on his tone. Anabel looked up at the mountain above them and saw the primitive reptilian people. There had to be over twenty of them, and they were quickly scaling down the rock face as if it were the easiest thing to do. She realized now that she had at least one answer to a burning question: the aliens could have easily found and reached her cave.

All of them were male except for two. They reached the ground first and created a protective perimeter, keeping the females in the semi-circle between their bodies and the mountain. The males drew their spears and looked ready to attack.

Anabel studied what was obviously an older alien woman. She had what appeared to be a white crystal embedded near the top of what passed for her forehead. Her coloring was different from that of the others. Most were shades of darker green, but the woman was noticeably paler. Some of the scales of her exposed "skin" appeared thinly cracked.

None of them had hair. The aliens looked like the love child of a thick-bodied lizard that didn't have a tail, and maybe a living tree...since their limbs, up close, reminded her of thick branches. Even their necks were thick and ridged, as if their heads had grown from a stump.

The female stared at Prasky first. Anabel hoped he didn't terrify the alien woman, though she didn't appear fearful. She ran her dark gaze over Bruck next, before glancing at Raze.

She hissed something to him.

If snakes had a language, Anabel imagined that's what it would sound like.

Raze shocked her by hissing back. He bowed his head for a moment and used his free arm to touch a fist to his chest. Then he hissed more. Whatever he said made the pale woman push the males out of her way and she came closer.

Anabel didn't like it when the woman stopped only about eighteen inches away from a very naked Raze. The woman reached out her thickly scaled arms and cupped his face. Her claws appeared deadly. Anabel tensed, wanting to shove her back.

"Stay still. She is greeting me," Raze rasped. "We are allies. She remembers Veslors."

The alien hissed, her black gaze staring directly at Anabel. Her scales darkened slightly.

Raze gently pushed Anabel behind him, then Bruck was suddenly there, gripping her hips and yanking her farther away.

Anabel tensed, but Bruck's hold on her tightened, as if he sensed she wanted to protect Raze. He lowered his head and whispered, "The lisssa says humans murdered some of her people and kidnapped one of their young females. She asked why he hasn't killed you. Raze is explaining that they were criminals from your world, and you are a law-seeker sent to kill them."

The woman alien moved slightly, staring at Anabel before hissing at Raze again. Whatever she said was long.

"Translate," Anabel urged softly. "Please."

Bruck complied. "She's telling him that small ships fell from the sky and she sent some of her tribe to give them aid. They know how it feels to be stranded here. Her tribesmen were murdered. They've kept an eye on the invaders since, but the humans roamed a lot during the day." He lowered his voice even more. "Their eyesight from a distance isn't good during daylight. The watchers lost track of the males killed here today."

Raze answered.

"He's telling her that your freighter was destroyed in space and that criminals escaped. You have been killing them." Bruck paused, listening to the exchange. "You were spotted by her watchers, but you move fast and were too hard to follow at a distance. She claims most of the bodies they found were killed by animals or plants."

"It's an effective way to get rid of bodies," Anabel muttered. "I used the planet to dispose of their bodies, and even to help me kill them sometimes. Like drawing the shredders with weapon fire or luring the idiots into plants that would crush them."

Bruck listened, then translated again. "She wishes for us to contact other Cobona to send ships. Their life here has been extremely difficult since they crashed. They lost all their technology. Approximately two thousand, six hundred survived a crash nearly seventy years ago, when they encountered a space anomaly." He paused. "An unstable wormhole. It damaged their ship and shot them out over this planet. They couldn't regain control for a landing and hit the deepest part of an ocean. Those who could, managed to escape the sinking ship and swam to land."

Anabel's was saddened by the news. "Two thousand, six hundred sounds pretty good, considering what they went through, right?"

Bruck's hands on her hips squeezed gently. "Most Cobona ships hold about ten thousand lives. Sometimes closer to fifteen thousand. Over half of them would have been hibernating during travel. Those ones wouldn't have stood a chance of survival. It takes them days to come out of hibernation and be fully alert."

Anabel closed her eyes, her heart breaking for the aliens.

When she opened them again, she continued watching Raze and the alien woman hiss at each other. She really wished she could understand and speak the language.

Thank god for Bruck. "She is sharing how difficult life has been for them on this planet. Most of the survivors were what you would consider children. They were too young to be in hibernation. Few mature adults survived the crash, or the first few years while they learned the dangers of the planet. They did their best to teach the young ones how to survive...but they weren't sure how to do that themselves." He paused. "Cobona are a highly sophisticated race," he told her. "Heavily dependent on technology. It's a testament to their intelligence that any survived this long."

The thought of the extremely wealthy Adler, Thomas or Bits families ending up stranded on a primitive planet was enough to make Anabel flinch. They were the three families who'd benefited from the tech business on Earth the most. To imagine them trying to figure out how to make clothing or weapons, or even to cook their own meals, gave Anabel a bit more perspective.

"We're going to contact their people to let them know the Cobona are here. They'll send a rescue." Bruck paused. "She is extremely grateful."

What happened next had Anabel reacting quickly. Or trying to. Bruck yanked her tight to his body, his arms wrapping around her when Anabel attempted to lunge forward, jealousy consuming her.

The alien had pressed her scaled lips to Raze's, then had the audacity to push her body tight to his front.

It looked like she was trying to seduce him.

Bruck could stop her body. But not her mouth. "Bitch, back the fuck off him!"

Anabel's harsh words had the alien woman jerking away from Raze and hissing at her. She even tried to step around him to come toward her.

Anabel fisted her hands. She was more than willing to fight.

Raze moved, hissing again, and got between them. The alien bitch paused. Raze waved a hand at Anabel and touched his chest, then shook his head and kept hissing.

Anabel did some hissing of her own. "Tell me what's being said!"

Bruck almost sounded amused when he answered. "He's explaining that your culture is very different, and only copulating couples touch mouths and bodies while nude." He paused. "That you meant no offense when you yelled at her. You were just...alarmed."

"I totally meant offense. She's making a pass at him!"

"She was showing him her gratitude, Anabel."

Bruck's explanation barely sank in as Anabel realized she shouldn't *care* if Raze wanted to fuck someone else—but she did. There was no denying it. He'd been with her right before they'd left the ship. What happened between them had seemed special...but maybe not to him.

She sealed her lips together and dropped her gaze as the alien bitch put her claws on Raze's chest. It was too painful to watch.

Which just pissed her off more. Raze wasn't hers. They hadn't made any commitments. He was an alien. Maybe he thought it was fine to fuck one woman, then turn around the same day and screw another. Maybe he'd even do it right here, in front of everyone.

She'd lose her shit. That was almost certain. She'd rip his damn dick off the first chance she got if the alien's pussy scales didn't do it first. Then again, maybe that super-secret miracle drug they possessed could make his missing appendage grow back.

Bruck's hold on her tightened more, causing her to look at Raze again, wondering what was happening *now*. Both had their backs to her, the alien bitch standing at his side. They were looking up at the mountain. Anabel followed their gazes.

"Shit. Are we being attacked?" Hundreds of the Cobona had appeared on the mountain and were quickly climbing down.

"No. The lisssa must have sent word to another with a transmission node that we are allies and it's safe to come."

"A what?" She glanced back at Bruck.

"The stone on her face. It's a transmitter, allowing her to mind speak to others with a node."

Anabel shouldn't be surprised, but she was. "They can talk telepathically because of some alien stone?"

"It has technology imbedded," Bruck explained. "They can communicate by focusing on who they wish to speak to, hear words inside their heads."

Anabel did a quick estimate of the incoming aliens. It had to be over two hundred.

Motion from the corner of her eye had her turning her head. More of them were walking out of the trees on both sides. She amended her number to about five hundred. Just over a third of them were women, at her best guess.

The lisssa of their people moved away from Raze to go speak to another pale alien with a stone attached to his forehead. Anabel saw her chance, now that Raze stood alone with his back to her as he watched the Cobona leader interact with a male wearing a fur skirt.

She elbowed Bruck hard in the stomach without warning. He grunted and his hold on her loosened. She lunged forward.

Raze must have heard her coming, because he turned. She refused to meet his gaze, but she did lift the long shirt, grab the rolled waist of his underwear-like shorts, and loosened them. Then she shoved them down her legs, the large leg holes easily stretching over her boots. She straightened and thrust the material at his stomach—hard. Okay, it might have been a punch. "Put those on."

He hesitated. "You're angry."

"Nudity offends me," she snapped, then punched him again with the fist holding his black underwear. "Put. Them. On."

He took them from her. "We will talk later."

Anabel spun, marching back to Bruck. She stopped at his side and crossed her arms over her chest. She no longer had pants on, but the shirt covered her girl bits. Part of her was tempted to strip out of it, if Raze didn't put those damn underwear on. She'd like to see *his* reaction if she stood naked in front of the hundreds of male aliens approaching.

She didn't have to risk it, because Raze put on the underwear and pulled them up. They fit him like a glove, not hiding the shape of his damn fine ass or the big bulge of his dick. It might be soft at the moment, but it was still noticeable.

Anabel looked away. They wouldn't talk later. She'd finish killing the remaining crew and ditch his ass. It was the only option, anyway. She couldn't let Raze or his grouping return her to the fleet. Not if she wanted to protect her baby sister.

Chapter Twelve

The trip back to the ship was a long one. Raze and the alien bitch had hissed at each other the entire way in the snakelike language. Anabel had been left to walk between Bruck and Prasky, about ten feet behind the chatty pair. Prasky had remained on four legs. She figured he probably didn't want to strut around naked like Raze had done, until she'd given him the underwear she'd stolen from his cabin.

Bruck couldn't translate for her anymore. He was too busy speaking to a few of the excited and happy-looking aliens surrounding them. Anabel felt a little nervous about the entire situation. The Veslors didn't seem alarmed at all that they were absurdly outnumbered and leading unknown aliens directly to their ship.

What if the Cobona attacked them to steal the ship? In her experience, people killed for a hell of a lot less. Being stranded on a planet for decades, knowing that ship was finally a way off, would be tempting for anyone. Even the nicest or most honorable of people.

Prasky surprised her by bumping his large body against hers. She looked down at him. Even on four legs, the top of his back reached her midsection; the top of his head nearing her throat. His sheer size reminded her of an Earth bear, if it had leathery skin instead of fur. She reached out and lightly brushed her hand over his back. His skin felt as leathery as it looked.

He gave a low growl, and she jerked her hand away. "Don't bite me," she muttered at him. "I'm already having a bad day."

He bumped into her again and turned his head. His golden gaze almost looked as if it held sympathy for her. She didn't want or need it.

Her gaze returned to Raze, his full attention on the lisssa. He was smiling, listening to the alien bitch hiss on.

Anabel hated the jealousy she felt. It wasn't something she'd ever dealt with before. Not where a man was concerned, anyway. When she'd been younger, the only excessive emotions she'd suffered had more to do with envy when she spent time around anyone who'd had parents and a normal life. The only anger tied to that emotion occurred when someone complained of having to spend time with siblings, or their family being too smothering. Such complaints made her want to throat punch the one speaking. She'd have given anything to spend time with her sister.

They finally reached the big empty field of long grass. Raze lifted his wristband and touched something on it, and the large ship suddenly appeared.

The aliens around them hissed, some of them lifting their spears as if they planned to attack the ship, but most of them just came to a dead stop, seemingly astonished. Bruck hissed loudly at the aliens closest to them. Anabel was pretty sure he was trying to tell them not to be alarmed.

The alien bitch turned and hissed at her people loudly while making some hand motions. As a large group, the Cobona broke into clusters. The females gathered and took seats on the ground. Males surrounded them with spears drawn. Two of the paler male aliens with stones imbedded in their foreheads followed Raze as he led their lisssa toward the ramp of the ship.

187

Bruck turned to her. "Raze will contact the Cobona. We will have to go into space to strengthen the signal and possibly deploy a..." He snarled something, then paused. "I believe a human term would be small missile, that heads toward a better location to transmit."

Anabel corrected him. "Missiles blow shit apart. *Boom*."

"Not missile." Bruck smiled. "A capsule that is fully automatic."

"That, I understand." She was hurt that Raze hadn't even bothered to say goodbye before entering the ship. She'd wanted to beat the shit out of an alien woman over him, proving she'd become way too attached at a speed that alarmed her. It was for the best, really, if she got away from the Veslor as fast as possible and never saw him again.

Leaving her on the planet even for a few hours would give her time to find a hiding spot until all the Cobona were rescued. Bruck had fucked up by mentioning deep caves could hide life signs from their scanners. That was information she'd use to her advantage.

"Well, have a good trip into space."

"You are coming with us." Bruck scowled at her. "We are not leaving you here."

"The Cobona know I didn't hurt any of their people, right? They won't attack me. I sure as hell won't attack *them*. This will give me a chance to return to my cave to grab some of my stuff. I'll pack up what I want and be back by the time you return."

Bruck reached out and gripped her wrist before she could step away. "You need a medical scan. Raze told you that you may not have healed properly. I will make certain."

"I should wait until we're back with the fleet, have them do that. They know human biology. Are you a doctor?"

Pain flashed over his face. "Hern was our medic, but we have all learned enough to survive without him. Don't fight me, female. You are getting that scan, and a second injection if you need one. Raze has entrusted me with your care. He must give all his attention to the lisssa right now. He's our grouping leader. She is their ruler here. It would be an unforgivable insult to the Cobona otherwise. Come, Anabel."

He headed toward the ship, pulling her along. Even Prasky bumped into her with his large head to prod her forward. She twisted, shooting him a glare. "Don't touch my ass."

He growled and bumped into her lower back. She got the message. They were going to force her onto their ship. "You *are* coming back here, right? There are crew still out there."

"We are returning. The hunt for the bad humans is only delayed. We'll find them all as soon as the Cobona have been evacuated."

At the ship door, Prasky turned away. Anabel watched as he ran toward the trees. Bruck tightened his hold on her arm and gave it a slight tug.

She looked up at him. "Where's Prasky going? Isn't he coming with us?"

"No. Some of the humans might still possess your Earth weapons. He's going to patrol the area to take any of them down if they approach the clearing while we're gone. We've accepted responsibility for protecting the Cobona until their rescue ships arrive."

She looked at the very large group of aliens in the clearing. "That's probably a good idea. This must be an entire village of them. What about the others? There are over ninety thousand on this planet."

"Their lisssa sent runners to go to other villages and tell them to prepare for rescue. It will take time to reach them all."

"Lend me a few of your weapons and I can stay to help defend the ones here. That's a big job for Prasky to do alone." Anabel really didn't want to leave the planet.

Bruck snarled and pulled her up the ramp, giving her no choice but to go with him back to their version of Med Bay. Once they entered the room, he lifted her to the bed and ordered her to lay flat.

Anabel sighed, doing as told. He ran a scan and used a handheld pad to see the results. No hologram appeared above her like they did with fleet med beds. "Well?"

He set down the pad and met her gaze. "The small bones weren't fully broken but three were fractured. I can see the newly healed areas. You are fine."

Anabel closed her eyes, letting that sink in.

"All trauma to tissue and nerves seemed to be repaired. Raze downloaded human anatomical information into our healing center's computer."

She opened her eyes and looked up at him. "That was nice of him."

"You are the sibling of a Veslor mate. We were asked to hunt and return you to the grouping that hired us. Raze worried that we'd find you severely injured if you had managed to survive long enough for us to arrive. He wanted to be able to keep you alive."

"Enough to give me your top-secret drug, apparently."

"Yes." Bruck stepped back to lean against the wall and crossed his arms over his chest. "You tested a mating with Raze. Your scents are mingled. He admitted that he hasn't told you what that means."

Anabel sat up and frowned. "We had sex. It doesn't mean anything."

Anger transformed Bruck's handsome face. "You were only curious then?" His upper lip curled back to flash his fangs, before he snarled and pushed away from the wall. "You are as callous as our own females. I will return you to Raze's sleeping place. Do not test a mating with him again. I won't allow you to hurt him, relative of a mate or not. We have suffered enough pain."

Anabel slid off the bed and stepped into his path to block the exit. His words didn't make sense to her. "Whoa." She held up her hands, before dropping them. Bruck stopped, glaring down at her. "I have no idea why you think us having sex was callous, or how I've hurt Raze. Why don't you explain this to me so I *do* understand?"

He took a step back. "We're hunters."

"I know that. Bounty hunters."

"Our females refuse to mate with males that travel off our worlds. They wish for mates who remain permanently on the surface. They believe cubs should never be raised on ships or taken from the planets."

"Okay. I follow that. You see that as callous?"

191

"Yes. Because they test matings with males despite having no intention of agreeing to bond. It is cruel. They only do it out of curiosity or to brag to other females that they were brave enough to copulate with *undesirable* males."

Anabel realized she'd stepped into some emotional Veslor shit without even meaning to. "But how is it cruel? I'm trying to understand, Bruck. On Earth, people have sex just for the enjoyment. It's about the physical pleasure found in the act, and wanting to be close to someone for a short time. Is it not like that for Veslors?"

He hesitated for so long that she wondered if he would answer at all.

"We're meant to have mates." He touched his chest. "It is a tremendously deep instinct to bond to a female. To care for her. To have cubs and spend our lives together. We aren't complete without one. That pain of loneliness grows stronger the older we get." He lowered his hand. "We know in our heads that every time one of our females test a mating with us that she will reject a bond, but it doesn't lessen the pain. Our hearts still feel hope. It is crushing." He paused. "Every time."

Anabel didn't know what to say.

"Raze felt hope. We always do. Appeasing your curiosity of what it would be like to copulate with a Veslor wasn't worth causing him pain."

"Stop right there. First off, he initiated it. Not me. Second, he didn't seem...*pained* in the least."

"His heart hurts, Anabel. You didn't ask him to bond after he demonstrated his ability to pleasure you."

She frowned. "You mean ask him to make me his mate?"

192

"Yes."

"I didn't know that was expected with sex."

"When a female approaches us, we prove we are strong enough to protect her and show her we're able to give her pleasure. Immediately after we copulate, that is when they accept or reject us."

"Maybe Raze had sex with *me* to appease his curiosity about humans. Did you ever think about that? He probably just wanted to get off."

Bruck snorted, giving her a dirty look. "You know nothing about Veslors."

"I don't," she agreed. "So tell me about your kind."

"We do not copulate to only seek pleasure. We can do that ourselves. No female is needed. Using our hand to release our seed is satisfying and doesn't cause pain to our hearts. We copulate with a female to bond. Do you understand? To give her pleasure and to show her that she needs us. That we can be whole together, instead of alone and empty apart."

His explanation left her reeling. "Raze doesn't want me for a mate."

"He wouldn't have tested a mating with you if that were true. He's not a human. I am saddened for your entire race if your males only copulate with females to use their bodies. Raze is drawn to you, and his heart feels the pull to yours. He wouldn't admit it to you, but you made him feel pain by not asking him to bond to you. We are proud." He lifted his chin and puffed out his chest.

"Fuck." Anabel turned toward the bed and rested her hands on the surface. They'd had sex right on that very med bed. "I didn't know that's what it meant when we...you know. Raze said nothing. And we were interrupted immediately after by his communicator. There was literally no time to reject or accept *anything*."

"Now you have that knowledge. Do not give Raze hope again, or you will hurt him deeper. Veslors can lock onto a female and he will always want you. Even after you are long gone from his life."

She turned back to Bruck, studying his face. He appeared utterly sincere. And sad. "Raze seems to have gotten over his pain already. That alien lisssa, as you call her, kissed him and had her hands all over him. He didn't pull away."

Bruck's eyes widened as if what she'd said stunned him. "She was not attempting to copulate with Raze. The touching of mouths is only that."

He suddenly stepped forward, gripped her upper arms and leaned close, pressing his lips to hers for a heartbeat before pulling away.

"I do not wish to copulate with you. That was the Cobona way of saying that she trusts Raze, and allowing her to get so close proved that he trusted her. He believed she wouldn't poison him, and she had faith he wouldn't attempt to kill her with his fangs. To pull away from her would have indicated that we weren't still allies. It is the same for you. You didn't fight me just now because deep down you must know I wouldn't hurt you." He released her and backed away.

"Poison?"

He nodded. "Cobona can poison others with their mouth spit and claws." He showed her his hands. Sharp claws grew slowly out of his fingertips, and he flashed his fangs. "The lisssa knows we aren't defenseless in this form. Veslors have been allies with their race for over a thousand years. Through touch, Raze and the lisssa proved the trust still exists between our races."

"Oh."

"We're not compatible to copulate with Cobona."

She wasn't so sure about that part. The females were reptilian, but they still had humanoid-shaped bodies.

Bruck seemed to read her doubtful expression. "Their females have protective exterior spikes that would physically harm a male's rod if he tried to copulate with one. Their males have tough scales. We don't. The Cobona also do not birth young the way our women do. They lay eggs."

That concept was tough to imagine. "Really?"

He nodded. "They lay three to six eggs at a time, normally. The females go into heat twice a year. Their fertility cycles last for approximately twenty years. They bond two males per female, which also makes them not compatible with us. A Veslor would kill another male who attempted to copulate with his mate."

"Oh." It was all Anabel could say. She was still trying to wrap her mind around aliens laying eggs. It also explained how twenty-six hundred survivors turned into ninety thousand in the span of seventy years, since their crash. With that kind of birth rate, she was surprised there weren't more. But then again, it was a killer plants planet. They also had no technology. That would mean a major lack of medical intervention if any of them grew ill, got severely injured, or needed advanced surgeries.

"Veslors are possessive," Bruck stated, pulling her back into the conversation.

"I got that impression when you said one of your kind would try to kill another guy who tried to fuck his mate."

Bruck flashed his fangs again, but this time it looked like more of a smile. "Raze would have attacked me if he'd seen me press my lips to yours. We should not mention that I did so to demonstrate his mouth contact with the lisssa. They did not tangle tongues. That is a human version of your kissing, correct?"

"Yes. Do Veslors...tangle tongues? Is that even a thing for your people?"

"Yes. Though you humans seem to tangle tongues even if you aren't mated or testing a mating. Veslors are different."

"I'm getting that."

Seconds of silence ticked by, both of them seemingly lost in thought, before Bruck pointed at her. "You felt possessive of Raze. You yelled at the lisssa, believing she wished to copulate with him. It wasn't truly your human culture being offended by nakedness and touching in public, was it?"

Anabel debated on whether to answer or just ignore his question. Ultimately, avoidance wasn't her way. "It's pretty rude to have sex with someone, and then touch another woman right after. I did get mad over seeing that."

Bruck's pale blue eyes narrowed as he watched her. "You wanted to challenge her for Raze." Then the big bastard had the nerve to chuckle. "You feel the pull of his heart to yours."

"I didn't say that."

"You are not denying it, either."

"We should change the subject. When are we taking off?"

"We have already left the planet."

She frowned. "No. I haven't heard the engines or felt us lift off."

"This is our healing center. It is built to be quiet and stable." He walked around her and opened the door. The sound of the engines immediately filled the previously quiet space. Bruck stepped out and pressed his hand on the wall. "We are breaching orbit. Remain here until it is done."

She didn't take that advice, instead stepping out of the medical room. The second her boot touched the floor, she felt heavy vibrations beneath her. There was a sudden jolt, and it would have knocked her over if Bruck hadn't gripped her arm, his other hand still braced on the wall.

"We normally strap in. It should be over soon. You should take my advice next time, foolish female."

Within a minute, the engine sounds lowered in volume until they were just a dull thrum in the background and the floor no longer vibrated. Bruck released her arm and pushed away from the wall.

"I am going to the bridge to help Raze. You should get something to eat." He turned, walking away.

Anabel hesitated, then followed him. She wanted to know what was going on, as well. Bruck glanced back but didn't seem to care that she tagged along. They entered the bridge to find Raze seated in a big chair, the lisssa in another nearby. The two Cobona males with crystals in their heads weren't present. She wondered where they were.

The front viewscreen was massive and it revealed mostly dark space. They must have flown to the dark side of the planet, since the sun wasn't in view. There were two moons and a dead planet showing in the distance.

Raze turned his head and their gazes locked. Then he looked away to growl something to Bruck. The male responded in Veslor. Raze nodded and faced forward again.

"Sit, Anabel," Bruck quietly ordered. "I'm going to my station."

She hesitated but then took a seat in a vacant chair. One good study of the console to her right convinced her it was a weapons station. The Veslor ship had four consoles. The one in front of Raze had two sides, which rose up to lock together over his lap. He seemed to be piloting the ship from it.

Bruck took a seat to Raze's left. Raze and the lisssa started hissing at each other again. Anabel hated not being able to understand what was being said. The strange vocals made them sound like they were arguing but their expressions didn't show anger.

A good twenty minutes of hissing passed. Anabel finally couldn't take it anymore.

"What's going on?"

Raze stopped hissing and turned his head to peer at her. "We don't have a direct link from this solar system to any containing Cobona. Bruck has launched a transmission relay."

"Relay," Bruck muttered. "Better word than missile."

Raze scowled, glancing at him.

Bruck shrugged. "I couldn't think of the human word to tell Anabel that we have the ability to extend our communications with a flying capsule that leaves a trail of transmitters."

Raze gave Anabel his attention again. "We have the ability to send out a communications relay. It will leave behind signal extenders as it seeks a connection to our people or the Cobona we wish to speak to. We don't like to use them unless it is an emergency."

"Why not?"

"We may attract the attention of other races."

She didn't like that idea, either. "Like the Kriror?" Those were the aliens she feared the most. The Elth were bad but they just seemed to want to capture human women for breeding experiments. The Kriror killed any humans they came into contact with. The retrieved logs from various doomed vessels indicated the aliens had ignored their pleas of surrender. Hadn't even tried to dock with them, but instead just blew them apart. No one survived a Kriror attack. They even destroyed any escape pods launched from threatened ships.

"Yes." Raze appeared grim. "They shouldn't bother us. We don't have conflict with them."

It still made Anabel uneasy.

More time passed, maybe an hour. She was bored, frustrated at her inability to understand the Cobona language, and starting to get hungry. Just when she considered leaving the bridge, a ding sounded though the room and the viewscreen switched from outer space to wavy static.

Raze did something and the console over his lap split into two, each side lowering to the floor. He growled something at Bruck. The male nodded, his hands flying over the controls in front of him.

The wavy static cleared, and Anabel sealed her lips as the face of a Cobona female suddenly appeared. The signal quality wasn't the best, but it was enough to make out the alien's face. She was dark green in color and had one of those clear crystals imbedded in her upper forehead. She also wore a crown of sorts, but it wasn't jeweled. It appeared to be a technological device. She wore a uniform that nearly matched her skin.

Her black eyes darted around the bridge before fixing on the lisssa.

The lisssa stood and started hissing frantically. Anabel could read astonishment on the other alien's face, her eyes growing wider, the black revealing a flash of red. Admittedly, that was a little disturbing to see. If Cobona had pupils in the center of their eyes...the younger woman's seemed to be bleeding a little.

Raze started to hiss when the lisssa finally stopped. He fisted one hand and placed it on his chest. The alien woman on the screen responded, nodding frantically enough to make her crown bump around on her bald head. She looked to her left, hissing something, and then hissed directly into the screen.

It probably lasted for four minutes before the transmission ended. The lisssa collapsed to her knees, head dropping, weird noises coming from her. It almost sounded like a squeaky whine. Raze slid out of his chair and crouched next to her, putting a hand on her back.

Anabel rose, wondering what she could do.

Bruck got out of his chair and crossed to Anabel, speaking softly. "A rescue will come within days. The Cobona we were able to contact were deeply stunned to know there were survivors from that long-missing ship. They are happy and grateful that we found them. Their lisssa is changing course and sending other ships to converge on this planet. Raze has offered for us to remain with them until they arrive. We'll return to the planet until then."

"Is she okay?" Anabel looked past Bruck, also keeping her voice down, even knowing the Cobona woman couldn't understand her. "Where are the two male aliens who came with her? I saw them board the ship."

"She's overwhelmed with emotion. They had given up all hope of ever being reunited with their people. Her bonded mates were taken to a guest sleeping place."

"Will the Kriror or the Elth attack Cobona ships when they do come?"

Bruck shook his head. "They fear the Cobona. They will avoid contact."

That was very telling for Anabel. If the Elth and Kriror were terrified of the Cobona...

Gemini, a United Earth company, had tried to slaughter their people.

"Shit." Anabel lowered her voice even more. "Some of those assholes from *Soapa Six* killed some of their people. Will their leaders go after Earth in retaliation?"

"No. Raze told them the human males were escaped prisoners that you asked us to help you hunt." He paused. "It may be best to blame the destroyed Earth vessel on the prisoners, if asked about it. When they arrive, be very careful of anything you say. It is likely they will already understand your language. Even the lisssa will eventually learn it after hearing it spoken enough. The node, even as outdated as it is, helps them learn languages quickly."

"Got it." Anabel took the warning to heart. "Thank you."

"Bruck," Raze growled loudly.

He turned away from Anabel and she saw that Raze and the lisssa had stood. Raze appeared angry. "Please escort the lisssa to her bonded males in the largest guest sleeping place. She needs their comfort."

Bruck went right to the lisssa and hissed softly to her. The female reached out, placing her hands on his chest. Then she pushed her body against his and Bruck lowered his head, accepting the kiss when the alien pressed her lips to his. They left the bridge.

Anabel watched the interaction with new understanding, now that Bruck had explained the meaning of the physical contact.

Raze strode to her once they were alone on the bridge and stopped a foot away. "I'm not allowing you off the ship when we land. Bruck and I will hunt the remaining humans."

"That's my job," she reminded him.

"Not anymore."

His arrogant tone didn't sit well with her. "That's not how it works."

He inched a little closer, his blue eyes narrowed. "You could have died," he snarled, his voice extra gruff.

She knew he was upset, but that didn't justify him trying to keep her prisoner aboard his ship. "I'm fine."

"You will stay in my sleeping place until I am able to return you to Roth's grouping. *I* will go after the humans."

"You can't just lock me in your cabin until then," she reasoned. "I have some things on the planet that I want to collect." The lives of certain asshole humans included, but she wasn't going to admit that part. "Belongings that I left in my cave."

"I will retrieve them for you."

"I'll have to show you where the cave is." And find a way to escape when she did. She didn't truly care about anything left in the cave.

He grumbled, not looking pleased. "After the humans are dealt with and the Cobona have been evacuated from the surface."

She nodded. "Thank you."

"You should eat. I need to wait for the communications relay to return and then land my ship back on the surface."

"Are you hungry? I could bring you something."

He shook his head. "I will eat soon. You should go."

Anabel didn't need to be told twice. He clearly didn't want her company.

The bridge door opened at her approach and she went to the Veslor kitchen. She needed time to think and plot her escape. Unfortunately, her thoughts circled around to what Bruck had told her about Veslor males and mates.

Had Raze wanted her to be his mate? The idea should have scared the hell out of her, but instead, all she felt was sad. She couldn't have been his mate regardless. But especially if Raze returned her to the fleet or anything controlled by United Earth. They owned her ass. No way would they allow her out of her contract early.

Or ever, honestly. People like her didn't get to walk away. Not alive. She'd lost all hope over the years of living a long life with her sister.

But...what if Raze *did* want her as a mate, and they stayed far away from other humans? His grouping didn't seem to like her people, after all. It was an option...

No. People like her didn't get long-term happiness.

Still, the longing she felt caused her heart to hurt just a little.

Chapter Thirteen

Bruck joined Anabel in the kitchen as she was still trying to figure out how to make something to eat. All the food in their cold storage was foreign to her. The packaged food was written in Veslor, which she couldn't read.

He chuckled as he gently gripped her arm and jerked his head toward the table. "Sit. I will make us something."

Anabel took a seat. "Thank you. How's the lisssa?" She no longer considered her an alien bitch, since she now knew that she hadn't been hitting on Raze.

"Emotional. She shared that she became lisssa just weeks after the crash, when her mother died from her injuries. She wasn't fully mature at that time but was being trained to lead."

"Lisssa means ruler, right? How does that work for the Cobona?"

"Lisssa means ruler of a large group. The Cobona own what you would consider six solar systems full of planets. The ship was taking them to a new world that had been terraformed for them to move to. They create new cities as their generations grow. Their ship encountered what she said was an unstable wormhole that sucked them in and spit them out over this planet. She was on the bridge when it happened, with her mother. Their ship was severely damaged and they couldn't regain control."

Anabel inwardly shuddered. It must have been hell to experience. To feel such helplessness as the ship fell and hit the ocean. The utter chaos afterward, trying to get out of a sinking ship. Then trying to make it to land and surviving on a foreign planet.

"They saved as many hatchlings as possible. Most of the adults were hibernating." He warmed some food in the cooker. "It's common for Cobona adults to sleep during travel to save on space and life support. Hatchlings aren't able to hibernate until adulthood."

"Hibernation is like sleep?"

"Yes. They lower the temperatures. Cold slows their breathing and the beats of their hearts. They drift into a very deep sleep. I believe you would compare it to a coma. Heat revives them, but it is a slow, delicate process."

"And hatchlings meaning kids?"

"Yes. Out of the six hundred adults manning the ship and overseeing the care of hatchlings, only about a hundred and fifty survived."

Anabel tracked his meaning. "Shit. So the majority of the survivors were kids."

"Yes. The lisssa said over two hundred of the surviving young were near maturity, like her. Between the adults and the older hatchlings, they managed to raise the younger ones to adulthood. They began to thrive in numbers as bonds formed and new hatchlings came along. She made the decision to form various villages to support their numbers, to make certain there were enough food sources."

Anabel's respect for the lisssa increased. "That's a hell of a lot of responsibility for a teenager to take on. No wonder she broke down on the bridge after seeing someone from her world, and knowing they were coming to get them. I can only imagine the shit she's been through and seen."

Bruck removed the food from the cooker and plated it, bringing both to the table. He placed one in front of Anabel, getting them drinks before he took a seat. "I'm grateful that we found them." He met her gaze. "Hunting you was very fortunate."

"I keep thinking about what would have happened if Gemini had succeeded in wiping them all out. The Cobona probably would have destroyed my entire planet in retaliation."

He hesitated. "They would never have known."

There is that. Anabel sighed. "Well, at least you can tell my sister that she helped me save over ninety thousand lives and got them back to their people when this is over, since she committed treason to find me. That might make her feel better when... When the fleet punishes her," *And when I don't come back*, she silently added.

His light blue eyes narrowed. "You can tell her yourself."

"Right." She looked away, digging into the food. It consisted of thick noodles of some kind and meat that tasted like pork. It was good.

"Your fleet will do nothing to the mate of a Veslor. They wouldn't dare."

She snorted and took a sip of her drink before holding his gaze. "Let me tell you something about the people who control my planet. They do a lot of stupid shit. Some of the United Earth ruling committee and the big bosses of fleet can be extremely vindictive. They don't like to be told what to do.

"Your king sounds like a great guy, Bruck. I can't say the same for all the people in charge of United Earth or our fleet. They'll want to punish Jessa for hacking into their top-secret files to find my location, and they certainly won't give a fuck if they piss off Veslors by taking her away from her mate. That's the reality. Their fear of what she might share will overrule everything else. Even angering an ally."

He just watched her.

"Tell this Roth to get my baby sister the fuck off *Defcon Red* immediately. He and his grouping need to sneak her away from the fleet vessel they're on and make her disappear, somewhere no other humans can find her. She's under U.E. contract just like I am. Unless those Veslors plan to stay with the fleet for the next nine years, until she's finished her contract...the U.E. will *not* let her go. Those bastards never do. They'll send someone like me to track her down if she runs. Their orders will be to bring Jessa back alive, but if that's not possible...they'll kill her."

His eyes widened.

"They'll want to interrogate her, to find out what she's shared, but if they realize they can't get to her—kill order. I am absolutely serious and certain of that fact."

"They wouldn't dare."

"They would. They *have*." Anabel had lost her appetite. "You have no idea what kind of orders they've given *me* over the years. Some I was able to circumvent by doing what I felt was the right thing, but not always."

"Circumvent?"

"Not always follow orders the way they wanted. Sometimes an order was given that just wasn't right. A control freak on a power trip who wanted someone dead, for example. And I might help them get away if they didn't deserve to die. That's why I know that grouping needs to get my sister away from *Defcon Red* and take her where no one can find her. You need to tell her that—"

"Bruck, leave us. The communications relay has returned. Land us back on the planet."

Anabel startled at the sound of Raze's husky voice. She slowly turned to find him standing by the door. Bruck rose to his feet without a word and left the room. Raze sealed the door and took the seat next to hers, his expression grim.

"How long have you been here?"

"Long enough for you to ask Bruck to speak to your sister. To tell her things. Repeatedly. You have no intention of allowing me to take you to her." It wasn't a question.

It was tempting to lie, but staring into his captivating blue eyes...she couldn't do it.

"No. It will get my sister killed or locked up at some black site for the rest of her life if you take me back. Some of my bosses will be afraid of what she might have discovered. Not all my missions were something the fleet or United Earth can allow to be shared with others. They'll view Jessa as a threat if they even *suspect* she's seen my file and the things they've had me do. She'll just disappear, and her mate will be told she died. I can't let that happen to Jessa. I refuse to be proof for the fleet that she committed treason to find me."

"I'm not leaving you here."

"You *can't* take me back!" She turned in her seat to face him. "So what other options are there?"

"You could stay with me."

Her heart raced. "Are you asking me to become part of your crew...or more?"

He leaned in close. "Do you wish to become more?"

"It depends on what you're offering."

Raze stood and held out his hand to Anabel. She didn't hesitate to take it. He pulled her to her feet, then surprised her by releasing her hand, lifting her easily, and draping her over his shoulder. He spun, storming out of the kitchen and down the corridor.

He growled when they reached his cabin. Anabel twisted and saw why he'd come to a halt. The table she'd used to block the doors remained. Raze lifted one leg and used his boot to kick it hard. The table broke and the doors started to close, until he slammed his hand against the scanner pad. Raze entered when they opened, sealing the doors behind them. He carried her to his bed and dropped her on her ass, where she bounced.

"Strip," he demanded.

She scrambled to her feet. "Are we officially testing a mating?"

"Yes. I will explain what that means, but later. I want you *now*."

It was tempting to inform him that Bruck had already filled her in, but she was too eager for him. She started to remove the shirt she wore but decided to get rid of her boots first. She tossed them aside, then stripped off the shirt. Once she was nude, she lay back. He only had to strip out of the underwear she'd given him to wear.

God, he had the best body. All male, muscle, and pure sexy. His cock was hard and impressive to look at. He took a step closer and leaned forward, pressing his hands on the mattress. He climbed on the bed over her. Anabel spread her legs and bent her knees.

Raze stilled, his gaze trailing down her body. "You are beautiful. So pale and pink."

She smiled. "Not pale. Wait until you meet my sister. Then you'll know the real definition. I had my handler spy on her from a distance more than once. Jessa hardly ever sees sunshine. The fleet tends to keep her working onboard vessels. I've gotten three months of planet living that has given me a bit of a tan."

Raze went for her mouth first. His velvety plush lips brushed against hers. The tip of his tongue teased her next. She opened to him, and the kiss deepened. He didn't just explore her mouth. He savaged it.

Anabel clutched at his shoulders, pulling him closer. Raze went willingly, his weight pinning her to the bed. She wrapped her legs around his waist, wanting...*needing* him closer. His taste and scent combined with the feel of his muscular chest against her breasts had her nipples stiffening. Especially when he moved, rubbing the tiny bit of furred skin against them. She moaned against his tongue and he growled. It was hot as hell.

His hand slid into her hair and he fisted a handful, giving it just enough of a tug to make her gasp. He broke the kiss and their gazes locked. She could get lost in the blue of them, the exotic sight of his vertical pupils. Not that he'd let her. He pulled on her hair again, forcing her chin up. He lowered his face and went for her neck. His kissed her there, licked, and whispered his fangs against her skin. It revved her need for him even more.

"Raze," she moaned, clawing at him with her nails, possibly digging them in enough to scratch him. She also wiggled her pussy against his body, wanting him inside her. She ached, she was so ready. He had to feel how soaked she'd become. "Fuck me now."

He nipped her with those fangs and growled. "Be still and patient. I'm learning you."

"Learn my body while you're fucking me."

He nipped her again, that time a little harder. It didn't hurt but was almost enough to break skin. "Don't test me, Anabel."

"That's what we're doing, isn't it? Testing a mating? Don't torment me, Raze. I want you inside me."

"Demanding female." He moved quickly, demonstrating his strength when he slid down her body, easily breaking her tight hold on his waist. He trailed wet kisses down her skin until he reached her breasts.

"Fuck," Anabel moaned, arching her back as Raze sucked on her nipple.

His hand trailed down her bent leg to the inside of her thigh. Then he cupped her pussy, teasing her with his thick finger by inserting it inside her.

"I'm going to come if you do that," she panted.

He sucked hard on her nipple as he applied pressure against her clit, rubbed against it, fucking her faster with his finger. Anabel lost it and did just as she warned. Her body seized as she came, crying out his name.

Raze released her nipple and pulled his hand from between her legs. He adjusted his body quickly, moving the mattress in his haste, and rolled her onto her stomach as she recovered, shoving one of his legs between hers to spread them farther apart. He came back down over her, pinning her body beneath his.

It reminded her of when they'd first met. He'd had her flat on the ground, trapped under him. Now there was no clothing between them as he got his other leg between hers and spread her legs more. She felt his cock that time, but it wasn't wedged between her butt cheeks. It pressed against the opening of her pussy. He fisted her hair again and lowered his face until his lips brushed her ear. His hot breath fanned her neck.

"Do you want me inside you?"

"Yes!"

That was all Raze needed. He pushed into her, making her cry out again. He was thick and hard. Big. No one had ever taken her pinned down flat before. She'd had sex in the doggie position but it was very different like this. She spread her legs more to make room for his hips as he drove inside her. Pleasure and pain mixed, but she didn't care. It all felt incredible. Especially when he started to thrust fast and that bumpy part of him rode her clit with every move of his hips.

Anabel lost her mind. It was too much pleasure for her already oversensitive body. She tried to buck him away, so she could match his rhythm, but she couldn't even move. Raze had made sure of that with the way his body wrapped around hers. All she could do was feel.

Another climax tore through her. It didn't end. The ecstasy just kept coming.

Raze snarled, and she felt it when he came deep inside her. Heat and pressure blasting her insides. Raze slowed his thrusts to a slow grind, as if he wanted to give her every drop by milking it out. He also lifted his chest off her back enough for her to breathe a little better.

"Yes!" she panted.

Raze went utterly still over her. "Yes to what?"

"I accept your claim...or your offer. Whatever you call it, the answer is *yes*. Bruck said this is the time that a woman decides if she'll accept or reject a mate. Right after sex."

Anabel felt nervous but she twisted her head, bracing her arms enough to get leverage on the bed and meet his very shocked gaze. "I wanted to beat the shit out of the lisssa when I thought she was coming on to you. I don't want anyone else touching you. For the first time in my life, I don't want to keep my distance. I want to stay with you, live with you, work with you...hell, grow *old* with you."

Raze just kept staring at her with wide eyes, appearing stunned. He did release her hair though, pulling his hand away.

A stabbing sensation pierced her heart and her pride took a massive hit. "Shit. Bruck was wrong, wasn't he? You don't want me as a mate. Just forget I—"

"No!" Raze nearly roared.

Anabel flinched. She wiggled a bit, trying to convey that he should let her go.

"*No,*" he repeated softer. "Bruck wasn't wrong. I will not ever forget that you have agreed to become my mate. I'm bonding us. You're mine." His voice deepened. "I'm *yours*. For life. Tell me yes again, Anabel."

"Yes."

An almost savage expression crossed his face. "You need to accept all of me for us to be fully bonded. But you are my brave female. You can take it."

Now that she knew they were on the same page, that she hadn't made a horrible mistake by thinking he wanted her as much as she wanted him, every ounce of tension left her. Anabel smiled. "I *am* taking all of you. You're balls-deep inside me still."

He leaned in closer until his mouth brushed hers. He didn't kiss her though. He peered deeply into her eyes. "That is not what I meant. Do you trust that I would never hurt you?"

Anabel didn't have to think about it. She wasn't someone who did anything half-assed, either. "I'm all in with you. I trust you." She paused. "Fair warning, though. If you ever cheat on me or break my heart, I'll probably cut yours out."

He smiled, showing fangs. "Fierce mate." His cock inside her flexed, seeming to grow even harder and thicker. "I wouldn't expect anything less from you. Terms accepted, but I will never cause you pain or betray you."

She believed him. "I swear the same. I'll never cheat on you or betray you." Then she chuckled. "You've convinced me that I'm never going to get better sex with anyone else but you."

He looked pleased. "I feel the same. I'm going to bond us now. Trust me, Anabel. You will enjoy it."

She couldn't help but glance at his fangs. "Does it involve you biting me?"

He shook his head and very slowly withdrew his cock from her. She hated the separation. Especially when he lifted completely off her body. That's when she became aware that they were both a little sweaty. Or she was. The air felt chilly on her slightly damp skin. Raze started to scoot down toward the end of the bed.

"Where are you going?"

He climbed off the mattress and grabbed hold of her ankles. She gasped when he dragged her down the bed. "Hey!" She tried to hold on when she realized he was going to pull her right off the end.

Raze dropped to his knees and leaned close, pinning her again. He positioned her until only her upper body rested on the bed. "Spread your thighs. I'm going to bond with you."

"You mean fuck me again? I'm all for that."

He positioned her a little higher. "Comfortable?"

"Yes." He had a tall bed, and her bent knees didn't quite reach the floor, but with Raze's larger body pressed against her, she didn't worry about slipping. She turned her head to study him, wondering why he'd changed their position if they were just going to have sex again.

Raze placed one of his big hands on the center of her back, applying enough pressure to hold her in place as he put a little space between his hips and her ass. He used his other hand to position his cock against her slit, rubbing the blunt tip of it against her before he pushed inside, going deep.

Anabel moaned. "You feel so good!" She wanted to ask about that hard, bumpy part of him pressed against her clit, but figured it wasn't the best time to play twenty questions. They could do that later, when she explored every inch of the man she was committing to be with for the rest of her life. She had no complaints regardless of what it was, since it helped give her the best orgasms of her life.

Raze leaned forward, pressing Anabel against the mattress. He really liked to keep her mostly immobile, but she found his dominating ways in bed a major turn-on. It heightened her other senses when she couldn't move, could only feel him fucking her.

"Anabel," he softly growled against her ear. "You need to accept both sides of me." He started to languidly fuck her in deep, slow strokes. That bumpy whatever body part of his teased her clit. "You will carry my scent, telling all others that you are mine. They will know I'll kill them if they even think about touching you or causing you harm."

Anabel moaned, deciding her life as an operator for the fleet must have twisted her in dark ways, since his words made her even hotter. Raze would kill for her. She fisted the already rumpled bedding, since she couldn't grab hold of him. His arms had hers trapped where they were braced against the mattress.

"I will kill to keep you safe or die," he growled, his tone gruff. "You must accept both sides of me." He started to pound into her, fucking her hard. "Do you trust me?"

Anabel moaned, knowing he was going to get her off again. "Yes!"

217

"I need to transform."

He was snarling enough that it made his words difficult to understand. He also fucked her even harder, and she came again. But she'd heard his words. If she had any doubts, the feel of his body over hers, against hers, had changed. His leathery skin rubbed against her back and ass.

She opened her eyes, glancing at his arm braced on the bed. It had a huge-ass paw on the end instead of a hand. She spotted his deadly claws dug into the bedding.

Hot wetness and pressure filled her from inside, and Raze made a noise she'd never heard before, almost a growling groan. He stopped fucking her, and she felt his skin texture softening. Now that she wasn't distracted by her orgasm, she heard his bones popping. It happened so fast. The paw shifted into a hand, and he brushed his fingers over her skin reverently.

"Mate," Raze breathed. "We're bonded."

Anabel didn't freak out. Her heart raced, her mind grappled with the reality of what they'd done...but then her quick wit surfaced. "Humans have a saying about wanting to be fucked like an animal. I guess I can check that one off my bucket list."

Raze suddenly slid his fingers into her hair, grasping a handful, something she realized he loved to do. He gently tugged and she twisted her head to stare into his eyes as he leaned in close.

"I'm *not* an animal. I'm a Veslor. We have two forms but one body. One mind. My people mate in battle form. It is the only way to form the bond. You will carry my scent now."

Anabel wanted to kick her own ass when she saw pain in his eyes. She'd caused that with her flip comment. "I know. I'm sorry." She wiggled her body under his.

He gave her some room to move by taking some of his weight off her.

She turned to face him and reached up, cupping his cheek. "It was my terrible attempt at a joke. Humans do that sometimes. I wouldn't have you any other way, and I accept you just as you are."

The hurt faded away and he smiled. "That's good. You're my mate for the rest of our lives." Then he grew solemn. "I'll die without you now. You are everything to me. Never question my devotion or need for you."

"I won't. I never want to be without you, either."

"Your heart is drawn to mine, the way mine is to yours."

"Yes. I'm falling in love with you, Raze. Hell, I *am* in love with you."

He leaned in and kissed her. "My mate is the reason my heart beats. I live for you."

Anabel wanted to cry. Happy tears, though. She really had fallen for Raze. He was irresistible, and she'd never stood a chance from the moment he'd captured her. "Same." She swallowed so she didn't get choked up.

A soft buzz sounded in the room.

Raze grumbled. "We've reached the planet and are descending. We'll be at the landing site soon."

He didn't need to say more. Raze was the leader of his grouping and had responsibilities to attend to. Just like she had some humans to kill before she could walk away from her last assignment.

"We should shower and get dressed. The lisssa needs your attention. We've got a shitload of aliens to babysit until their people come."

He kissed her again. "We'll celebrate our mating once we get the Cobona evacuated and take care of the bad humans."

"Yes, we will." She had the thrilling feeling that her and Raze were going to work out. "Now if I could only get clothing that fits me."

He smiled. "We'll get you some soon. For now, I will get you more of the spare clothing we keep for prey. You can alter them however you wish."

Chapter Fourteen

The amount of Cobona in the clearing had vastly increased. Prasky had to clear some of the aliens out of the way for them to land the Veslor ship. Anabel guessed that the number had gone from about five hundred to nearly a thousand. Some had set up large animal-hide tents and the smell of cooking meat filled the air.

She followed Raze and the lisssa down the ramp into the clearing. The two tall male Cobona with stones in their foreheads followed Anabel, which made her a little tense. They were big and possessed claws that could do serious damage to her body if they struck her. And she figured they might; humans had killed some of their people, after all. She was relieved that Bruck stayed close to her side.

He had taken the news of their mating a bit weirdly. When Raze told him, Bruck had loudly sniffed at them both, his eyes widening and his mouth gaping open, and then he'd practically fallen to his knees at their feet. He'd slammed his fist to his chest, kept his chin tucked low, and growled softly.

Raze had reached out to touch the top of Bruck's head, almost like a caress, and growled back. Bruck had risen to his feet and immediately gone to her side, where he hadn't spoken since, even avoiding her gaze. She didn't have time to question him before the lisssa and her two males joined them to disembark.

"Are you cool with us being mates?" Anabel spoke softly once the lisssa started to loudly hiss at her people at the bottom of the exit ramp.

"Cool? No. I am astonished. I feel many things, but cold is not one of them. I am happy for Raze. I also am worried about how Prasky will react."

Anabel made a mental note to either cut back on Earth slang or teach the meanings to the Veslors. "I figure he won't be thrilled since he doesn't trust women."

"He'll adjust."

"I hope so."

"Prasky will have no choice. You are a part of our grouping now."

A loud cheer came from the assembled Cobona. Anabel figured the lisssa had just informed her people that they'd be rescued soon. A lot of the aliens dropped to their hands and knees, scooping up handfuls of dirt and grass and tossing it into the air.

"That's unique."

Bruck chuckled. "They are thanking the land that has supported their survival by releasing it into the air. To give it freedom as well."

"Okay." She covered her mouth and nose since their display of gratitude had made the air dusty. "What's up next?"

"We wait with them until the first of their ships arrive."

"Wouldn't it be better and easier if they returned to their villages to wait?"

"They are showing us their gratitude by waiting with us and preparing a feast. Can't you smell it?"

"Sure. I just thought they were cooking to feed this horde."

"This is for us, otherwise they'd just eat the meat instead of roasting it first."

Anabel gulped. "That implies they don't cook their meat. Am I right?"

He nodded.

"Gross," she whispered.

Bruck chuckled. "They wouldn't bother to cook the meat even for us, if Raze hadn't dressed in an urga when the first wave of Cobona saw him with their lisssa. They are respecting this form instead of our other one."

She was confused. "He wasn't dressed. He was naked."

"You made him wear his urga."

Bruck's reply just made her more confused. The only thing she'd made Raze wear was his underwear so his dick was covered. "So wearing underwear means cooked food? Okay." That made zero sense to her.

A smile widened the Veslor's mouth. "That wasn't an item to wear under clothing the way you humans do. An urga is what you would consider a uniform to wear during formal meetings of our people. We mostly wear what you'd consider wraps or loincloths. They slide easily off our hips when we go from one shape to another, instead of tearing apart. A form-fitting covering such as an urga is considered formal and respectful, so we do not accidently expose our rods to other aliens. That offends some races." He paused, looking way too amused. "The Cobona are not one of them, since they wear little on their worlds as well."

Anabel tried to wrap her head around all that information. "Okay. Well...I can't eat raw meat. It would make me sick. Cooked food is good."

Bruck nodded. "It smells delicious. I'm hungry."

"You just ate not too long ago."

"We're Veslors." He grinned. "The feasting will continue until their ships come."

She decided to change the subject, watching Raze walk around with the lisssa and her two-man entourage, speaking to various groups of Cobona. "The next few days are going to feel really long with all the socializing I'm assuming will be expected from you guys." Since she couldn't speak the language, she'd prefer to go hunting for the rest of the Soapa Six crew. "Are you still running life sign scans?"

"I haven't checked the updates from the robot scout recently." He shot her a suspicious look. "You are not hunting the humans."

"I didn't say I was going to. Call me curious about how many of the Soapa Six crew remain alive."

He snorted, glancing around the area. "It's what you *don't* say that makes me suspicious, Anabel. You have a plotting mind."

That was true, but she wasn't about to admit it.

"You are forgetting one thing."

She looked up at Bruck when he spoke again and arched her eyebrows.

"It is not just our males who must socialize. You are a part of our grouping now, too. We all are responsible for these Cobona until their ships arrive. The remaining humans will be dealt with after these people are evacuated, unless they come too close. Then we will end the threat the humans pose to our allies."

Anabel studied the clearing full of aliens, then glanced back at the ship. "Any humans still alive are already coming this way," she informed Bruck. "Unless your ship was cloaked from sight while landing, they'll have seen it. It's broad daylight. Even if they realize it's not from Earth, they'll think their company paid you to come rescue them." She paused. "Or they'll just try to kill you to steal it."

He growled but nodded, lifting his wristband. "We weren't cloaked, as you call it." He tapped the band.

Anabel saw Raze lift his wrist to tap his own band, then turn to stare their way. Bruck snarled into his communicator. Raze's expression hardened and he gave a sharp nod. His mouth moved but Anabel didn't hear a response. Bruck lowered his wrist and turned to her.

"I'm going to shift and go find Prasky. We'll prevent any humans from reaching the Cobona. You stay here. Do you understand? We have shields that protect us from weapon fire. The humans can't hurt us."

"How did you hear what Raze said?"

Bruck reached up and touched one of his ears. "Receiver." Then he waved the band on his wrist. "Tracker, communications, and it provides us with body shields. Stay here, Anabel. Your mate has ordered you to do so." He spun and hurried up the ramp, back into the ship.

Less than a minute later, a huge, leathery-looking alien panther rushed out of the ship. Bruck in his shifted form. He didn't slow, only increasing his speed as he headed toward the tree line to find Prasky.

Anabel turned her attention to Raze. He and the lisssa were still together, speaking to various groups of her people. He probably had to stick close to her side until the rescue. Bureaucratic crap that she didn't want any part of. Raze glanced her way and she forced a smile, then pointed up the ramp and made an eating motion.

He paused, then nodded. Anabel hated to deceive him, but she still had a job to do. She entered the ship, heading for the kitchen. She had no plans to eat. The Veslors had sharp implements in there since that would make great weapons, since she didn't have access to their armory. She did find one of their data pads left on the table. It wasn't password protected. She accessed the robot scout and found just six targets still alive.

"I'm coming for you, assholes," she muttered.

Five minutes later, she peeked out of the ramp. Raze had walked even farther away from the ship, his back facing her as he spoke to the lisssa. Anabel quickly rushed down the ramp and made her way around the other side of the ship, hoping Raze didn't glance her way. Once she felt the ship would block his view, she ran toward the trees, leaving the clearing.

There was no doubt in Anabel's mind that any living humans would be heading toward the Veslor ship if they'd seen it come down. They'd kill any Cobona they encountered, since that was their job. Hers was to stop them.

She picked up the pace and ran in the direction where most of the pods had come down. She also activated her ear to enhance her hearing.

She just hoped she didn't run into Bruck or Prasky. They'd be pissed that she hadn't followed Raze's order to stay at the ship.

"I never took orders well," she muttered, running faster.

Raze was furious. He'd caught sight of Anabel running around the *Satrono*. He wasn't surprised. She was a rebellious female. He was also slightly impressed. She wasn't docile enough to do everything he demanded. Life with her would never be boring.

He addressed the lisssa, lowering his voice. "We must speak privately."

She met his gaze and then led him away from her people. Her bonded males stayed close. "What is it?"

"The criminals would have seen us land. My males and mate have gone to prevent them from harming more of your people. I would like to join them with your permission."

"I will send hunting parties to assist you."

"The humans have advanced weapons. Please have your warriors guard the perimeter of the clearing and bring your females and hatchlings closer to our ship, where they will be safer. We'll handle this enemy."

She gave a nod. "I will trust your judgement. It would be unforgivable to lose more of our lives so close to our return home." Then she stepped closer. "You trust your mate to hunt her own people? Do you not worry that her loyalty rests with them instead of us?"

He hid his anger at her doubt. "My mate is a law-seeker. The other humans on this planet are law-breakers. She's already killed many of them, including two of the males who attacked your female right before we met. Anabel's loyalty is to us." He touched his fist to his chest. "To me. On my honor. I am certain."

The lisssa studied his features but then gave a nod. "You have my trust, and therefore I will trust your mate."

"Thank you. The faith is not misplaced. Anabel is completely honorable. I will join the hunt."

Raze quickly walked away to return to his ship. He retrieved a data pad and linked it to the robot scout. There were only six humans besides Anabel showing. He checked the locations and quickly left his ship, closing the ramp behind him.

It wasn't that he didn't trust the Cobona. He did. They wouldn't steal it. There were young in the clearing, though, and he didn't want them exploring his ship and possibly causing any damage to the *Satrono* or to themselves. He was responsible for them for the time being.

He rounded his ship and took off after his mate. Anabel's scent had faded with the slight breeze but she hadn't tried to hide her foot trail. Her haste had left an easy enough path to follow.

He wasn't certain if he'd yell at her or not when he found her.

His mate's footprints deepened and were spaced farther apart once she left the tall grasses in the clearing. He knew she was fast once she got going. The direction she headed was directly toward one of the human prey. He grit his teeth and ran faster. She didn't have weapons.

Regret filled him at that thought. He should have coded her into the armory, to give her access. She was part of his grouping, even if she refused to take his orders.

Minutes later, he halted, inhaling the stench of what he felt certain was an unwashed human male. He ducked behind a tree and narrowed his eyes, all senses on alert. He activated his shield. The soft electric current washed over his skin.

228

He spotted slight movement in a treetop about fifty yards to his left and peered up. A snarl locked in his throat as he watched his mate walk along a thick branch about thirty feet in the air. Her gaze appeared to be locked on something he couldn't see from his position. He heard a twig snap and his heart stopped.

Anabel kept moving along the branch, away from him—then suddenly jumped.

He rushed around the tree as a loud grunt sounded. The sound of flesh being struck was one he knew well. He raced around a thick, tall brush, his claws unleashed.

His mate had a human male on the ground, straddling his hips. She ripped a laser rifle away from the male, tossed it aside, and punched him in the face. Raze wanted to pull her away but he refrained. The human was now unarmed and Anabel would probably grow angry with him for interfering. His mate was fierce.

The male, much larger than Anabel, managed to roll them both. Anabel threw her head forward, slamming it into the male's chin.

"Fuck!" The human flinched back.

His mate drew up a leg tight to her chest, placed her boot on the male's shoulder, and kicked out, sending him flying. He landed hard on the dirt, one arm striking the trunk of a tree. Bone snapped and the male screamed.

The human recovered faster than Raze would have expected. He grabbed a knife from his belt and stood.

Anabel had already risen. Raze couldn't believe it when his mate smiled and pulled yet another cooking spike from the kitchen out of her belt.

"There's a fucking alien ship!" The human cradled his injured arm but kept his knife pointed at Anabel. "I saw it come down. I'll let you live if you help me kill the crew and take it over. We can get a distress signal to Gemini. Then you and I can work out a deal."

"Fuck no, asshole."

The male threw the knife without warning. Raze roared his rage as it flew toward his mate. Anabel swiftly ducked the knife as the human dove for his laser rifle.

Anabel rushed toward him, the cooking spire raised to strike the human.

Raze had seen enough. He reached the male first and used his claws to tear out the male's throat as he turned, attempting to lift the weapon. Raze realized his mate had stomped on the human's arm, to keep the weapon down, but she needn't have bothered. The male died in seconds.

Their gazes met. Anabel took a deep breath and reattached the spire to her belt. "How pissed are you?"

"Very."

"You're supposed to be with the lisssa."

"You're supposed to be eating on our ship."

"And I've only told you a million times that this is my job."

Raze had to leash his claws before he touched her. He gripped her shoulders, looking her over for injuries. He smelled a little blood and found the source. He crouched, staring at her knee in her baggy pants. There was a tear in the material and a small bloodstain.

"It's already healed. I think I cut it on the bastard's belt when I jumped on him. I made sure my legs took the brunt of the impact."

He rose to his feet, glaring at her all the same. "We're going back."

"There's five more of them out there. He admitted to seeing your ship land, Raze. I'm betting the others did too. They'll be heading for it. We need to stop them before they reach the clearing and all those Cobona."

"Bruck and Prasky are hunting."

"So am I!" His mate appeared frustrated and angry at the same time. "I didn't need your help. I would have stabbed him before he made the shot, but you got in my way."

He reached down and tapped his finger against the spike attached to her belt. "With something we use to cook meat strips?"

"I work with whatever's at hand when I don't have access to high-tech weapons." She moved to his side, bent, and tore the laser rifle from the dead human's hand.

He watched her check it over as she straightened.

"It's got over half a charge left." Then she smiled. "Is this better? Do you approve?"

He growled, not sure if he wanted to kiss her or roar at her.

"You can snarl at me later. Let's finish this. Five more to go unless your males already ran into a couple of them. How fast does the robot scout update again?"

"Every hour."

She pulled out a data pad from the back of her shirt, tapping it on. Then she pointed. "Two more that way. Are you coming with me or not?"

"We will talk later about this, mate."

"I'm sure we will." Anabel smiled again. "You know I'm probably as stubborn as you are, don't you?"

"I'm starting to understand that."

"Veslors mate for life, right?"

"Yes."

"Then you're stuck with me, sexy." She winked. "Now let's—"

He deactivated his shield and lunged, grabbed her around her waist, and took her to the ground. They landed behind a thick tree. Laser fire missed them by inches, hitting the trunk. He rolled, stayed low, and searched for the threat.

"Fuck!" Anabel rolled as well, crawling forward to peek around the trunk. She raised the weapon and fired toward another tree.

A human male fired back. Anabel jerked back and met his gaze. "Shift and leap. I'll fire at him while you distract him."

"I have a shield. *Stay.*" He activated his shield, feeling infuriated, and stepped from behind the tree. Laser fire immediately hit his shield but didn't penetrate. He roared and stomped toward the human.

The male gasped as he fired again, then quickly realized his weapon was useless. He turned to run. Raze unleashed his claws, wanting blood. That male had nearly ambushed and shot his mate.

Raze didn't get the chance. Anabel fired, hit the male in the back of the head, and the human went down. He was dead by the time Raze reached him.

Anabel approached and took the human's weapon, checking it over. "This one's almost fully charged."

Raze glared at her.

"Two weapons are better than one, right? Two down, four to go."

"I am going to tie you to my sleeping place again."

"I look forward to it." She smiled and then marched away from him.

He followed. "Female..."

"Four more, Raze. Then we'll go feast. I'm sorry that I didn't realize what an urga was, by the way. I just thought I was borrowing your underwear."

"You have a lot to learn, mate." The first thing he'd teach her once they took care of the threat is that she should never put herself in danger, despite her impressive skills. It was his duty to protect her and keep her safe.

Anabel suddenly stopped and raised her weapon. Raze raced forward to put himself in front of her, silently promised to get her a shield as laser fire struck his own. Anabel darted from behind him and fired.

A human male fell from one of the tree branches and hit the ground with a thud.

"Willis. He was a smart one."

Raze was confused.

Anabel rounded him and approached the fallen human. "This is Whitmore Willis. He was an engineer who served nine years for killing his ex-wife and her new husband. He liked to brag about how he got the charge dropped down to manslaughter." She checked his weapon, then dropped it with a sigh. "It broke when he fell."

"Why do you believe that male was smart?"

"I'm betting he was following the other guy to see any danger coming. The idiot I shot in the head was his bait. And Willis kept to high ground by climbing into the trees."

Raze snarled. "I want to take you back. Let Bruck and Prasky take care of the other humans."

Anabel ignored him, pulling out the pad to check the last known locations of the other humans. "I love you, but I'm finishing this."

"Stubborn female."

"Guilty. And I'm all yours." She jerked her head in a direction to their left. "Let's go."

He followed but stayed very close to his mate. It was tempting to throw her over his shoulder and take her by force back to the ship. He didn't though. Anabel drew him *because* she was spirited. She'd always do her own thing. He'd just have to remain close to keep her protected.

"We're doing a job for the Brani soon."

"Remind me who they are?"

"The ones who gave us our shields. I'm getting you one."

"I can't wait. Does it hurt at all when the laser fire hits you?"

234

"No. It just gives off a very mild jolt of electricity where a weapon impacts."

"So cool!"

They didn't run into more humans. The robot scout updated, and Anabel's lips puckered out. He'd never seen that expression on her face before, and inched closer to get a view of the data pad screen.

There was only one human life sign. It was Anabel's.

"My males were successful."

"Yeah..."

"Why are your lips doing that?" He turned off his shield and gently gripped her chin, forcing her to face him. "Do they hurt?"

"It's called pouting. I really wanted to take out those males." Then she smiled. "My job here is finally over, though. Bright side. All the humans are dead."

"All but the one in our holding cell. That life sign wouldn't show."

Her lips pushed out again. "Don't remind me about Brandson. You should've let me kill him. He's going to be nothing but a pain in your ass until you dump him on the fleet."

Raze lowered his head and kissed his mate. "So bloodthirsty."

"Just over people who shouldn't still be breathing."

"The Cobona await. Let's feast."

She nodded, giving him another kiss.

Raze felt relief as they headed back to his ship and the clearing.

Chapter Fifteen

Anabel snuggled closer to Raze's warm body. He lay sprawled flat on his back with his arm around her, Anabel pressed against his side. Both were recovering from marathon sex after waking up.

The past few days had been busy, mingling with the Cobona, but at night, they secluded themselves inside his cabin. Her new mate had stamina to spare, and was extremely talented at making her come.

A beep sounded, and Raze growled softly, extricating himself from her to sit up. She watched as he tapped his wristband and growled into it. She really wished she spoke his language, or they'd revert to standard Earth, since all of them knew it. She figured it was probably Bruck telling them to get their asses out of bed and go outside for another day of feasting. She couldn't tell Prasky or Bruck's voices apart in growl.

He tapped his band again and met her curious gaze. "Three Cobona ships have entered this system. They should be sending transport shuttles to the surface within twenty minutes."

She quickly sat up. "I thought they wouldn't be here for a few more days?"

"I never underestimate the Cobona. They've probably improved the speed in which their vessels can travel. They are highly evolved and intelligent. I wish they shared their technology with us." He got out of bed, moving toward the bathroom. "We must meet with the first representatives who land."

Anabel climbed out of bed, following him. "Well, now is probably the best time to ask if they could at least help you upgrade your engines. You did just save thousands of their people."

He paused just inside the bathroom to look at her. "We would never expect compensation for something like this. They are our allies. It was an honor to discover the Cobona trapped here and reach out to their people."

I mated a saint. Anabel just nodded, entering the bathroom, too. "Of course. My bad. I'm too used to thinking like a human. We're big on trading a favor for a favor."

He chuckled as he started the shower and stood under the warm water. "Now you're a Veslor."

But she certainly wasn't a saint, since she itched to run her hands over his body as he soaped up. Raze had turned her into an addict when it came to sex. She couldn't get enough of him.

He seemed to read her mind when he smirked and shook his head. "I want you, too, but we must be responsible."

"I hate that word right now," she admitted, trading places with him under the flowing water to scrub down her body. Aliens tended to have amazing senses of smell. It would probably be rude to meet with a Cobona delegation reeking of sex.

"I do too," he admitted, helping her out with her back. His big hands felt good on her skin as he soaped her up.

"Tease."

"I will please you this evening."

"Then don't slide your hands any lower." She moved out of the water and cleaned her lower half herself, while he did the same. Soon they were dressing. All the spare clothing the Veslors kept onboard for their prisoners were more like pajamas. They were comfortable, but she missed clothes that fit and didn't have stretchy waists on the pants.

"I might be the first human the Cobona meet, and I look ridiculous," she admitted, using a thin strap to tie her hair into a ponytail. "Upside, they might not see us as threatening in any way because of it."

"You look adorable."

She turned away from the reflective portion of the wall Raze had shown her how to activate, glaring at him. She hated being called that. Kids and pets were adorable. Not fully grown women. Her annoyance quickly fled when she caught a glimpse of Raze dressed in black, form-hugging leather pants with matching boots. His looser long-sleeved shirt was white and a good portion of his chest was revealed with the low slit in the front. He reminded her of one of the characters in those space pirate vids she'd seen from Earth, only an alien, much-hotter version.

"I want to strip you naked and lick you right now."

Raze's blue gaze locked with hers and he growled, flashing fangs. "Behave."

A shiver went down her spine, but the good kind. The way his voice deepened, that slight growl to it, always turned her on. So did the sight of his fangs. She knew intimately how good they felt when he applied them to her skin. "I'll try, but it's hard."

He reached down and adjusted the generous bulge betraying his reaction to her words. "My rod is hard now, thanks to you, mate."

She turned away and waved her hand over the sensor to make the wall in front of her no longer reflective. "Do all Veslor ship cabins have these? They're neat."

"I had that one added."

Anabel faced him again, grinning. "Is there anything in particular that you like to watch yourself do?" She glanced down at the front of his pants.

He growled, advanced, and clasped her hand. "I can't meet the Cobona representatives with a hard rod. *Behave*." Then he led her out of their cabin and through the ship to the ramp. "I added the reflective wall because I sometimes hold meetings with our king. I don't want him to see me looking undesirable."

That had her eyebrows arching and she shot him a look. "Do you want him to feel attraction toward you?"

He snorted. "'Undesirable' means a Veslor who doesn't take care of his appearance. Rough. Unkempt. As though living in space has made us forget who we are and where we came from."

"Got it." She bit back a laugh. "Just making sure."

Prasky and Bruck were already outside. The lisssa and her two bonded males were with them. The temporary tents and cooking pits were being disassembled by the Cobona. It seemed word had already spread that some of their rescue transports were about to land.

Raze stopped, holding her back. He lowered his voice as he leaned in, putting his mouth close to her ear. "Remember to watch what you say at all times. The Cobona coming will more than likely understand every word. They can instantly download languages."

239

"Got it." He was reminding her to stick to the story he'd told the lisssa. Her job title was law-seeker, the crew who made it to the surface were escaped prisoners, and they were the ones that blew up *Soapa Six*.

Raze squeezed her hand and they met with the lisssa. The tall Cobona smiled, but she appeared nervous. Raze hissed at her, and she hissed back, speaking in her language. Anabel again wished for a translator. She made a mental note to ask Raze if she could have one implanted, since he'd stated she was a Veslor now. *He* might not ask for upgraded tech, but she had no qualms in doing so.

Her gaze went to his cool black wristband. She wanted one of those, too. It would help her work with them on their bounty hunting jobs. She fully intended to be a part of their grouping in all ways. That also reminded her that she needed to learn all about their food, and how they prepared it, so she could take her turns at kitchen duty.

There was a slight booming noise, and everyone raised their heads to peer up at the sky, including Anabel. A shuttle streaked into view, giving off a bright red trail of exhaust. For a second, she worried that something had gone tragically wrong, but no one else seemed alarmed when she glanced at Raze and the lisssa.

She pressed up against his side and whispered, "Is that normal? Smoke means fire where I'm from. Usually it's black, though."

"It is a representative vessel. They tend to make it clear that attacking their ship would bring blood and death," he whispered back.

"Got it." She watched as the shuttle grew larger, heading right for them. It circled over their heads about five hundred feet up, still releasing

240

red smoke. Then it stopped, and the shuttle lowered, landing next to the Veslor ship. They had it uncloaked for the occasion.

Raze pulled her tighter against his side. "Stay with me. You're my mate. We're one unit."

She gave a sharp nod, knowing her years of training would pay off. She was used to throwing herself into all kinds of unusual situations.

Raze moved them toward the alien shuttle, the lisssa on his other side. Her two bonded mates followed behind. They stopped and waited as the seamless ship suddenly revealed a large door. It slid open sideways and a ramp lowered.

The delegation consisted of two female Cobona and eight heavily armed males. All wore very dark gray, except for the leading female. She wore black. Their uniforms appeared military. All of them wore those technological crowns, resting just above the nodes imbedded in their foreheads.

"Bow your head," Raze whispered, doing just that.

Anabel lowered her chin but refused to take her darting gaze off all ten.

Boom. Boom. Boom. Boom. Boom. Boom.

She startled a little. Raze's arm around her tightened. "More transports," he whispered. Then he straightened.

So did Anabel, looking up. It wasn't just six shuttles in the air, as indicated by the booming noises—but over fifty. At least. They'd sent a small army. It made her nervous, but she was easily distracted as the black-uniformed female rushed forward and hissed at the lisssa.

The lisssa hissed back and ran forward as well. Both women embraced. It wasn't a brief social nicety, more of a bear hug, as if the two were old friends seeing each other after a long separation. That guess was confirmed when they broke apart, and the younger alien cupped the lisssa's face. They stared at each other but didn't speak.

"They are family by blood," Raze whispered. "Their mothers were sisters."

"One looks so much younger." Anabel kept her voice low, to avoid offending anyone.

"They have lived here without medical assistance," Raze explained.

She could understand that. Humans also lived much longer with medical intervention to slow their aging, and remove signs of it.

The two Cobona turned to Raze. Anabel put on her game face as the uniformed woman stared hard at her. She wasn't sure of their protocols, so she didn't offer her hand to shake. It might be insulting. The woman turned her attention to Raze.

He released Anabel and put his fist to his chest, then hissed at her.

The woman hissed back before looking at Anabel, hissing.

Raze responded.

The woman stepped closer. "You are a law-seeker?"

Her standard Earth was impeccable. "Yes."

"Why did some of your people kill ours?"

"They were law-breakers who escaped from an Earth freighter, and made it to this planet. I've been tracking and slaying them for their crimes."

The alien's black eyes grew red in the center. It still freaked Anabel out a little, since it looked like blood was leaking out. "Your planet leaders didn't sanction this attack on the Cobona?"

"Absolutely not," Anabel said firmly. "We immediately execute our people for the crime of killing innocent aliens. Humans are only allowed to kill if it is in self-defense, to protect themselves from certain death. That wasn't the case here."

The Cobona woman stared at her intensely. It almost felt like a test.

Anabel blinked first, not wanting to piss her off, in case it was. "Our leaders aren't even aware of your kind," she admitted. "When I first saw the Cobona living here, I believed that they were the indigenous inhabitants of this planet. I'd never seen them before. I eliminated the humans who murdered the Cobona. They paid for their crime with their deaths."

"Our scouts witnessed this woman killing one of her own," the lisssa admitted. "She allowed the other to run free, but followed him to where other humans were camped. Then she attacked them."

Anabel hid her surprise. First that the lisssa could suddenly speak her language, and second, because she hadn't realized the Cobona were shadowing her. They were damn good; she'd been vigilant, trying to avoid them.

"It's my job to take out threats." Anabel carefully chose her words, not wanting to overshare more on that subject. "They were a threat to everyone living here."

The black-uniformed Cobona addressed her next. "Your race is truly unaware of ours?"

"Yes. I travel in space often for my job, and kept apprised of races that come into contact with my kind." She gestured toward Raze. "We are allied with Veslors." She hoped that helped smooth things over with the woman, who still seemed a bit on edge.

The uniformed Cabana growled at Raze next. It seemed she knew Veslor language, as well.

He growled back and reached out, taking Anabel's hand. She figured he was backing her up and possibly stating they were mates. Either way, the alien woman in charge seemed to relax her stance as he continued to growl.

The woman turned to Anabel when he finished. "Your job here is done. We sent trackers out to locate the remaining humans. Their deaths will be swift, without pain. We are a merciful people."

Anabel wasn't about to argue or point out that there were no remaining humans left alive, besides herself and the one locked up in a Veslor cell. Six of their people had been murdered. It was their right to seek vengeance. She wondered if the "swift, without pain" would have actually been the case if there were any humans left to kill...but she didn't question it further. The crew of *Soapa Six* would have deserved whatever the Cobona dished out. "Of course."

The woman lifted her head, staring into the distance seemingly at nothing, then focused back on Anabel and flashed her fangs. "I have just received a report. You are the last of your kind breathing here this day, mate of Raze."

She turned away and hissed at the lisssa. Then the two linked arms, walking amongst the other Cobona. Their delegation followed.

Anabel waited until they were a good distance away. "Do you think they'll go after Earth in retaliation?"

"No. The lisssa's testimony of you killing your own kind to seek vengeance for the deaths of the Cobona will prove your people have honor."

"Has the lisssa always known standard Earth?"

"No. Their nodes allow them to share data. The link is instant."

"So, they like...sent a language program mind to mind?"

"Yes."

"Cool." Anabel was pretty certain she wouldn't want a stone imbedded in her forehead to gain the ability, however.

"Are you angry that they planned to kill the remaining humans?"

Anabel looked up at Raze. "No. We have a saying on United Earth— an eye for an eye. Those assholes killed some Cobona. It would've been only fair if they'd died at their hands. Do you think they really would have taken them out fast, if any had remained, or made them suffer first?"

"Instant death." He shrugged. "The Cobona aren't into torture or suffering. It's considered abhorrent and perverse."

"So they're way better than humans," she muttered. "Got it."

He chuckled. "I wouldn't say that. Just different and more cultured than most races."

"So what now?" She watched as the lisssa and the delegation kept moving around the large groups of Cobona, speaking to them. "Is there going to be another feast?" She reached down and touched her stomach.

"Because I have to admit, I'm never going to get used to putting down that much food just to avoid insulting someone."

"No more feasting. We're free to go."

Anabel let that information sink in, trepidation creeping in. "You can't take me to *Defcon Red*...or anywhere else where the fleet is established. They'll report that I'm alive to United Earth. That would be bad for me, but worse for Jessa, if anyone suspects she had anything to do with getting me off this planet. They'll arrest her. And I'll be considered a fugitive for not returning to duty."

Raze released her hand and cupped her face. "No one is taking you from me."

She stared into his beautiful blue eyes. "They're sneaky and underhanded, Raze. I should know. I was one of them. I've pulled off all kinds of impossible retrieval missions over the years."

"I will think of a safe way for you to visit your sister. I gave my word to Roth and his grouping to bring you to them."

"There's no safe way to get me onboard a fleet vessel. They have face scanners that would identify me instantly and send out alerts. I'm considered missing by now, so they'll be looking for any sign of me surfacing anywhere."

"Then we won't have you enter their vessel. We will visit Roth's grouping and invite them onto *Satrono*. I will keep my vow to Roth to bring you to them, but you'll be staying with us when we leave."

"*Defcon Red* has the best tech available. They'll scan your ship and detect a human onboard."

He touched his wristband. "This tech is better than your Earth's."

"But I don't have one of those."

He smiled. "You will. The humans will not know you are with us when we visit Roth's grouping."

Anabel was still afraid. A lot of shit could go wrong. "That grouping really needs to get Jessa the hell away from fleet if she's taken a mate. I told you that they have contracts on us. Once they learn she's married, they'll pull Jessa's ass off that ship and make her disappear."

Raze growled and anger creased his handsome features. "Stay here."

He started to walk off but she grabbed his arm. "Where are you going?"

"To ask a favor of the Cobona. Their transmitters are more powerful than ours. They could send a message to Roth and his grouping faster than we can. We're too far from their location. I'll tell Roth to prepare to leave with us, and why."

"Be damn careful. The fleet might have them under surveillance."

"We're allies."

"Yeah. Well, humans are paranoid. Would Roth's grouping know the Cobona language?"

"Yes."

"Send it in that. As I said, we didn't know about them. That means we won't have any way to decipher their language unless you mix standard Earth words in there, which they could possibly use as keys to unlock some of it."

He gave a firm nod. "Understood."

"And shorter is better when you send that message. It will give the linguists less to work with."

"Agreed." He spun and strode to the Cobona in the black uniform.

So much for Veslors not asking for favors. "I'm a bad influence on him," Anabel muttered.

"You make him happy."

She startled, turning to peer up at Prasky. Yet another Veslor had managed to sneak up on her. "Are you angry about our mating?"

"I don't understand his attraction to a female so delicate, but you are his mate. It is done." He sighed. "Don't hurt or betray him, female. I will hunt you like prey if you do."

"Fair enough." She smiled at him. "I'm falling madly in love with him, Prasky. Raze is amazing. I never thought I could have what he gives me. If you don't believe me, one thing you can count on is that I'm not a fucking moron. I'm never going to screw up what we have."

He studied her face and his features softened. "Your vow?"

She lifted her fist to her chest and lightly thumped it. "My vow."

That made Prasky smile. It shocked her a little that he actually *could*. "Good. You have my blessing, Anabel. Be good to him."

"I will."

More shuttles landed, and large groups of Cobona began to board. After only an hour, all of them were gone.

Raze returned to Anabel after the delegation left last. He smiled at her. "The squadron lisssa agreed to send my message. She's already transmitted it to her vessel in space, and they are forwarding it to others in the closest vicinity to *Defcon Red*. Roth and his grouping should receive it within the hour."

"That's fast, considering we're so far in the black."

He took her hand, leading her toward the ramp of the *Satrono*. "They have shielded scout ships everywhere. They could get a message directly to your planet if they wished. They have long been aware of humans."

"They have?"

He nodded. "They enjoy studying other races."

"But not to interfere," Bruck added, walking beside them. "They don't stay to watch, but send out scientific teams randomly to gain information as different civilizations evolve. Veslors were deemed a good ally. It's why they made contact with us long ago."

In other words, Earth hadn't been deemed worthy, Anabel thought. It didn't surprise her. "What message did you send?"

"I kept it short." Raze closed the ramp and led the way toward the bridge. "We are coming, and be prepared to leave with us."

Anabel let Raze buckle her into the seat next to his. "That's all?"

"Yes. You said to keep it short."

"Right. That's definitely short. Did you mention that I'm with you?"

He took a seat and activated the console that folded over his lap. "No. It is implied. We were sent to hunt and return you to their grouping. We wouldn't come for them unless we had you, and they'll assume we have information that they're in danger by my insistence they leave with us."

"Okay." She'd trust Raze's take on the short message, and that the other Veslors would understand. They'd worked together in the past. It meant they'd probably developed a rapport.

Bruck and Prasky were also on the bridge with them. Her seat vibrated from the engines coming online, and Anabel felt a little excitement as they lifted off the surface. Emotions also choked her up a bit.

She'd gone to KP thinking it would be the place where she'd die. Now she was safely off it, with a mate, and her entire future had changed. She wouldn't be returning to service. It would make her a fugitive if United Earth or the fleet found out she was alive...but Raze was worth that risk.

As they entered the upper atmosphere, the sight of four massive alien ships had her eyes widening. They were dark green, shaped like two thick tubes, with countless connectors between them. She'd never seen ships built that way before. "How many Cobona fit into those vessels?"

It was Bruck who answered. "They each house up to about ten thousand."

"Are they transport vessels like the one that crashed here?"

"No. This is their version of military vessels. But similar to the transports, a good portion of them will be hibernating. They keep large numbers in case troops are needed for any reason. Coming out of hibernation fully still takes a day or two, but they would plan a battle in advance, if fighting is necessary."

Again, Anabel felt United Earth had dodged a huge bullet. Or total annihilation, really. The Cobona were not an alien race to mess with.

They flew past the vessels and soon she spotted the remains of *Soapa Six*. What appeared to be hundreds of small shuttles were swarming over the wreckage.

"What're those?" She hoped the Cobona hadn't sent teams inside to retrieve any information on the freighter. They'd figure out fast that most of the things they'd been told were fudged a bit, with plenty of details left out.

"Those are salvage robots," Prasky informed her. "They are stripping materials from the wreck. They'll cut it, melt it down, and repurpose it for the Cobona. A lot of races take advantage of discarded vessels in that way."

Anabel turned to shoot Raze a worried look.

He shook his head. "They won't be interested in any of Earth's technology. It's too primitive by their standards. Just metals and materials they can repurpose. They won't investigate how the vessel was destroyed or who lived on it."

She breathed a little easier. It also reminded her... She lifted her leg and crossed it over her knee, shoved up her pants, and applied her fingers on the pressure point to activate the hidden compartment.

Anabel stared at the data chip.

Raze snarled. "You're bleeding."

"I'm done with my old life. Everything on this was already sent to my handler." She smiled at him. "I'm going to destroy it."

He glanced at her leg, then nodded. "Don't do that again. I don't like you harming yourself."

"The skin is already healed." She tugged down the pants and lowered her leg. "That's the last time I'll ever have to open that compartment."

"Good."

"How long do you think it'll take to reach *Defcon Red*?"

Bruck was the one to answer. "Five days, if they've remained where they said they were traveling."

Raze suddenly separated the console and stood. "Take over, Prasky. We're going to strengthen our bond."

Anabel unclipped her belt, grinning. "Lots of sex?"

He took her hand, grinning back. "Lots of sex."

Bruck groaned. "Go. Copulate. Forget that your two males have no females."

"You could find some," Anabel called back as Raze quickly led her off the bridge.

"Never!"

She laughed. "Prasky is *really* against mates. But at least he's cool with us being together."

Raze suddenly grabbed her, threw her over his shoulder, and his big hand cupped one of her ass cheeks. "We will convince him that mates bring happiness, and he will seek his own."

Anabel wasn't sure about that, but she wasn't going to think too hard on it, either.

Raze carried her into their cabin and gently set her on her feet. "Strip. You said you wanted to lick me." He tore at his own clothing.

"I so am."

Chapter Sixteen

Raze waited for the communications to link. They were only hours away from reaching *Defcon Red*. It was tempting to have contacted the grouping leader earlier, but he wasn't certain how closely the humans monitored the Veslors living onboard their military vessel. It was best to be closer to the other grouping, in case they needed help escaping from the fleet.

It would be an unexpected tactic to suddenly arrive if the humans were keeping a close surveillance on the fighting Veslor grouping. The fleet would expect to have plenty of time to prepare a trap if they wished. They also would have heard Roth offering his hunter grouping the job, and Raze's promise to send word immediately if they found the female, if the humans monitored Roth's communications.

It wasn't Roth, but Gnaw who showed on the communications vid. The male appeared to have just woken.

"Raze." Gnaw touched his bare chest. "How went the hunt? Roth and my grouping are on duty, but I remain with our females in our home."

They spoke in Veslor. Raze wasn't certain of how much the humans had learned of their language, with the other grouping living on the vessel. He switched to Juba. They were an alien race who only had contact with Veslors for trading. They lived one solar system away. All his people knew their language. "We must be careful of our words, friend."

Gnaw's gaze sharpened and he sat up straighter. "Understood," he replied in Juba. "Why this language?"

"The people you live with will not know it."

Gnaw gave a sharp nod. "But why the secrecy? Did you find—"

Raze cut him off before he could say Anabel's name. "Watch your words. Nothing that will give away what we speak of in case someone hacks or overhears our communications. Our hunt was successful. We have the female. She is healthy and fine. But she has sworn anyone knowing she is alive will create danger for her sister and your males. Understood? She fears others of her kind in power will kill them both, but make it appear as an accident. Did you receive our message? The female believes you need to leave your ship immediately."

Gnaw appeared grim. "Yes. We've had some warnings about the female you hunted."

Anger filled Raze. "She is an honorable female! Who said that she wasn't? They are being dishonest!"

"Not that." Gnaw leaned closer. "We were warned that the people she worked for might harm her if the female you hunted was returned. We were told to take her far from her people, for her safety.

"Your message said we need to leave with you. Is this still correct? We had planned to contact another grouping to pick us up, after the sister was returned to us. We didn't bring a ship for this job. Our king was worried our technology might be studied and duplicated without permission. These people are mostly good...but not all."

"It is best if you come with us. Our ship has technology that their sensors can't track if we don't want them to. We will arrive within a few hours. Be prepared to leave."

Gnaw appeared a little surprised again, but he gave another sharp nod. "I will inform my grouping. Thank you for the offer to pick us up. We'll be leaving sooner than imagined, but we have two mates pregnant with cubs. Do you have a healing center on your ship? Neither are due to birth soon, but their health and safety must come first."

That news shocked Raze. Bruck had shared that at least one Veslor male had bred cubs with a human, but he hadn't been aware any of the males in Roth's grouping had been that fortunate. "We have an excellent healing center and *Satrono* can accommodate up to twenty people. We're currently four. I hadn't heard that any of your grouping expected cubs. Blessings to your males and mates!"

Gnaw smiled. "My mate has already given me two cubs. Roth's mate is carrying one." He paused. "Do not share this with the female...but her sister is carrying at least one cub as well. She wishes to give her that news herself when they are reunited."

Raze reached up and placed his fist to his heart. "My vow of silence. A great yearning has come true for your males. Many blessings."

"Yes." Gnaw's smile widened into a flat-out grin of joy. "Our king has given us territory. It is on a growing planet, but he knows we do not wish to be farmers. It is a small continent, ours alone, with much to hunt by land and sea. The weather is always fair. It will be a good place to live with our mates and raise cubs."

"My grouping is happy to assist you, your mates and cubs to get home."

"The female you hunted is truly well?"

"Yes." Raze gave a smile of his own. "She is a tough, fierce female." He had another question. "Do you feel any resentment for returning to our territory? You will have to give up traveling and fighting."

Gnaw chuckled. "No. It was good to fight, and we may one day venture back into space again, in the far future, but to raise our cubs on land has become our priority. It grows more difficult to do jobs while leaving our mates and cubs for any length of time." His expression turned solemn. "Mating bonds change everything. We will be happy to return to living on land."

Then he smiled again. "It is easier to accept, too, since no farming will be expected. We hated that. Though we will plant small food gardens to feed our grouping. My mate's family are farmers, and they love it. They have offered to plant and tend to our growing needs."

A little envy crept into Raze. His grouping had taken to the stars after being banished from their home planet. They'd decided to live and work in space, rather than relocating to another planet in their home world. The false accusations against them had been spread among their people. Groupings near any territory they settled in likely wouldn't trust them after hearing the lies told by Yendo. It had just seemed best to start an entirely new kind of life. They did enjoy the hunting.

Raze halted his thoughts. He needed to stay in the conversation, not review his life choices. "Should we stay at this distance until you tell us when to come?"

Gnaw shook his head. "There is no reason to delay. I will contact Roth now and inform him that your grouping is close. The sisters have been separated long enough. We've been prepared to go with you since receiving your message from the Cobona. We'll be thirteen in numbers."

Raze did the math. Four males, their mates, and two cubs equaled ten. "Did you allow more males to join your grouping?"

"We have three additional humans coming with us. I mentioned my mate's family. Her parents and a sister will settle with us. Her two brothers have decided to stay on *Defcon Red* until they meet females to bond with, before joining us at our new home." Gnaw hesitated. "We didn't see any hope that a Veslor female would choose a human male as a mate."

Raze couldn't disagree with that assessment. Human males wouldn't test well against their females in battle. "We'll prepare extra guest sleeping cabins for your mate's family. It will be crowded, but we'll manage. Be careful when you speak to your grouping around the people there," Raze reminded him. "I don't want anyone to learn that we have the female onboard. Her safety is a priority to me."

Gnaw's gaze sharpened again.

Raze smiled, making a quick decision. Since Gnaw had shared a secret with him. He would do the same. "She has her own news to tell her sister."

Gnaw appeared surprised but recovered fast. "She found a mate amongst your grouping?"

Raze nodded. "Me."

Gnaw fisted his hand to his chest. "I am happy for you! You are blessed."

"I am. Please don't tell her sister."

"I won't. We will prepare for your arrival. Your ship will be welcomed by the fleet. Contact their bridge. Tell them you are our Veslor transportation."

"Done. We'll remain onboard until the members of your grouping join our ship after we dock. It will be good to spend time with your grouping again. Tell your males we have fresh meat from hunting. The food served during our travels will be good. Raze out." He cut communications.

Bruck watched him from his seat on the bridge. "I don't like taking Anabel so close to the human fleet."

"I don't either, but their fleet won't be able to see her on their sensors."

Bruck frowned. "Are you certain? We're not familiar with their technology."

He nodded. "I gave her my shield and have already masked her life sign." He flashed his bare wrist. "Nothing the humans have can compare to Brani tech."

His grouping male gaped at him. "You gave Anabel your band?"

"She's my mate. Her safety is my priority. I'll have one made for her as soon as we drop Roth's grouping off in their territory. Then I will contact the Brani to offer our services."

Bruck gave him a curious look.

"I want my mate to have her own shield."

"Agreed."

Raze held his gaze. "Perhaps we should trade for a few extra shields...in case you and Prasky find mates. That way we will have them ready and waiting."

"I'm not taking a human mate. No offense to Anabel. She is a fine female. Brave. Vicious. Just too small and delicate to appease my sexual needs."

The snorted laugh that burst from Raze surprised even himself. He was that amused. "You are very wrong. My mate is many things, but delicate isn't one of them. Anabel would be insulted if she heard you use that description. You would quickly understand if you got a human female bare beneath you."

Bruck didn't appear convinced in the least. "Do you resent having to control your aggression? I refuse to believe your female seriously challenges you before copulation. I could smell that you'd tested a mating in the healing center. There was no damage in there. She didn't make you fight her. You must have been extremely gentle."

"It's best when there is no challenge beforehand. Much more pleasurable." Raze stood, grinning. "*Much* more. The best. I don't feel any aggression with her. Only possession and tenderness."

The confused look on Bruck's face had Raze feeling even more amused.

"Trust my words. I would never deceive you. Humans are different but in extremely good ways. I'm grateful that Anabel is not a Veslor, now that I know the difference."

Bruck turned to his station, giving Raze his back. "You should share the news with your mate that we have contacted Roth's grouping. I'll be sure to send the human fleet a message that we wish to dock with them."

"Call me when we're within viewing range. I don't trust any humans besides my mate."

Raze left the bridge and returned to his sleeping place. Anabel was curled up on their bed, napping. He stripped quickly before climbing in with her. He loved to hold his mate.

"Where did you go?" She turned her head as he curled around her back, pulling her tight into his embrace.

"I reached Roth's grouping. We're a few hours from *Defcon Red.*"

Anabel cursed and wiggled away. He hated to let her go, but did. His female could use her small elbows to cause him pain by jabbing him in various places. He'd learned that quickly.

She sat up, her exposed breasts distracting him. He licked his lips.

His mate chuckled. "Don't look at me like that and keep your tongue in your mouth. You're too damn tempting. I need to shower, get dressed and prepare for shit to hit the fan. What if the fleet commander of *Defcon Red* demands a tour of your ship?"

"They will not. Veslors are allies to the fleet. It would infuriate our king if we were treated as hostile enemies. I have already programed the shield to hide your life sign from their sensors."

She lifted her ankle. His band wouldn't shrink small enough to fit on her wrist. His mate had small bones, so he'd attached it there. He'd promised her that their grouping would take a trip to the Veslor home world to get her one that fit. For now, wearing it on her ankle worked.

"Are you sure this thing works for me?"

"Yes. I asked many questions while the Brani added the shield and other functions to my band. One function is hiding life signs. I was assured it would work on anyone wearing it. The Brani tend to use small devices attached to their clothing to hold the technology. That didn't work for us."

"Because you lose your clothing when you shift?"

He nodded. "But not our bands."

"I remember. Because your people made them for shifters. It adjusts with you."

"Yes. They are also impossible to remove except by the person it was made for."

That made her frown. "You mean I can't take it off?"

"No. It will only release when I tell it to, after you're safe from the fleet finding you."

"Is it functional for me the way it is for you? Can I talk to your grouping?"

He nodded. "I activated that function for you as well. The band also identifies you as a Veslor to any allied races. All our males wear them when traveling from our planets. Some even wear them on our world. The bands help us keep in touch with not only our own grouping, but others within transmission range. Some prefer the bands over keeping a stationary communications device inside their homes." He chuckled.

"Especially if they have cubs. When I was one, I broke ours playing with it."

His humor fled when he thought of his parents, and their betrayal.

Anabel distracted him by leaning forward to brush her mouth over his. "Don't be sad. Though, I get it. I'm sometimes reminded of good times from my childhood, but then realize I'll never see my parents again. Yours are still alive. Maybe one day they'll apologize for picking the wrong side and see what assholes they were to you and your grouping."

"They must feel shame, but they have much pride. The truth is widely known. It is just painful for all who trusted Yendo's lies to acknowledge that they were deceived. Our birth grouping will avoid us, and always will."

"It's their loss. You're amazing. I'm not just saying that because you're hot as hell and all mine." She smiled. "You're a great guy, Raze. I'm damn lucky you hunted me."

He chuckled. "I am the blessed one." His gaze darted down to her breasts. They were so very tempting. Everything about his mate was.

Anabel suddenly flipped around and crawled toward the edge of the bed. "No! Don't even give me that titillating sizzling look. We'll celebrate me not getting caught by the fleet after we get the hell away from them free and clear with my sister and your people. I need to get my game face on. That means showering and putting on clothes. Not letting you spend the next hour or two distracting me with multiple orgasms. My brain is always mush afterward."

He felt proud of his skills pleasing his mate and sat up. "We have one hour to play."

"After." She fled. "I'm relieved I'm officially retired. You'd get me killed, Raze. I can't think about anything but you when you're naked. Put some clothes on." She entered the bathing room to shower.

Raze was tempted to follow and seduce her. He'd learned how to tempt her easily, but he redressed, this time in leathers and typical Veslor gear. He might be facing the enemy soon. It would depend on whether the fleet humans attempted to board his ship.

He reached for his band to contact Prasky but touched bare skin, forgetting that it wasn't there. He sighed and walked to the wall, using the ship's systems. Prasky responded immediately.

"What are you doing?"

The confusion in the other male's voice amused Raze. "I gave my mate my band so she can use it to hide her life sign. Prepare for docking with the human military vessel in two hours. We will pick up Roth's grouping and fly them back to our home sector of space."

The male growled. "Good. We can get rid of the human prisoner. Finally. I hate that male and have had to fight the urge to kill him often."

Raze had mostly forgotten about the male who'd surrendered to them on the planet. "We will leave that male to their human justice."

"I hope that is death. He whines and attempts to deceive me every time I feed him. I've never met anyone more dishonorable."

"We'll be rid of him soon. Two hours."

"Are these fleet humans going to act like allies or enemies?"

"We'll find out. Prepare for the worst but hope for the best."

"Humans," Prasky snarled. Then he ended the coms.

Anabel wore yet another oversized outfit. She really needed clothing that fit her, but it wasn't like she could stroll onto *Defcon Red* to hit up their shopping district. Fleet battle vessels were about as close to a self-contained floating city that one could get off-planet. They contained not only everything the military needed, but they employed civilians to work shops, restaurants, and even a large hydroponic garden. It was because they were mostly deployed in deep space.

She opened the bathroom door to see Raze waiting for her. "Can you contact this Roth's grouping again and have them pick me up clothing?"

His eyebrows rose. She'd surprised him.

"I'd like some actual pants and tops that fit me. Maybe a bra."

He grimaced. "Your breasts are freed for good."

She laughed. "Okay. I'll pass on the bras. I *would* like pants and shirts that fit, though. Maybe a spare set of boots, since these ones have seen way too much action. Socks, too, because yours are too big."

"I can go to the bridge to contact one of the males in Roth's grouping again."

She rattled off her sizes and made him repeat them. "I'll pay the other grouping back for whatever they spend. I can access accounts I've set up if we stop at an Earth station, or any colony with humans."

He growled. "You're my mate. I will provide for you."

"Do you have Earth currency?"

"No, but I am returning one of their criminals. Perhaps the human male has a bounty on him. I will collect it. If not, I will pay Roth directly in our currency. I also will return what he paid me to hunt you."

She frowned, thinking about that. "I have money, but it's not going to do me much good unless we go somewhere I can access it from Earth."

"We have done well hunting. There is no need to think about it. You need nothing. I will give you everything."

"My hero." She went to Raze and gave him a hug. "If I can't access my accounts, I guess I'm now officially broke. I'm glad that you don't seem to mind being my sugar daddy."

He chuckled, holding her. "I don't know what that means, but you're my mate."

"I'm totally working with you guys on your next hunt to earn my keep."

He growled, obviously not liking that concept.

"It's a done deal. We're not going to waste time arguing about it. I'm kind of excited. I bet I'm going to meet a lot of aliens that I've never seen before."

He spun her in his arms, curled his body around hers, and placed his hands over her stomach. "Perhaps not. You could be carrying my cub."

She twisted her head to peer into his eyes. "I have an implant. Sorry. I'd have to remove it before you're able to get me pregnant."

Amusement gleamed in his eyes. "We have a healing center."

"I want to hunt with you for a while. Then we'll talk about having babies."

He sighed and kissed her cheek. "I will reach out to Roth's grouping about your clothing and new boots. Meet me in the kitchen? I will cook breakfast for you."

"Deal. I'll watch and learn. I *do* plan to earn my keep. That means I'll take a turn providing meals just like the rest of our grouping."

He released her. "Stubborn female."

"Don't you forget it."

She noticed that he was smiling, though, as they left his cabin. They split apart at the kitchen and she went in. There were a few dirty dishes on the counter. Those, she knew how to handle. She opened the machine that cleansed them, loading it to run a cycle, her mind turning to her baby sister.

Soon, she'd see Jessa.

Tears filled her eyes but she blinked them back. It had been way too long. Having someone take vids of her sister from time to time wasn't the same as seeing her in person. She couldn't wait to be face to face with her after so many years, and to hear all about how Jessa had mated to another Veslor.

Though, she now understood it perfectly. Veslors were gorgeous aliens with killer bodies and amazing sex skills. Her sister probably hadn't stood a chance.

Anabel could relate.

Chapter Seventeen

The three Veslors led their prisoner through the ship. Anabel kept in the shadows to make certain Brandson didn't see her. The last thing she needed was for the loudmouth criminal to mention that she was onboard the Veslor ship.

She'd asked Prasky to purposely avoid bringing up her name anytime he'd dealt with the prisoner since leaving the surface of KP. Brandson would spill his guts about everything and anything once he found himself in the fleet brig, in hopes of making a deal that would save his life.

"I know where lots of hot women are." Brandson's tone got louder and whiner. "You can fuck the hell out of them. I'll pay! I have money. They'll suck your dicks, too. Ever had that done before? Just put me back in the cell and fly us to Redding Station. I'll make sure you get the best damn pussy they have. The brothel owner owes me a favor."

"Silence," Prasky snarled.

"I demand amnesty with you aliens! My own people are going to kill me. Don't you care about that? I'll be your slave. Hell, *I'll* suck your dicks. It beats being dead. I'll do all three of you."

Raze snarled at Brandson and gave him a shove that would probably leave bruises. "Silence, or we'll kill you. Your people will be kinder than Prasky. He really wants to rip you apart with his claws after listening to you for too long. You will pay for your crimes. Stop trying to bribe us. It is an insult."

Anabel had to hang back farther when the group was about to exit the ship. The exterior door on *Satrono* opened and Raze had to drag the prisoner forward, down the already extended ramp. Both of his grouping followed and left her sight.

She turned, activating the small vid screen that Bruck had shown her. It was connected to one of the surveillance feeds from a camera on the exterior of the hull. The commander of *Defcon Red* had given the grouping permission to land inside one of the massive hangars that were usually reserved for visiting dignitaries or any bigwigs from United Earth. It spoke of trust...or a trap. Anabel hoped for the former.

The commander had formally suited up and pinned on his medals to meet the Veslors. That sight made some of her worries fade. The fleet official had also brought a few high-ranking officers with him. The one that made her nervous was the tactical team leader. From the cut of his uniform and the multiple patches...he was top dog of all the teams.

There were only two regular security officers, and both stayed way back. They were at a relaxed stance, hands away from their weapons.

The commander approached first, smiling. Anabel wished for sound as the man spoke, his lips moving. He extended a hand to Bruck.

Raze moved in front of that male and extended his hand. He was probably introducing himself as their grouping leader. The two men shook hands, and Raze stepped back, waving toward their prisoner. In under a minute, the fleet commander's mood shifted, his expression one of anger. He turned and gestured, then the security officers moved forward. They grabbed Brandson, one of them cuffing his hands behind his back, before hauling him out of the hangar.

Anabel had made Raze swear he'd tell whoever he handed Brandson off to that he'd tried to murder defenseless aliens. It seemed he had kept that promise, considering how angry the commander looked. That information would piss off any decent fleet personnel. The commander's smile seemed forced when he faced Raze and his grouping again, speaking.

"Thank you for bringing us the criminal. May I ask how you came across him?"

The male voice speaking English startled Anabel, until she realized it came from the band Raze had given her. She glanced at the screen and saw Bruck look directly at the camera. He flashed her a brief smile before facing the humans.

She wanted to hug Raze when she heard his response to the commander.

"We were in that section of space and discovered missing Cobona on an uninhabited planet. They are a highly intelligent race with impressive technology. Once we landed, we learned some humans on the surface had killed a few of their people. It would have caused a war with your planet that you wouldn't have been able to win, if we hadn't intervened. That male was the only human who surrendered to us. The others fought to the death. A group of them even captured a female Cobona to use as a hostage. It didn't end well for them. We learned while on the planet that the crew of *Soapa Six* had gone there to murder the Cobona on behalf of their company, which hoped to mine it for resources. I believe the company is named Gemini."

269

Anabel was impressed. Raze had told the truth. He'd just…left a lot out.

The fleet commander swore, seemingly outraged. "Thank you. I can't begin to express our gratitude. I assure you, wherever they went, it was without fleet permission or knowledge. We owe your grouping a great debt. Does anyone remain on the planet?"

"No. Our robot scout can track various races. There are no humans or aliens remaining on the planet." Raze hesitated. "It was our privilege to protect the Cobona. Their ship had crashed there decades ago, stranding them without technology. We contacted their people and they came to retrieve their missing. Our king is very pleased. Cobona are one of our closest allies."

The commander looked a little pale. Anabel could imagine he must be about to shit his pants, knowing Gemini had risked causing an interstellar incident that could have put Earth and the fleet at war with a deadly alien race.

"He'll be executed. We don't condone invasions on other worlds *or* harming aliens. I give you my word," the commander swore. "Please assure your allies that his death will be swift."

"I will," Raze stated.

"I'd like to invite you and your grouping to have dinner with me. Having Veslors on *Defcon Red* has been a privilege. I've grown very fond of Roth, Gnaw, Drak, and Maith. They are well-respected and liked here."

"We are blessed to hear that, and I am honored to be asked to share a meal, but I'm afraid we are on a tight schedule." Raze reached up and pressed his fist to his chest. "Our king is expecting us to bring Roth's grouping home. We need to leave immediately."

The commander nodded. "Of course. Are you coming back? Your king sent word that a new grouping would be assigned to *Defcon Red*. We're going to miss the current grouping, but look forward to having more Veslors onboard."

"We are hunters. Not fighters."

The commander appeared puzzled.

"We hunt criminals or missing aliens. It's what we do. We do not fight unless hostages have been taken. Then we track the offenders to rescue their victims," Raze explained. "Only then do we fight."

Bruck growled. "We've killed many Elth, since they are the worst offenders for kidnapping aliens."

"We've had issues with the Elth," the commander admitted. "They kidnapped and murdered some of our people from a transport shuttle. We were able to track them and get our survivors back, thanks to Roth's grouping."

"Roth and his grouping have a lot of experience with Elth," Prasky agreed. "We've worked with the fighters before."

A group of people entered the hangar, and Anabel studied the screen. It was four Veslors, four human women walking at their sides, and two of them were carrying...

Anabel blinked twice to make sure she was really seeing two smaller versions of Veslors in their shifted form.

They were Veslor children. Young ones.

Then one of the women immediately drew her attention. The blue streaks in the black hair were a dead giveaway. Jessa.

Her sister had one of the Veslor babies in her arms.

Tears blinded Anabel and she felt them slip down her cheeks. *Am I an aunt?*

Kurt, her handler, kept tabs on her sister for her. No one had mentioned her sister mating to an alien...or being pregnant.

Then again, she had no idea how long a pregnancy would take with a human and Veslor pairing. Once, she'd heard about a human who'd been kidnapped and knocked up by an alien giving birth in a matter of a couple of months. Tracking that missing woman down hadn't been one of Anabel's assignments, but word had spread when she'd been rescued. It was possible that Jessa had given birth while Anabel had been trapped on KP.

Anabel wiped at her tears, her gaze locked on Jessa. A big, overly muscular Veslor with black hair and green eyes walked extremely close to her sister. She had thought Raze and his grouping were big, but the four other males were even bulkier.

Her sister stopped when they reached the fleet commander and Raze's grouping. As if to verify he was her mate, the big male Veslor put his arm around Jessa, pulling her closer to his body. Anabel could tell by his stance that he was prepared to defend her baby sister if the need arose. His head turned constantly, gaze roaming, as if seeking any kind of threat. Anabel instantly liked him.

A black-haired Veslor advanced on Raze, and they embraced. A deep voice spoke in English. "It is good to see you, Raze."

272

"You as well, Roth. We are prepared to fly your grouping home. Shall we do introductions inside? Our king awaits to speak to you."

"Yes," the male agreed. He turned and approached the fleet commander.

Anabel watched in shock as each of the Veslors from the other grouping hugged the fleet commander, then the leader of the tactical team. Hearing their quiet words of goodbye, she realized all of them had become very friendly. One of the human women, the redhead, flat out threw herself at the commander and wrapped her arms around him.

"I love you, Uncle Howard! This isn't goodbye forever. It's just for now."

"I'm holding you to that, Abby," the commander said, kissing the top of her head fondly. "I've got months of vacation time stored up. I'm going to hitch a ride with your parents when they come to see you. Who knows? Maybe I'll ask the Veslor king if he'd allow me to retire there. It sounds like paradise, where you're going."

"Find a woman first." Abby laughed. "Unless you think you can impress a Veslor female enough to move in with you."

The commander chuckled. "I just might. I *do* keep in shape."

The other Veslor grouping were speaking to the tactical team leader. Roth cupped the shorter, smaller man's face. "You are welcome to retire there, too, Clark. We have plenty of territory. Bring a female with you. One that is too old to have cubs. I know that you don't want to chase them." He grinned.

"I'm going to really miss you boys." The tactical team leader sounded choked up. "I wish you weren't leaving, but I understand why you need to live on one of your planets. And I might take you up on that offer."

"You are welcome to live with us." Roth stared at the commander next. "Both of you. Always. Just contact us, and we'll send someone to escort you safely to our sector. The new fighter grouping should arrive within days. I know you will be just as welcoming to them."

The redhead was crying, and she hugged the commander again. She turned when she let him go, and one of the Veslors pulled her into his arms. He led her past Bruck and up the ramp. The rest of the other grouping followed, including Jessa. The male with green eyes kept his arm around her baby sister.

Three humans out of uniform suddenly appeared, pulling a cart full of luggage behind them. It was an older couple and a younger woman. They headed directly toward the ramp. It had to be the family members of one of the human mates; Raze had mentioned they would be joining them on the trip.

Anabel's heart raced when she heard soft voices enter the ship. She wanted to rush to the ramp, but held back. It was still open, and anyone near it in the hangar would see her.

She wiped her face again to hopefully hide that she'd been crying, took a few deep breaths, and glanced back at the screen. Prasky and Bruck were grabbing the bags off the cart to bring them onboard. The fleet personnel were leaving the hangar, the commander and the tactical team leader walking close, talking. They were the last fleet to exit.

"Where?" That was Jessa's voice.

"That way," Raze stated.

Anabel heard light running feet heading her way, and she sucked in a deep breath before peeking around the corner.

Her sister ran straight at her, the Veslor baby no longer in her arms. Anabel met Jessa's gaze, one brown eye and one bright blue.

Her sister plowed into her. The impact had Anabel staggering back a little, but she held her ground, hugging her sister while managing to keep them from falling. Her baby sister seemed to be attempting to give her the mother of all bear hugs.

"Anabel!" Jessa sobbed, burying her face against her shoulder. "You're real! You're alive! You're *here*."

Anabel closed her eyes and rested her head against her sister's. She was slightly taller and bigger than her sister, but not by much. An inch and maybe fifteen pounds of muscle. "I am. Was that your baby? What's his or her name? Am I an aunt?"

Jessa sniffed but laughed, her death grip not easing. "I was holding Rasha. She's Darla and Gnaw's daughter. But I'm pregnant. And I have a mate. He's a medic and he totally kicks ass. So you're *going* to be an aunt. Please don't be mad."

That had Anabel wiggling out of her sister's tight hold. Jessa resisted, but finally eased back. Their gazes met and locked. "Why in the hell would I be mad? I'm so happy for you. I don't know anything about babies, but we'll figure it out. You're a fucking doctor twice over and I'm a high-level fleet operator. Learning baby stuff should be a breeze."

Tears spilled down one side of her sister's face.

Anabel reached up and wiped them away. "You're so beautiful."

"So are you. You have hair!"

Anabel laughed. "Right. The last time I was able to send you a picture was just after they'd chopped it all off."

"I want you to meet my mate. I know I ruined our plans, but I love Maith. He's amazing. Can you forgive me?"

Anabel frowned. "There's nothing to forgive. Why would you even ask that?"

"We always had a plan. But I fell in love—"

"Shush," Anabel cut her off. "That plan was just something to keep us going, to look forward to. I'm happy that you found someone to love."

"You aren't even a little upset that he's a Veslor?"

"No. You made a good choice. Speaking of...I met one of my own. I took a mate, too. Are *you* pissed?" Anabel smiled to show she was teasing.

Her sister just gaped at her.

Anabel laughed. "Yeah. You never stood a chance of resisting if your Veslor is anything like mine. Thank you for sending Raze and his grouping after me." Then her humor fled. "But you *promised* me that you'd never hack into my file. That was too damn dangerous."

"I didn't hack anything."

"Don't lie to me, Jessa. That's the only way you could have known where I was marooned."

"A woman came to see me. She told me where you were."

It was Anabel's turn to gape.

"She said you once saved her life. She wasn't part of your mission but she'd been captured. Someone sent her to *Defcon Red* and gave us the idea of asking for Veslors to go after you."

Anabel closed her eyes, letting that information sink in. Emotion welled in her chest and she fought tears. Kurt and the few trusted friends she'd made over the years had risked everything to try to save her. To help her. It was the only answer. "Fuck."

"Anabel?" Her sister sounded worried and touched her face.

Anabel opened her eyes and smiled. "I should be pissed that they'd risk their lives for mine...but I'm not. I've done the same for them. What did she look like?"

"Tiny. Maybe five-one. She wore a wig but her eyebrows were light. Maybe blonde. She—"

"I know who you're talking about." Anabel wasn't surprised that Kurt would send her. She was a good operative, and very loyal.

"The woman said she always wanted to save your life after you'd saved hers."

Anabel smiled. "Well, Jane did."

"Jane?"

"The woman who came to see you. Forget that I said her real name."

"Our contracts are void," Jessa blurted. "The Veslor king pressured the U.E. and fleet to let us go. Of course, that woman said they'd try to kill you. That's why our grouping decided to leave *Defcon Red* once you were found. Plus, we're going to have more cubs in our grouping as soon as

Vera and I give birth. But legally, we are no longer owned or obligated to serve."

The surprises kept coming. Anabel sucked in a deep breath and blew it out. "The big bosses would feel the need to send someone after me, make me have an *accident*. I know too much."

"No one but us knows that you've been rescued. I was supposed to give them a ten-day notice to quit on a civilian contract, but I made a deal with them. I also used the excuse of finding out I'm pregnant."

"What kind of deal?" Anabel was leery. The big bosses were rarely reasonable.

"I might have given them a sedative I created that will take down the Elth in seconds, and shared my current research on how to nullify Ke'ter saliva from spreading and causing more damage in a victim. I promised to keep working on that second project and send them updates if they let me go immediately. They agreed." Jessa paused. "I also figured it might make anyone pissed off about letting me out of my contract early rethink wanting me dead, if I'm still kind of working for them, even though I'm going to be living on a Veslor planet."

Anabel was impressed. "I knew you were smart."

Loud footsteps came closer, and Anabel looked past her sister. It was the dark-haired Veslor with green eyes. He hesitated, staring at her.

Jessa turned, hugging the big male. "This is Maith. He's my mate and the baby's daddy."

"It's an honor to meet you." Anabel smiled at him and extended her hand.

The male took it and then tugged her closer. "I am very happy to meet you, sister. We are overjoyed that you are with us."

Anabel didn't resist as Maith pulled her close and hugged both her and Jessa.

A low growl came from somewhere—then two big hands gripped Anabel's hips, tugging her away. She glanced behind her and laughed. Raze was possessive.

"This is Raze. Raze, meet Maith and my baby sister, Jessa."

Raze released her to press his fist to his chest. "It is an honor to meet my mate's sister." He looked at Maith next. "This makes us family."

"We are family now," Maith agreed. "You and your grouping are welcome to live in our territory. Roth extended the offer as soon as he heard you had mated Anabel. Gnaw kept his word by only telling our males." Maith glanced down at Jessa. "Your sister wanted to share her news with you first, and now she has."

Raze's body tensed against Anabel as Maith spoke. The other Veslor didn't seem to notice anything was wrong. He kept speaking. Anabel glanced back. Raze's features had frozen, as if he were trying to hide his reaction to whatever seemed to have put him on edge.

"The king gave us a small continent. It is large enough to support dozens of expanding groupings. We could become one together, or live as two, but be close enough for our mates to visit daily. Think on it." Maith glanced between Jessa and Anabel. "They have been separated for too long."

"The 'small' continent their king gave us is about half the size of Australia on Earth," Jessa clarified for Anabel. "Most Veslors on that planet don't want to live there, because it's not overly close to other land masses. Which they view that as a bad thing, since they like to roam to meet mates. I'm sure you already know, our guys don't interest Veslor women."

"My grouping will discuss your generous offer," Raze told Maith. "It is an honor to be asked. The decision is not mine alone to make."

"Agreed." Maith nodded.

Anabel's guess that something was wrong was confirmed by Raze's tone. It didn't take a genius to figure out what it was. It was generous of Maith and his grouping to invite them to live on a Veslor world, but it was possible they didn't know why Raze and his grouping had left the planet they'd been born and raised on.

She turned to her sister and Maith. "Give us a moment alone, please?"

Jessa frowned.

Maith nodded. "We'll go find out where we are to sleep."

"I'll catch up in a few minutes." Anabel smiled at her sister. "I have so much to talk to you about. So much I want to hear."

She turned to hug her mate and lowered her voice after her sister and Maith had walked around the corner. "I love you just as you are, Raze. I wouldn't expect you to change—or move to a planet for me. Let me spend some time with my sister for a bit and then we'll talk more. Okay?"

Raze nodded, holding her gaze. "I should help our guests get settled and go to the bridge. Roth and I need to discuss where his new territory is located so I can plot a course to the correct planet."

She reached up and cupped his face, tugging him down. Raze lowered until their faces were inches apart. "I wouldn't ask you to live there. This ship is your home. *Our* home. I'm excited about being a hunter with you. We can visit my sister and her mate often, but we don't need to live with them all the time."

He tried to hide his relief but she was getting to know him too well.

It caused her to laugh. "I love you."

"You have my heart."

"Okay. Let's get all our guests settled and then I'm going to spend a few hours catching up with my sister."

"Go. Spend time with her."

They parted, and Anabel found the other grouping. She couldn't help but stare at the small Veslor babies. They were cute even in four-legged form.

Jessa chuckled. "Adorable, aren't they?" She used her finger to point. "This one is Roshi. He's the more aggressive of the twins. This one is Rasha, who I was holding when I boarded the ship. She's a bit mellower."

Anabel smiled at the couple holding the babies. "They *are* adorable. I don't see too many kids. My apologies if I'm being rude by gawking a bit."

"Did your mate tell you that Veslors are born in battle form and don't start to transform until they're about a year old?" Jessa appeared thrilled about sharing that information as she put her hands on her belly. "I'm going to birth a *cub*. Not a baby. And I can't wait! The cubs are a lot tougher in their battle forms. Which is good, since I figure I'll be a nervous mother. It will help knowing this baby can take a lot of bumps and falls without causing serious injuries. They also learn how to walk, run, and leap way faster than a human baby would."

"Wow!" Anabel said. "Raze and I haven't really talked about kids, beyond the fact that I have an implant that'll need to be removed before we can conceive."

Jessa released her stomach and stepped closer. "Standard capsule implant injected into your arm?"

Anabel nodded.

Jessa bit her lip, her expression becoming comical as she glanced at Anabel's stomach. "Um…"

"Um…*what*?" Anabel asked, suddenly uneasy.

"Are you officially mated?"

"I'm not sure what that means. I accepted Raze as my mate."

"Did he change? Transform during sex?"

Anabel rolled her eyes at her sister. "I'm not talking about my sex life." She glanced at the other couples and babies, before looking back at Jessa. She didn't know her baby sister well, but she hoped Jessa got the hint. It wasn't the time or place to have an intimate discussion like that.

"You're a part of our grouping now," the redheaded human woman said. "We're a tight, close-knit family. Privacy is a thing of the past. Hi, by the way. I'm Abby Thomas. It's great to meet you, Anabel. We've all been worried about you since my old friend came for a visit." She winked.

Anabel felt confused.

"The woman your handler sent," Jessa supplied. "She was using the identity of someone that Abby used to know."

"Oh." Anabel peered at Abby, studying her. "Shit. You're *that* Abby Thomas, aren't you? From D Corp? I didn't recognize you right off. Your hair is a bit longer, you wear less makeup now, and you aren't dressed in business attire."

"One in the same," Abby admitted. "Life in deep space is way more relaxed."

Anabel gave a nod. The Thomas family was extremely rich and well connected. She suddenly had a suspicion. "You're the reason the big bosses cut Jessa and me free from our fleet contracts, aren't you?"

"No. I was willing to use our family connections and make some threats to sway them, but it wasn't needed. The Veslor king scares *everyone*." Abby smiled. "And Veslors supply a large portion of food to outlying space stations. No one wanted to blow that trade agreement. Imagine the riots that would take place if food supplies were cut off. It's been pretty peaceful and has saved the U.E. and the fleet a lot of time and money. That fact was pointed out to them during negotiations to get you and your sister free from all obligations." She pointed at Jessa.

Anabel looked at her sister, impressed yet again.

"You can still get pregnant," Jessa suddenly blurted.

Anabel just stared at her.

"If you officially mated by letting Raze fuck you in his other form, the implants don't work. In battle form, Veslor sperm overrides the chemicals the implants release, makes them stop working. Veslors also share hormones during sex," her sister informed her softly. "You should know that. I brought my med kit. It now includes a Veslor pregnancy tester. Do you need a test?"

Anabel couldn't find words; she was too stunned. Anger trickled in as she recovered. "Raze failed to mention that."

"He wouldn't know," Maith said. "Jessa discovered it, but she hasn't shared that information with anyone but our grouping. She's had unlimited access to my body since we mated. I've allowed her to run various tests."

"The hormones they produce while aroused in battle form basically start ovulation in human women almost immediately. Their sperm is up to ten times more fertile than that of a healthy human man in his prime," Jessa said excitedly. "It's fascinating!"

Anabel took a deep breath. Then another. "I love you, baby sis. Even if you are weird for being thrilled about learning that kind of info."

Maith growled, not looking happy.

Jessa smiled at her mate. "She's not wrong. It's an A.R.S. thing." She winked at Anabel. "It *is* cool though. Do you need a test?"

"Let's talk about this later." Anabel didn't want to think about the possibility of being pregnant. She'd been on the implant since she'd turned sixteen. The fleet had made sure of that. Every ten years, she had to get a new one. She'd had the current one for two years, with eight more to go.

"Pregnancies are shorter. We can have—"

"Stop." Anabel held out a hand, cutting her sister off. "Too much info, and this isn't the place." She glanced again at the other people surrounding them.

Jessa still looked happy. "Like Abby said, you're part of a grouping. Forget privacy. Everyone learns everyone's business. But I get it. We've always been alone. You'll adjust to having a large family quickly. Trust me."

Anabel nodded. "Give me time. I'm still adjusting to having a mate, realizing that the U.E. and the fleet are no longer in charge of my life, and that I'm never going back. Just let me focus on being with my sister for right now."

"I can do that," Jessa promised. "But there is one thing we're doing for sure within the next day."

"What's that?" Anabel asked, curious.

Jessa glanced up at her mate before grinning at Anabel. "We're going to use the medical bed on this ship to run a scan." She placed one hand over her belly. "Maith and I have waited until you and I were reunited to find out if we're having one cub or two." Tears filled her eye. "I wanted my older sister to be there with our grouping when we take a peek at our cub or cubs."

Tears flooded Anabel's eyes as well, and she had to blink them back, completely touched. "Thank you. I totally want to be there for that."

Prasky walked up to them. "We're about to lift off and exit the fleet vessel. Raze and Roth have the bridge. Let me show you where you'll sleep. I've already taken your belongings to rooms. Then Bruck will serve us a meal. We were gifted a lot of fresh meat from the Cobona on the planet where we located Anabel. It's good eating."

Anabel was grateful for his interruption. She was very happy to see her sister, but she needed a few moments to compose herself.

Jessa was pregnant with an alien cub.

The fleet had voided her contract. They'd still want to kill her, but she was legally a free individual.

And she might be pregnant.

It was a lot to take in.

A lot.

Chapter Eighteen

Anabel felt nervous as she stood in the crowded healing center. It wasn't a big space to begin with, but now it contained five large Veslor males and four other human women. Raze wrapped his arm around her waist. She leaned against his side, grateful that he was there with her sister's grouping.

Bruck had offered to occupy the cubs' attention by feeding them in the kitchen. Prasky remained on the bridge flying the ship. Roth, the other grouping leader, and his human mate were standing next to Anabel and Raze.

"Are you ready?" Maith had helped Jessa up onto the medical bed. He held her hand and placed a data pad on the edge of the mattress.

Her baby sister smiled at him. "Run that scan. Let's see if we're having one or two. I'd also like to know the sexes if the cubs are positioned so we can take a peek."

Anabel glanced at the other couples. Gnaw and Darla were grinning. Drak and Abby were holding hands, appearing excited. Roth and Vera did too. It sunk in that those people really loved her baby sister. They seemed equally invested in finding out what the scan would reveal.

Jessa met Anabel's gaze and grinned. "I'm so glad you're with us."

"Me too," Anabel admitted.

"Activating the scan," Maith announced. The bed hummed and light ran over and under her sister. Unlike fleet and U.E. med beds, it didn't instantly flash an image of the person overhead. At least not until Maith tapped something into the data pad with his free hand.

A hologram appeared, hovering over Jessa. An image of her body, minus skin, showing her sister's insides. Maith tapped at the screen again and the midsection of Jessa's hologram enlarged, and kept doing so as her mate adjusted it.

Jessa gasped, staring up in wonder. Maith leaned over her sister, kissing her.

Anabel studied the hologram, not sure what she was looking at.

She glanced at Raze. He appeared just as confused. Then she raised a brow at the other women. Darla shrugged. Abby frowned at the hologram, seeming to study it. Roth and Vera stared at the hologram with confused looks, too.

Anabel couldn't take it anymore. "What are we looking at? I can pack a wound to stop bleeding and put a tourniquet on a severed limb, but I can't read those damn scans for shit."

"You never do anything easy, mate," Maith chuckled to Jessa.

"Don't blame this on *me*." Jessa laughed. "This is *your* fault, with your overpowering hormones and super-sperm."

Raze suddenly sucked in a gasp. Anabel looked at him.

He released her and lifted his hand, holding up three fingers. Anabel just stared at those digits. "No way," she whispered.

"We're having triplets!" Jessa loudly announced. "Ha! We've got you beat, Darla and Gnaw!"

Her baby sister sounded a little hysterical to Anabel. She would be, too, if she found out that she was carrying three babies. Her gaze locked on the couple, kissing again. When Maith finally lifted his face away from Jessa, they both were grinning.

"I'm glad we decided to move to our territory," Drak muttered. "We're going to be overrun by cubs."

"And you bitched because I decided to wait," Abby whispered back.

"Better you than me," Vera added. "I was glad to find out I'm only carrying one."

"Maybe the next time we'll have multiple cubs," Roth, her mate, teased. "I do want more cubs with you, after you birth this one for us. We could try for four at once."

"I love you—but no," Vera blurted.

A few of the people in the room laughed. Anabel didn't see the humor. "Is that safe? Three...um...cubs?" She really didn't know anything about having babies or pregnancy.

Jessa turned her head and met her gaze. "Yes. Humans have triplets. And believe it or not, Veslor cubs are smaller than human infants at birth. Besides, I'm an A.R.S. and I'm mated to a medic. We've got this covered. It's going to work out great. I promise."

"Okay." Anabel calmed after hearing that. "Good."

Maith turned off the overhead hologram and helped her sister sit up and get off the medical bed. Anabel studied the couple closely. They were truly in love. It showed in their every expression. She was grateful that her sister was so happy.

Jessa pulled away from her mate and hugged the other people in the room. When she reached Anabel, they hugged as she said, "You had to make me an aunt three times over at once. Nice shock factor there, Tinker."

Jessa chuckled. "I love it when you use my nickname. And it's all Maith's fault that we're having three."

"I heard that," he grumbled.

Jessa released her. "Okay. Everyone out except Maith, Anabel, and Raze." She clapped her hands.

The other Veslor and humans left the healing center. Anabel waited until the door closed before holding her sister's gaze. "What is it? Is something wrong?"

"Nothing's wrong, except you're not used to being a part of a large grouping yet. I knew you'd refuse if I didn't make them leave. Get up on the medical bed. I'm going to scan you next." Jessa glanced at Raze. "To see if you got my sister pregnant."

Anabel felt him tense beside her. She hadn't mentioned what her sister had told her about the possibility. He had already been freaked out over the offer to live on a Veslor world again. "Jessa..."

"No," her baby sister snapped. Then she addressed Raze. "I've done a lot of research, and here's the bottom line. Human birth control implants don't work if you shifted into battle form and officially mated my sister. Did you?"

Raze nodded.

Jessa nodded back. "There's a good chance Anabel could be pregnant. When you're aroused and in your battle form, not only is your sperm super-efficient, but you secrete some very strong hormones that override the chemicals in that implant. It actually triggers ovulation in human women." She pointed to her stomach. "Exhibit A, B, and C. I was on the implant. Yet—three babies." Then she turned to Anabel. "Now get on the damn bed. That's an order."

Anabel hesitated, afraid to even glance at Raze. She was worried that he'd be upset.

He gently pushed her toward the bed. "I would be happy to have cubs with you," he rasped. "We need to know if you are pregnant. You tend to rush into danger. I'd like to know if I need to tie you to my bed or not."

She snorted a laugh when Jessa sucked in a sharp breath. "He's mostly kidding."

"No, I am not," Raze argued. Then he swept Anabel off her feet and put her on the medical bed. He also took her hand.

Anabel was still worried. Raze and his grouping liked to hunt. Could they still do that with a baby onboard the *Satrono*? Would he feel trapped if he felt the need to live on a planet for their baby's sake?

She knew Prasky would definitely throw a shit fit. That was one male who hated change, and he was just starting to get used to her being a part of their grouping.

Anabel wasn't even sure if she'd make good mom material. What would she teach a kid? How to kill?

291

Her heart pounded as Jessa lifted the data pad that controlled the bed and tapped at it. Lights lit up under and above her. She locked gazes with Raze.

"It will be fine either way," he swore, looking calm and sincere.

She tightened her hold on his hand and closed her eyes. She didn't want to stare at the hologram since she couldn't read the thing anyway.

A good minute passed in silence.

"Fucking fleet!" Jessa spat.

Anabel forced her eyes open to stare at her obviously pissed-off baby sister. "What?"

Jessa turned off the hologram and slammed the data pad down. Then she stepped closer. "They *really* wanted to make sure you couldn't get pregnant."

Anabel's entire body went cold. "They sterilized me?"

Jessa put her hand on Anabel's stomach. "No. Thankfully. But they not only gave you a birth control implant, they inserted a Klessiona device. You didn't know?"

She was relieved that her doctors hadn't permanently made sure she couldn't have kids. "I don't even know what the hell that is," Anabel admitted. "No one said anything to me. I just knew about the implant in my arm. I had to have it replaced two years ago, when the first one expired."

Jessa took a deep breath but she still appeared infuriated. "They're named after the doctor who invented it. Birth control implants release a chemical that keeps you from ovulating. A Klessiona device is inserted

292

inside your uterus." Jessa gently tapped part of Anabel's stomach. "It basically releases a chemical if it detects sperm, to kill it, and any egg or eggs present inside the uterus."

Anabel stared at her sister, speechless. Her mind was a whirl. Some doctor had done that to her without her knowledge? She was mad, upset, and feeling extremely violated. "Is it harmful to me?"

Jessa hesitated. "Klessiona devices are usually used for patients with severe medical conditions where a pregnancy is life threatening. The good news is that I see no damage to your uterus. Long-term use of the devices is not advised. That would be no more than five years max, to be on the safe side. It can cause permanent damage after that time."

Jessa released Anabel's stomach to use the pad, putting up the hologram and enlarging something on it. "From what I'm seeing, I doubt you've had it in there for long; this wasn't a regular method of birth control they used on you. The drug the device releases has a color dye to show if it's working. I can tell by how dark the device is that it's still full. They whiten when they're low on doses. This one is very dark, almost as if it's new."

"I don't have sex often, and I made the few partners I had wear condoms. Diseases," Anabel muttered. Then she looked at Raze. "You're the only one I've had sex with bare."

"I can remove it," Jessa offered. "It's an easy procedure that I can do right here. I highly suggest removing it. I wouldn't want that inside me. You can't get pregnant by just having sex with Raze, he'd have to shift into his battle form to be fertile, so you can control when you get pregnant.

Abby and Drak haven't officially mated by him shifting into his battle form because she didn't want to get pregnant while living on *Defcon Red*."

"Remove it, and the other implant," Raze demanded.

Anabel arched her eyebrows at him. "I think that's a discussion we should have. Instead of you telling my sister what should be done with *my* body."

Raze suddenly stepped closer and leaned forward, lowering his face close to hers. "I don't trust the humans that you've claimed want you dead. Anything they've put inside you should be removed."

She considered his words carefully. Then she looked at Jessa. "You're sure about me not getting pregnant unless Raze shifts into his other form?"

"One hundred percent...unless you're ever captured, he becomes enraged, and you're forced to have sex over and over because whoever captured you threatens to kill you if you don't fuck like bunnies."

Anabel gaped at her sister.

"Long story," Jessa sighed. "Please let me at least remove the Klessiona device. It worries me that they put it in you without mentioning it. Especially after what that woman your handler sent had to say about who you worked for and how dangerous they are. What if they're dosing you with a different chemical that will permanently sterilize you over time? Or worse, kill you at some point?"

"Please." Raze squeezed Anabel's hand.

She stared deeply into his blue eyes and nodded. "Take it—and my birth control implant. But I'm keeping my legs."

"I just wish I knew how to turn off whatever shielding program they used, since both of your legs are reading one hundred percent real on the scan. I'd like to make sure they didn't hide something else you don't know about." Jessa paused. "It worries me, not knowing."

"I have the access codes to shut the shielding off and turn it back on. Kurt, my handler, stole them from my medical file for me, in case I ever had to go on the run. That way I could get my synthetics fixed if they needed to be repaired."

"I want those codes." Jessa met her gaze. "I'm really curious to see what they've done to you." Her sister touched Anabel's knee, giving it a gentle squeeze. "The skin here is clone-enhanced, isn't it?"

"Yes. I also want to know everything the doctors did to *you*," Anabel admitted. "Did they add more shit to your body besides that brain implant and your eye?"

"One enhanced ear." Jessa pointed to it.

"I have one of those too." Anabel pointed to hers. Then she glanced at Maith, before looking at her sister. "Can you remove what you need to alone? No offense, but I don't want your mate to see me naked if I have to strip down and spread my legs to get that device removed."

Raze growled, glaring at the other Veslor.

Jessa glanced between the two men, then rolled her eyes. "I don't need assistance. Why don't you two go do something somewhere else? This won't take long. Let my sister and I handle this alone."

Raze tightened his hand on Anabel's. "I don't want to leave you."

"I'd be more comfortable with just my sister. Trust me, she's a very overqualified doctor." Anabel gave him a smile.

Raze didn't look happy. "Is my mate in any danger during these procedures?"

"No," Jessa swore.

"Please," Anabel whispered.

Raze met her gaze, growled, but released her hand. "I'll wait outside." Then he stomped to the door.

Maith hesitated.

"I've got this," Jessa told him softly. "Go."

Both Veslors left, and Anabel sat up a little. "Is there anything you didn't tell me?"

"No. You'll learn I'm really blunt these days."

"What do you want me to do?"

Jessa turned away and open a cabinet, looking through them. "Give me a few minutes to acquaint myself with their healing center. I've got their version of a med bed down. Maith wanted me prepared for what we'd have available once we left the fleet."

"Are you freaked out even a little about having three babies?"

Jessa spun and nodded. "Hell yes! But don't tell Maith."

That answer caused Anabel to tense.

Her sister seemed to read her mood. "Not for a bad reason. He's wonderful, but he's also super overprotective. If he even suspected I'm a little anxious, he'd stick to me like a second skin around the clock. He already tries to feed me all the time, and if I even look a little tired, he refuses to let me walk." Jessa chuckled. "It's going to be fine though. We all help with Roshi and Rasha. The grouping will do the same with these three little ones after they're born."

"You're happy?"

"More so than I ever thought possible." Jessa stepped close to her side and studied her face. "I'm so glad we're together. We have so much catching up to do."

Anabel figured it was a good time as any, since they were alone. "I am too...but there's something you should know."

"What?"

"I'm pretty sure we won't be moving to live on a planet with you. Not right away, at least. We'll visit a lot, though. Often. My grouping are hunters who live on this ship. It's their way of life."

Jessa's eyes widened and her mouth parted.

Anabel rushed on. "The offer by your grouping to let us live with you shocked Raze. Him and his grouping suffered some trauma in the past, and it's why they decided to work and live in space. I think he needs some time to adjust to the idea. They all do. Please don't be upset."

"What kind of trauma?"

"It's a long story, but it involves a shitty grouping leader who did really terrible things that resulted in a Veslor woman getting killed, then that asshole tried to pin it all on Raze and his grouping. The king luckily realized it was bullshit, but Raze admitted his own parents believed the lies. I know it hurt him deeply. I mean, from what he said, it seems the entire planet he lived on bought that bullshit enough to banish them."

297

"Are you serious? My grouping *raves* about how great the hunters are. I got the impression they know them well from working together in the past." Jessa went from sad to mad.

"Yeah. I'm also pretty sure they worry that those lies spread to other planets in their world, and Veslors might not welcome them with open arms if they try to settle on a planet again. Raze basically admitted it. Give me some time to help them work through this."

Jessa nodded. "I want you to visit often though."

"You got it."

"Now—let's get this shit out of you."

Anabel grimaced. "Stirrups? Is it that kind of removal for the device?"

"Unfortunately."

"Shit."

Jessa chuckled.

"There's nothing funny about that."

"Yes there is. I missed seeing you. Now I'm going to see *way* more of you than we ever thought I would."

Raze paced. He was a little hurt that Anabel had asked him to leave her side. They were mates. He should be in the healing center, holding her hand. What if the procedure hurt her? He could assist Jessa with whatever she needed to do to Anabel, thanks to the medic training he'd taken since Hern's death.

Maith leaned against the wall, watching him. "Jessa is an excellent doctor. She wouldn't hurt her sister."

298

"I know that." Raze stopped to shoot a glare at the sealed doors. "How bad was it, living with humans on that fleet vessel?"

"Bad at first, but we made friends. We learned that most humans are good."

"Did they treat you like an enemy?"

"A few were highly disrespectful but that quickly changed. Abby made sure of it, even before she realized Drak was her mate."

"Drak is a good male."

Maith nodded. "Have you considered Roth's offer to share our territory? My mate doesn't want to be separated from her sister. I know you and your grouping tend to avoid going to our home planets."

"I haven't brought it up with my grouping yet. They've been busy."

"We all had our reasons for leaving home and becoming undesirable males. Life on a planet isn't for everyone."

Raze met his gaze.

"No one will attempt to make you into farmers." Maith shuddered. "We won't do that. Darla's human family loves working the land and looks forward to creating a large food garden to feed our grouping. We hated it. It's why we left. But the fresh air, roaming room, and hunting will be a nice change after living on ships for all these years."

"Farming wasn't the problem."

Maith nodded. "I'm aware."

Raze tensed.

"I know only a few details. I have a male cousin who mated one of our king's sisters. What happened to your grouping shouldn't have. We trust all of you. You were the first grouping Roth thought of when we needed someone to search for Anabel. Our king sent you to assist us on Tesina planet when the Elth began to steal their people. You're the best hunters. Those were *his* words. Are you worried that we are only making the offer to share territory because of who your mate is to mine? That's not it."

Raze wasn't convinced.

"We've also made the offer to a trader grouping. They have currently declined, but agreed to one day join us. Only one of the six males has mated. Our king gave us a large enough piece of territory to support many groupings. Dozens, with room to grow after our children mature and if any have an urge to start their own."

"Are you closely aligned with the traders?"

"Abby is friends with Brassi's mate. He's the grouping leader of the traders. He was the first that we're aware of who bonded to a human. My grouping has discussed it at length. More males like us might find human mates. They should have territory to call home if they have cubs they don't want raised in space. We learned what it is like to be different while living on *Defcon Red*. The humans adjusted to us, but it took time. We want our mates and cubs surrounded by people who will openly accept them."

Raze understood. "You offered us territory because my mate is human."

"We also like your grouping." Maith smiled. "But yes." Then he grew solemn. "Take the territory offered. Claim it. That way it's yours when you're in need of fresh air and a safe place for cubs to grow, when you're not living on this ship taking hunter jobs. It would also be nice to know you'll agree so our groupings are located close together for our mates."

"The loss of Hern has damaged us even more. Especially Prasky. We're no longer fit to be sociable."

"Who says you have to be?" Maith shrugged. "We've been traveling in space for too long to be as we once were. There won't be any events held every few months so single Veslors can test matings, or the hosting duties that go with it. Our king gave us an entire continent to make our own. The only Veslors invited to live there will be like us." He paused. "The ones considered unsuitable and undesirable by other Veslors."

Raze liked that concept. "We still plan to hunt, but it would be nice to have a home to stay at during breaks."

Maith pushed off the wall and reached out, gripping his shoulders. "Good. We are family now, but we're also more. Friends." He released Raze and thumped his chest with his fist.

Raze did the same. "Thank you."

"No, thank *you*. My mate will be happy knowing she'll get to see her sister regularly."

Raze glanced at the sealed door. "What is taking so long?"

"Knowing my mate, she's talked yours into showing her what the fleet doctors did to her legs. I would never have guessed they were artificial."

"I wouldn't have either if Anabel hadn't told me. They bleed as if they are natural."

Maith appeared intrigued. Raze knew it was because he was a medic. Hern would have asked Anabel hundreds of questions if he were still alive. Healing and different medical technologies had always fascinated him.

He pushed the thought away. It hurt too much to think of the male.

The doors finally opened and Anabel and Jessa stepped out. Raze carefully studied his mate from head to foot. She seemed well and not in any pain.

"All done," Jessa announced. "All forms of birth control have been removed. I even got to take a peek and saved the scans of my big sister's amazing legs. It's some of the best limb work I've ever seen. That's why we were in there for so long. I was admiring the beauty and complexity of them."

Raze pulled Anabel into his arms, studying her face. "Are you in any discomfort?"

"No. Jessa shot me with some Veslor medicine afterward, and I healed up super-fast. The slight cramping I felt disappeared within a minute after she remove the device." She lifted her arm and tugged the material away from it. The skin was almost completely healed from a small cut. "The implant is gone, too."

"No sex until tomorrow, just to be safe," Jessa ordered. "At least not penetration." She winked at Raze. "Oral sex is fine and always highly encouraged."

Anabel laughed. "I remember when you used to be shy."

Raze lifted Anabel into his arms. "She's going to rest."

"I can walk," Anabel protested.

"Veslor mates," Jessa called out. "They love to carry us around. Get used to it!"

Raze hurried away, just wanting to get Anabel to their bed and cuddle with her.

"I'm okay," she assured him, resting her head against his shoulder.

"Thank you for removing them."

"Just don't knock me up until we're ready to have kids."

"Cubs."

She laughed. "Right."

Raze had never imagined having cubs before...but he suddenly couldn't stop envisioning them. One day, they'd try to make it a reality. Everything had changed since he'd taken a mate, and he had no regrets.

"You are my heart."

"You're mine, too."

Epilogue

Two weeks later

Anabel stared at the seemingly endless blue ocean in the distance. The view was breathtaking. Soft grass cushioned her bare feet where she stood near the edge of a cliff. Below, soft golden sand led to white cresting waves. Her gaze lifted to the two suns warming her skin from above. One was more distant but still in view. The pale blue sky was beautiful and fresh air blew against her skin.

The planet they were staying on reminded her a lot of how Earth might have looked once in the distant past, before humans had built massive cities and industry. Thankfully, the Veslors were more into preserving nature.

"There you are."

She turned, smiling at Raze as he walked around a large boulder on the path that led to where the landing field for space vessels sat. Her sister's grouping had a massive home built nearby before they'd even moved to the planet, to house their expanding family. It was farther inland, near a river of fresh water that joined the ocean by falling over another cliff in a beautiful waterfall.

Raze made it to her side, wrapped his arm around her, and walked them both back along the path to the valley where the *Satrono* and another smaller Veslor ship were parked. That one apparently belonged to Jessa's grouping. They'd been denied having it on *Defcon Red*, and it had been returned to them after they'd come home. It gave them a way to travel around the planet, and to others.

"We looked at the land a few miles upriver from your sister's home, in the wooded section again," he informed her.

Anabel's heart sped up. "And?"

"We went fishing. Prasky caught some impressively sized ones. He volunteered to cook this evening."

She paused walking, gazing up into his eyes. And saw the hint of a smile curve his lips.

"You talked him into letting a contractor grouping fly here to build us a home, didn't you?" That didn't surprise her. The wooded area that they'd viewed would be a perfect home, with tons of trees, fresh water, and hunting options. It was also beautiful.

He nodded. "Bruck sold him on us vacationing here when we're not hunting prey. He's in love with the territory Roth and his grouping offered us. We officially accepted. The contractor grouping will clear the ground in a couple of weeks. By the time we return from our next job, it will be completed. Our grouping just needs to sit down to give them the floorplans we wish."

Anabel snuggled into him. "Can we afford it?"

"Yes."

Pure happiness filled her. She was also a little suspicious, though, as she peered up at him. "Are you doing this mostly for me, so I'm close to my sister when we're on this planet between jobs?"

"It was actually something Maith said."

305

She waited.

"I spoke more with Roth's grouping about their plans for this continent. It's not only Veslors with alien mates who will be invited to live and claim territory here. This will be a place where all traveling Veslors will find a home."

"The undesirables," she said.

"Yes. We will be welcomed and accepted. So will our cubs, when we have them one day. We won't be shunned in any way for traveling when we come home. It will be an acceptable way of life to leave and return as we please."

"That sounds fantastic."

"It does. Our king heard of Roth's plan and was pleased enough to offer to pay for homes to be built for all groupings who decide to claim territory here."

That surprised her. "Wow, that's generous of him."

"Traveling Veslors are as important as the ones who remain," Raze said. "Our king knows this. He appreciates us."

"One day, I want to meet this guy."

He chuckled. "You will. Our king asked if it was possible for him to have a home nearby for a vacation spot. Of course Roth agreed. It is an honor that our king wishes to visit us from time to time. A small portion of the territory is reserved for him."

"So we're going to have a king neighbor?"

He grinned. "It appears sometimes we will. Our king believes it will help others of our kind grow more accepting of us claiming territory if he visits a few times a year."

"What is his first name? I've never heard it."

Raze frowned. "I do not know."

Her eyebrow arched. "You don't know your king's name?"

He shook his head. "We call him our king. Whatever name he was born with became irrelevant when he took over leading all our people, making the ultimate sacrifice for us."

"Is it really a sacrifice? I mean, he's your king. That sounds like a pretty great job to have."

"I am the leader of my grouping. It comes with great responsibilities. I can't imagine having the lives of every Veslor under my care and charge."

"I guess I almost feel bad for the guy, now that you've put it that way."

He nodded.

Anabel hesitated. "I have to ask something."

"What is it?"

"Are your parents and birth grouping on this planet somewhere?"

"No." He pointed up toward the more distant of the two suns. "They are on a planet close to that one."

Part of her was relieved. She didn't want anyone to visit who might possibly believe any of the lies once told about Raze's grouping.

"I have decided something."

"What's that?" She held his gaze.

"I am not going to allow what happened in the past to harm my heart anymore. I am blessed. You, our grouping, and the friends we've made who have become family are all that matter. My heart is happy, and my conscience is clear. It is *their* shame. Not mine. I will no longer carry it with me."

"You're pretty smart."

He chuckled. "I have a beautiful, loving mate. It is easy to forget the pain when every day with you brings pure joy."

Anabel's wristband vibrated lightly, and she looked down at her new black band with cool Veslor symbols on it. A Veslor grouping of medics had arrived a few days before to fit her for it. They'd also installed a small implant inside her ear to go with it.

Raze released her and tapped his band and hers. "What is it?"

Bruck's voice came through her ear. "Prasky wishes to start preparing his fish for our meal and is complaining that you are taking too long tracking your mate. He is snarling about how you could have just dinged her band and made her come to you, instead of going to find her."

Anabel grinned. One thing she'd noticed was the grouping argued more while on a planet. It was always about silly stuff that almost seemed to be a contest to make her mate lose his temper. She'd caught on quick to Prasky's game. Raze...not so much.

Raze growled. "We'll be there soon."

"He is impatient to eat these fish."

Anabel chuckled over Bruck's grumbling words. It *was* kind of funny. "We wanted him to like it enough here to agree to make it our part-time home," she reminded them, speaking into her band.

"We did," Bruck sighed. "Just hurry. He's grumbling about how his precious fish are best when cooked fresh."

"We're on our way. Raze out." He tapped off their bands and gripped her hand, leading them back to the landing field.

Anabel walked fast to keep up with her long-legged mate. "When's our next job?"

He slowed a little. "I felt we should take a few weeks off before we went on our next hunt."

"Actually, Jessa's settling into her new home and morning sickness has hit. She was puking when I visited her earlier today. Maith said it's normal and might last a few weeks. He also told me she needed rest. He wanted to give her a bath and put her to bed. It's why I went for a walk. He's mega-protective of her. Even from me."

"She's his mate and his instincts demand that he cares for her. Don't feel insulted."

"I don't. I was glad he nicely kicked me out. I love my sister, but it was gross seeing her toss up her breakfast. As I was leaving, she was yelling at him that she wasn't tired. He was snarling at her that she needed a nap." She paused, chuckling. "I think now would be a great time for our grouping to go away for a bit. She won't care as long as we're back before she gives birth. And our house will be close to completed, if we okay a floorplan quickly."

309

He laughed. "You don't want to spend the next few weeks watching her be ill and seeing the mates argue."

"Guilty. I knew you'd understand."

"We do need to earn some body shields from the Brani."

"Yes," she agreed. "And I really want to see what they look like."

He came to a halt and hauled her into his arms, lifting her. "Then that's what we'll do."

She kissed him. He deepened it, making her forget everything but him until both of their wristbands vibrated. They ignored them, but Prasky was able to activate their communications anyway, and his voice sounded.

"Tangle tongues later. Don't you two do that often enough? I have started to cook our meal. These fish are going to be delicious."

Raze snarled, breaking the kiss and gently putting Anabel back on her feet. He turned his head to glare at the extended ramp from their ship. She followed his gaze. Prasky stood at the top of it, glowering back, arms crossed over his chest. Then he threw up his hands and stomped inside.

It took a lot for Anabel not to burst into laughter. Prasky could be grumpy, but he always entertained her. "Let's go, sexy. We wanted him to be excited about being on a planet. Mission successful."

Raze grumbled. "Too much so."

"We'll lock ourselves inside our cabin later and make up for the interruption."

"You're a wonderful mate."

"So are you."

They entered the *Satrono* and found the two members of their grouping snarling at each other in the kitchen. Anabel took a seat. She could understand everything they said in Veslor now. The medics had also given her a translator when they'd added her ear implant and the band. She just sucked at speaking it, since her voice didn't go deep enough to make all the sounds they could.

Raze got between the males. "You're like children. We're here. Cook, Prasky. Bruck, stop teasing him. He did well today by catching many fish."

Anabel just smiled.

Raze turned, his blue gaze meeting hers. She could read the love in his eyes.

She had a mate, and two brothers of the heart that she adored. Her baby sister was safe and had her own family. They'd see each other frequently. They were both free from United Earth forever. One day, she and Raze would have babies together. Adorable ones. She couldn't ask for anything more.

About the Author

NY Times and USA Today Bestselling Author

I'm a full-time wife, mother, and author. I've been lucky enough to have spent over two decades with the love of my life and look forward to many, many more years with Mr. Laurann. I'm addicted to iced coffee, the occasional candy bar (or two), and trying to get at least five hours of sleep at night.

I love to write all kinds of stories. I think the best part about writing is the fact that real life is always uncertain, always tossing things at us that we have no control over, but when writing you can make sure there's always a happy ending. I love that about being an author. My favorite part is when I sit down at my computer desk, put on my headphones to listen to loud music to block out everything around me, so I can create worlds in front of me.

For the most up to date information, please visit my website. www.LaurannDohner.com

Made in the USA
Las Vegas, NV
11 September 2022

55074053R00184